D1269641

VOYAGE OF MALICE

Book Two of
THE HUGUENOT CONNECTION
Trilogy

PAUL C.R. MONK

A BLOOMTREE PRESS book.

First published in 2017 by BLOOMTREE PRESS

ISBN 978-0-9934442-7-2

www.paulcrmonk.com

Cover design by Sanja Gombar.
Formatting by Polgarus Studio.

BY THE SAME AUTHOR

Strange Metamorphosis

Subterranean Peril

In the Huguenot Connection trilogy:

Merchants of Virtue

Voyage of Malice

Land of Hope

Also in the Huguenot Connection series:

May Stuart

ONE

FROM THE FOREMOST cabin of *La Marie*, Jacob Delpech steadied himself as best he could against the brine-splashed frame of the porthole. He stooped to avoid hitting his head on the coarse timber beam, so low was the cabin where he and his Huguenot brethren were incarcerated. But the view was certainly worth the effort, he thought, as the French pink, a three-masted cargo ship, pitched and rolled into the Bay of Cadiz.

'So this is the gateway to the ocean sea,' he said, almost to himself.

Mademoiselle Marianne Duvivier, standing next to him, made a comment on the pageant of colour growing nearer and bigger. Indeed, the Spanish port's importance was attested by the multitude of foreign merchant ships anchored here and there, flying their colours atop their main masts.

It occurred to Jacob that they were now only one stop away from their Caribbean island prison. That is, provided the ship, more apt for coastal ferrying than sailing the great sea, did not turn turtle en route—for she bobbed like a barrel.

The passage from Gibraltar, though short, had been

1

rough enough to shake up the stomachs of the hardiest of seafarers. In fact it had finished off two prisoners in the cabin next door, which housed galley slaves too old or too infirm for service. However, miraculously perhaps, the eighty or so Protestant prisoners were none the worse for wear despite being at the bow of the ship, that part which took the full brunt of the waves. But unlike the poor lame wretches next door, at least they bore no visible chains. And most of the Huguenot men and women seemed to be gaining their sea legs at last.

To Marianne Duvivier's great relief, they could now spy *La Concorde*, the great ship that had accompanied them much of the way from Marseille, and which carried a greater load of galley slave labour and Huguenot prisoners. More efficient and faster than *La Marie*, she had sailed ahead from Gibraltar and was already at anchor in the ancient Andalusian harbour. Significantly larger and built for the high seas, she was also more stable and seemed to sit in the port waters like an albatross among chicks, hardly bobbing amid the ripples.

La Marie dropped her anchors just a gunshot from *La Concorde*, but not close enough for prisoners to exchange words, nor parallel so that they could see each other. Nevertheless, Marianne Duvivier was still standing at the gun port an hour after their arrival, hoping for her grandmother to show her head through a porthole of the great ship.

She turned to Jacob, who had joined her again. In her resolute and selfless way, she said, 'I am so glad it was my grandmother and not I who was sent aboard the *Concorde*.' She was referring to the cruel separation from Madame de Fontenay at the embarkation point in Marseille. Jacob had since fathomed that separating grandmother and granddaughter was certainly a ploy between guards so that the girl could be more easily singled out and plucked from the crowd. However, her ravisher had ended up drowning with the first mate and another seaman when the longboat he was rowing capsized in the port of Toulon, the day after his failed abduction. And by a strange twist of fate, or Providence maybe, his death had granted her protection, for sailors were deeply superstitious.

'Yes, quite,' said Jacob, nodding towards the Spanish quay. 'Otherwise she may have been leaving the ship earlier than planned.'

The girl followed his eyes to where the dead prisoners, bound in hessian sacks, were being hoisted to quay from the longboat, then unceremoniously dumped like dead pigs onto a barrow. It was still early morning. The harbour was just beginning to stir in the grey light, and they could clearly hear the vociferations in French and Spanish about the stench emanating from the bodies. The Spaniard made several signs of the cross before taking up the shafts of the barrow, then wheeled the dead men away to God-knows-where.

Delpech felt a pang of injustice for the galley slave, whom he had known to have been a God-fearing shoemaker whose only crime had been the illicit purchase of salt. His wife and children would not even be able to mourn his passing properly without the body, he thought. He inwardly prayed for the man's soul to accept a place in heaven, if it so pleased God.

'I would willingly miss three days' worth of rations for a place on board the Concorde,' said one white-haired gentleman, a surgeon named Emile Bourget.

'Can't say you would be missing much,' said Madame Fesquet, the middle-aged matron who had comforted Marianne after the attempted abduction.

'Let us not allow our regrets to undermine us, my dear Professor,' said Jacob, touching the man's arm. 'Instead let us spend our effort seeking God's grace in our misfortune.'

'Yes, you are right, Sir,' said Bourget. 'Forgive me my weakness.'

Madame Fesquet, in her matronly way, said, 'Praise be to God that we have arrived safely and have been granted this reprieve from the treacherous sea!'

Jacob thought she needn't be so loud; she might rouse the guards. But he bowed his head and said *Amen* anyway. After all, she was of goodwill and was only voicing her support of his remark.

Delpech had inadvertently become something of a moral touchstone among even these adamantly virtuous people. He had become their spokesman whenever their meagre rights of humanity needed to be reaffirmed to the captain, even though these demands were always made through the guards. The unsolicited honour no doubt had something to do with his forthright eloquence, his former position and fortune, and perhaps most of all, his standing up to the sailor who had one night tried to ravish the girl from the cabin.

Yet in truth, all Jacob Delpech really wanted was to lie low and get through this nightmare until he could find a way to escape the madness. And, with God's help, recover his wife and children.

The Huguenot ladies and gentlemen agreed to take advantage of the month-long stop in the Spanish port to swab the planks of their cabin, and to reduce the number of vermin. But undertaking the former required water and cloths, at the very least.

Jacob bravely accepted the task of go-between. He decided, however, to wait for the most appropriate moment when the soil buckets had been emptied, and when the least volatile guard came on duty. So it was not until after their noon slops—a mix of pellet-like peas and half-boiled fish—that he was able to put the question to the guard through the iron slats of the half-timbered door.

GUARD: What now?
DELPECH: We desire to speak to the captain.
GUARD: Cap'ain's busy.
DELPECH: It is a matter of hygiene.
GUARD: Don't care what it's about, mate, I said he's busy. And when he's busy, it means he don't wanna be disturbed, savvy?
DELPECH: Then would you please be so kind as to ask him if we may be supplied with extra buckets and some rope so that we can haul seawater into the cabin.
GUARD: So you can escape more like, cheeky bugger!
DELPECH: Not at all. We would simply like to clean the cabin.
GUARD: I'll give you a bucket, all right, a bucket of heretic shit if you don't watch out!
DELPECH: Then would you kindly supply us with the water yourselves? And some sackcloth? I pray that you put my demand to the captain, or at least to the first mate, should the captain be unavailable. Will you do that?

GUARD: Pwah. All right, but woe betide you if I get my arse kicked!

Jacob Delpech had become as inured to threats as he had to the revolting stench of the cabin, full of unwashed people and buckets of excrement. Over the past two years, from one prison to another, he had been threatened with hanging, perishing in damnation, being burnt alive at the stake, having his balls stuffed into his mouth, and finally, being sent to America. Only the last threat had so far been carried out, which enabled him to take the guard's colourful language with a pinch of salt, and to pursue his demands calmly and collectedly.

An hour went by before the key clunked in the lock.

'Where's the prat who asked for water?' said the guard, peeking through the iron slats of the door.

'I am the one who asked for water. And rope,' said Jacob, who was still by the door, imperturbable.

'It's your lucky day, pal. The captain sends his blessings!'

The door was flung open, and three men with malicious grins stood in the doorway, each holding a pail. Delpech instinctively held up his hands to shield his head as three columns of water drenched him and those immediately around him from head to foot. The men laughed out loud. Then the guard pulled the heavy door shut and turned the key in the lock.

Jacob prayed inwardly for the strength to continue to suffer humiliation, torture, and even death for his faith. However, at least the guard's threat was only partially carried out. Thankfully, seawater was all that was in the buckets.

Nevertheless, to state that Delpech was becoming weary

6

of the crew's scorn—scorn that he suspected was fuelled by a callous captain—was an understatement. But he kept it to himself, and prayed the day would come when he could escape to carry out his plan.

*

Captain Joseph Reners, thirty-nine, was a merchant. A strong leader and very proud of his person, he was as able with low life as he was with the elite, and he enjoyed the company in both the Old World and the New. He loved his occupation, buying and selling, which took him to places where a man could forget himself. What he disliked, though, were the bits in-between, the seafaring bits which were either extremely dangerous or downright boring.

He vaunted himself as being well travelled and delighted in thrilling the bourgeoisie in Cadiz, especially the ladies, with tales of peril at sea and man-eating savages called cannibals. Given his gregarious nature, he had acquired expert knowledge of parlour games and card playing. In short, he lived for the social life on land, and this latest venture transporting galley slaves and Huguenots gave him the means to indulge wholeheartedly in his passions, from Cadiz to the Spanish Main. Nevertheless, over the years he had traced a regular circuit and by consequence had a reputation to keep up, at least in Europe, if he were not to be shunned by his usual hosts.

Consequently, a day after the water-throwing incident, the crew's degree of crassness towards their prisoners slipped down a few notches, and their attitude became, if not respectful, at least more tolerable. The soil buckets were emptied before they were completely full, and the peas were cooked, so they no longer ended up in those buckets. The salted beef, however, remained as tough as boot leather, and the cold fish still resembled a kind of briny porridge. But most of all, the Huguenot detainees no longer ran the risk of being drenched by buckets of seawater whenever they knelt down to pray.

Jacob correctly supposed that this change was owing to the captain's desire to show a façade of respectability and humanity during his stay in the Spanish port town.

What is more, the shift in behaviour was sustained and even enhanced, thanks to a series of visits paid to the Huguenots during their stopover.

Dutch and English Protestant merchants who had settled in the Iberian port quickly got wind of the 'cargo' of Huguenots. It had become a normal occurrence to hear of lame slaves being transported to the New World. But how could respectable, devout Christians be stripped of their earthly possessions and dispelled from their homeland for simply remaining faithful to their religious conscience?

Despite Louis XIV's attempt to draw a veil over his religious purge and conceal it from the outside world, word had nevertheless percolated out of France. Tens of thousands of Huguenot escapees had taken with them to Geneva, Bearn, Brandenburg, Saxony, Amsterdam, and London tales of unfair trials, family separations, enslavement, and incarceration. French etiquette was quickly going out of fashion. It was losing its capacity to charm the breaches off the European bourgeoisie as the darker side of the Sun King was becoming apparent. And here in Cadiz was the chance to see the living proof.

The captains of neither *La Marie* nor *La Concorde* did

anything to prevent visits to their ships. On the contrary, Reners for one was astute enough to give orders not to impede such visits, as proof that he himself had nothing to hide, that he was only carrying out the King's orders. When asked at his hosts' table about his cargo of Huguenots, he would make a point of stating that the poor wretches on his ship were treated with humanity, even allowed to pray to their God, in spite of their disloyalty to their King.

On the morning of 22 October 1687, the second morning after the French ships' arrival, Mr Izaäk van der Veen and his wife were the first of the Protestant merchants to visit *La Marie*. The Dutchman was an influential broker with links to counters in Holland and the West Indies. He had done business with the captain on numerous occasions, usually for the purchase of barrels of French wine which went down well with the multi-cultured population of Cadiz, as well as his Flemish buyers.

Mrs van der Veen, a straight-faced and well-endowed lady with mothering hips, climbed aboard *La Marie*, taking care not to dirty her dress in the rigging. The Dutchman knew the ship from previous visits, although this time neither he nor his wife was there to choose barrels of beverage. This was just as well, as the space normally given over to wine and spirits had been converted for the captain's human cargo.

Both Mr and Mrs van der Veen were dressed with sobriety in accordance with their reformist beliefs. They were greeted by the second in command. This did not disgruntle the visitors in the slightest, as they knew of the captain's legendary distaste for dwelling on board his ship. The remaining crew were busy offloading cargo destined for

Cadiz. The visiting couple advanced carefully to avoid slipping on the wet decking, and continued past sailors swabbing the main deck.

Mr van der Veen followed the second mate down the scuttle hatch into the tween deck, and then turned to assist his wife. She immediately noticed that the open space that once spanned from the capstan to the windlass was now partitioned off into cabins. And thank goodness she had thought to perfume her handkerchief, which she now held to her nose. The savoury and sickly smell of food, urine, tar, and dank timber grew stronger as they advanced towards the galley slave cabin, where a large rat stood nibbling at a flat square of flesh—a prize stolen from an inmate's bowl. The rat had grasped that a man inside the cabin who carelessly placed his bowl on the ground had no chance of catching the rodent once it had scooted with the food under the door. But on the approach of the intruders, the hideous creature showed its teeth, jealously took up its prize, and indignantly scampered away.

Mrs van der Veen and her husband turned to each other with a look which said they were dreading to see the conditions in which their brothers and sisters in faith were being held captive.

Then the sound of a woman's voice rose up in song. It was spontaneously joined by a host of male and female voices, and the Dutch lady recognised a psalm that sounded beautiful, sung in the French language.

They hastened their step to the Huguenots' cell and stood to watch through the iron slats. The inmates nearest the door stopped their song, and for a suspended moment stood watching the couple staring back at them.

Mrs Van der Veen, who spoke some French, had prepared her introductory sentence in her head that morning. But it did not come out, so absorbed was she by the piteous sight of the scene before her. Instead she put her hands together in prayer. Her husband followed suit. Then gradually, like a wave leading from the door, the Huguenots also stood or knelt in silent prayer.

At last, the Dutch couple looked up, and their eyes met those of a slim gentleman with cropped hair who took a step from the crowd.

'Madame,' he said in French. 'Do not pity us but rather our persecutors. For we are the privileged few whom the Lord has graced with the chance to earn a place in heaven. There is no need to shed your tears for us.'

'Monsieur, please forgive us,' said Mrs Van der Veen. 'We were not prepared to see such injustice before our very eyes.'

The second mate who had accompanied them was standing sheepishly with the guard, three paces back. Mr van der Veen turned to them and asked in Spanish to open the door so that he and his wife could enter the cell. The second mate gave the nod to the guard, who opened the door, then locked it behind them.

The gaunt-looking man with the cropped head introduced himself. 'I am Jacob Delpech de Castanet,' he said. Other men and women huddled around them without thronging, and introduced themselves in the gentlest manner.

'Dear lady, your heart is noble and kind,' said one young lady who introduced herself as Mademoiselle Duvivier. 'But please do not be afraid to hold your handkerchief to your nose. We understand that the odours must be intolerable to someone unused to this despicable den.'

'Thank you for your consideration,' said Mrs Van der Veen, 'but allow me the honour of sharing a part of your humiliation and sufferance with you. It will make me nobler.'

Mr van der Veen said slowly in Spanish, 'If we can bring you any comfort at all, we shall be eternally grateful.'

Mrs van der Veen said in French, 'I shall bring you vials of perfume, which will at least sweeten the air around you, as well as other provisions. Please tell us what you need most.'

'You are kind, my good lady,' said one Huguenot woman.

'A splendid idea,' said Madame Fesquet. 'It will distance the bad smells that breed disease.'

Mademoiselle Duvivier said, 'The disease is also brought by the vermin, I fear. As Jesus tells us to travel through life in a clean body, we should very much like to embark on our voyage in a clean cabin.'

'We have been enclosed in this cabin for the past four weeks,' said Jacob. 'Alas, in spite of our demands, we are deprived of water and rags for swabbing.'

'I will ask the captain to see to it that you are equipped,' said Mr van de Veen, who then let his wife translate.

*

By the following morning, not only was the Huguenots' wish for water and cloth granted, but more visits followed from other Dutch and English contingents, and continued throughout the Huguenots' stay in Cadiz harbour. Each visit uplifted their spirits, like a rag of blue sky in an otherwise murky firmament. They saw each visit as a ray of God's love that galvanised their faith and filled their souls with new courage. It meant He had not abandoned them. Now they could embark on the long, perilous voyage across the great sea, secure in the knowledge that their place in heaven was assured. What, after all, was earthly suffering compared to eternal life?

The visiting parties also brought very earthly provisions: dried sausage, cheese, bread, fruit, clothing, writing kits. They even managed to smuggle in miniature Bibles and a few other books for the voyage, one of which would shape the course of Jacob's destiny.

The book in question was at first given to Professor Bourget by a rosy-faced Englishman with sparse white hair for whom Jacob acted as interpreter. Delpech still possessed remnants of English, having learnt it as a young man when his father had taken a position there in 1663 to learn about medicine. However, the book was of no use to the professor, a surgeon who knew only his mother tongue, German, Latin, and Greek. Jacob's father had been a physician and herbalist, and during previous conversations with Bourget, it had come to light that Delpech had always nurtured a fond interest in the Lord's natural world. So it was without regret that the professor gave the book to Jacob.

It was an old book that the elderly Englishman had kept since his younger days. He had spent half his career as a ship's surgeon for the East India Company. The book was *The Surgeon's Mate*.

*

On the twenty-first of November, one month to the day of her arrival, the pink lowered her sails and turned her prow towards the open sea.

Jacob Delpech was eager to reach the New World. Before setting out from the Bay of Cadiz, he had been able to converse in his broken English with a Dutchman by the name of Marcus Horst, who was familiar with the West Indies. 'There are a great many islands, large and small,' he had said. 'You must hold firm. It would not be so difficult to escape to an English settlement by cargo ship. From there you can gain passage aboard a ship bound for London or Amsterdam.'

La Marie and *La Concorde* were escorted by *Le Solide,* commanded by Admiral Chateaurenaud, chief of the French fleet. As they left the Bay of Cadiz, Jacob knelt with a group of fellow inmates to give thanks to God for the reprieve before the storm, and for the rays of light that had brought them comfort, hope, and their Holy Bibles.

The sound of the key in the lock made Jacob look up in time to see the door swing open. Next thing, he saw two men, two buckets, and a shaft of seawater.

'Enough of yer jabbering to false gods!' bellowed one of the guards.

'Or we'll come in and search yer all for fake Bibles,' said his mate. 'And if we find any, it's twelve lashes for heresy!'

TWO

JACOB HAD KNOWN about the perils of sailing near the Barbary Coast for a long time—which was why, as a merchant, he had always shipped goods overseas from the west coast via Bordeaux.

He was sure that, should by misfortune they be captured, the King of France would find no reason to send his ambassador to Mulay Ismail to part with wealth or Muslim slaves in exchange for a few Huguenot bourgeois, no matter what their standing in society had once been.

Understandably, then, Jacob and those who knew anything about international affairs inwardly gave praise once they had sailed clear of the Gulf of Cadiz, unmolested by Barbary corsairs.

But the moment *Le Solide* veered northward towards the coast of Portugal, *La Concorde* put all sails to the wind southwestward, and *La Marie* was soon left alone amid the vast expanse of the Atlantic Ocean. They would not encounter land for six long weeks. Six weeks of being rocked and tossed about at the bow of the ship—the worst part, the part usually reserved for animals—with nothing to engage the eye but sea and sky.

Noah had endured a similar voyage, Jacob often philosophised; the Ark could not have been any more seaworthy than this pink. So he resigned himself to patience and prayer, and surreptitiously read books and his Bible whenever the light and the swell permitted. But even this was made impossible much of the time by the roasting heat of the sun, augmented by the heat of the kitchen stove only six feet above their heads. It was like sitting inside a furnace and so insufferable at times that the men were obliged to remove their shirts and tunics, drenched as they were in sweat. To compensate for their natural modesty, women were given the areas out of the direct sunlight and furthest away from the heat emanating from the stove above.

The only resort was to remain as still as possible, which became increasingly difficult given the atrocious proliferation of fleas that feasted on legs and other body parts come nightfall. And the itchiness the morning after was always more intolerable than the precedent.

One stifling afternoon, three weeks out of Cadiz, despite a constant urge to scratch his fleabites, Delpech sat, knees forming a *V*, perusing *The Surgeon's Mate*. With a steady wind in her sails, *La Marie* was able to hold an even keel, which made a change to the sporadic blasts of the night before. Most of the cabin was in slumber. Jacob was trying to decipher the chapter entitled *Of Salts and Their Virtues*—which gave him cause for a rare chuckle given that they were surrounded by the stuff—when a terrible cry of despair broke the creaking, snorting, catnapping silence. Lifting his head from the page, he saw a young woman jump up in a dim corner across the cabin and scream out: 'I cannot go on, I cannot. I am being devoured. Oh Lord, have pity! God help me, please!'

He recognised Madame Gachon, normally a quiet, obliging lady, whose two children had been taken from her to be raised in the 'true' religion back in France. She then flung off her bonnet, stripped off her dress from neck to waist, and dashed topless to the porthole opposite where Jacob was sitting.

Jacob sensed in his bones what she was about to attempt. But the surprise of seeing the poor woman half-naked and the horrible seeping carbuncles on her upper body had him mesmerized. And for an instant he was unable to react to the impending tragedy. Before anyone else had fathomed what all the fuss was about, she had hoisted herself through the square porthole in an attempt to reach the solace of the sea.

At last, throwing his book aside and heaving himself up, Jacob called out: 'Grab her!'

An old man dozing close to the gun port sprang up like a coiled snake and managed to latch onto her ankles before she disappeared completely through the hole. With the help of another man, he managed to pull her back inside the cabin as she drummed her fists wildly against the side of the hull.

They were laying her down on the rough timber boards, careful to avoid her arms lashing out, when two guards came bustling through the door, buckets at the ready, as if to put out a fire.

'She tried to jump out the porthole,' said Jacob, who was at present struggling to hold down her arms while Mademoiselle Duvivier and Madame Fesquet were trying to pull up her dress to cover her bare torso. The tortured soul was now in tears, writhing like a captured beast and tossing her head from side to side in a frenzy, crying out for the peace of Christ.

'Shut your bloody bone box and move over, unless you want another hiding!' said one of the guards. Jacob edged back a step, but stood ready to intervene even if it meant taking a beating.

'I'll give her a mouthful of sea all right, if that's what she wants!' said the other guard.

With deliberate, almost lascivious slowness, they poured the contents of their buckets up and down the length of Madame Gachon's body, reducing the flow to a trickle when they reached her open dress, her rash along her white belly, and her half-bare breasts.

'For the sake of common decency, that's enough, Sir, I beseech you!' said Jacob. Huguenot men had positioned themselves ready to pounce should the situation deteriorate. Sensing they may have gone too far, the guards more hastily finished emptying their buckets.

But the debasing punishment of pouring seawater in Huguenots' faces, which still kept the thugs amused, now seemed to instantly quell the woman's delirium. She stopped crying out, only snuffled now as the cool water splashed onto her skin. She let her arms lie limp, so that the unwavering ladies could thread them into her dress, and cover her torso.

'She does it again, we'll bound her up and leave her on Dominica with the savages!' bellowed one of the guards, puffing out his chest. Looking around with his hand on his scabbard, he backed out of the cabin with his mate.

Dominica was a Caribbean island inhabited by ferocious savages known as Caribs. It was one of the places the guards repeatedly said they would leave women who refused to attend the Catholic mass once on land. The men would simply be hanged, they said. These were ongoing threats they had concocted to put the 'fear of God' into their captives. But what can these heathens know about Christianity, let alone the fear of God? thought Jacob, who had previously told his fellows to dismiss their menaces as mere hogwash.

The women took over operations as Madame Gachon began to come back to her senses. They helped her return to her place. Jacob went back to his book.

But he could not help revisiting in his mind the neat bands of weals on the poor woman's torso where the fleas had eaten into her flesh, and the large weeping carbuncles that had formed here and there. The excruciating itching and pain they must have caused her, along with the intolerable heat and the confinement of her clothing, would have driven anyone to distraction, which was why the poor woman had sought comfort in the wide ocean.

But what gave Jacob the most matter for reflection was the effect of the seawater. It had seemed to bring her instant relief and had visibly quashed the distress and itchiness of her sores. No, her intention had not been to kill herself—for that was a crime in the eyes of the Lord—but to instinctively seek a cure from the ocean.

Jacob turned back to the page where the author was praising the virtues of salt. He read: *All those which are vexed with any disease, proceeding of grosse crudity, or unnatural humidity, as rheumes, itch, scurve, ring-worms, or the like noysome greefes: let them make a bath of common sea salt.*

Delpech sat in wonder as the confirmation of his deduction hit home. He then explained his theory to Professor Bourget and a few others who cared to listen.

'Salt has indeed been used since ancient times for its virtues,' said Bourget, who had been seasick throughout the voyage so far, and was only able to concentrate his thoughts for minutes at a time.

'And it is all around us,' said Jacob.

*

That night, after the buckets were emptied and returned to the cell, instead of using them all for their usual purpose, they kept one back for their experiment.

Men tied their shirts together to form a line. To the end of this line, Jacob tied the bucket, which he lowered through the porthole until it broke the water's surface. Then he hoisted it back up. In this way they were able to discreetly retrieve the providential brine.

Delpech and Bourget applied cloth soaked in seawater to the men's sores. Mademoiselle Duvivier and Madame Fesquet did likewise for the women. And indeed, to everyone's amazement, after the initial sting, the itchiness subsided, and the fleas did not bite so much during that night. 'Why, bless me soul,' said Bourget the next morning. 'Dear Delpech, you are right. Fleas are averse to salt!'

Every night thereafter, they carefully retrieved buckets full of ocean water. They doused their wounds and swabbed the planks, and some even soaked their clothes in it. Salt is not comfortable, but the discomfort it caused from dryness was but a small tithe to pay for the protection it gave against the evil of fleas, and the horrible pustules they caused on the skin.

Jacob linked the series of events which had led to his revelation: Madame Gachon exposing her sores; her uncontrollable attraction to the sea; Jacob reading the very pages that spoke about salt; having the book in the first place; saving the poor woman; her being soaked in seawater; and Jacob falling upon the very paragraph that dealt with itching and the like.

Surely, then, the woman's momentary folly was a manifestation of God's grace, was it not? It had given them the cure to their greatest discomfort. And the ongoing voyage became more tolerable, or rather, less of a nightmare for it.

Whenever they were caught praying henceforth, they no longer felt humiliation at seawater being thrown into their faces. Instead they felt the grace of God.

*

The stench was intolerable at the best of times, what with the buckets of defecation seldom being emptied till evening. But at no time was it more asphyxiating than when the gun port flaps were closed, mostly due to big swells, but also due to the cruelty of the guards—although, in some ways, the dim light and the appalling smell were lesser evils than the blazing rays of the sun.

It was impossible to read once the wooden flaps were lowered, so Jacob found plenty of time for introspection.

He was going to die, no matter what, and so was everyone else. But where did the Christian soul go? He knew not; the Bible only gave a few lines in Revelation. Would the celestial city be anything like the one described in *The Pilgrim's Progress*? Since the stopover in Cadiz, John Bunyan's book had been passed round to the few who could understand English. Jacob had read it, and it gave him hope, especially when Christian was helped out of the Slough of Despond. Is that not where he and his fellow Huguenots found themselves now? Although their slough was an ocean!

Jacob Delpech often set to thinking about the coming of Christ, the birth of Christianity, the gospel, and the inception of the Holy Roman Church. He reflected on the ungodly crimes to which the Church had turned a blind eye, and the assassinations it had sanctioned. He mulled over the wars of religion, and the Saint Bartholomew massacre where French Catholics had cold-bloodedly slaughtered thousands of Calvinists. He thought about how the pope had congratulated the French king by sending him a golden rose. Pope Gregory had even issued a medal to commemorate the event. When, as a young lad, Jacob first learnt of the horrific binge of killing, he could hardly believe his ears. Then one day he saw one of these medals with his own eyes. On one side it showed the head of Pope Gregory VIII, and on the other an angel brandishing a cross and a sword while standing over a group of slaughtered Protestants. It was struck with the words *Ugonottorum strages 1572*, which meant '*Slaughter of the Huguenots 1572.*' And so here was proof of the pope's benediction, and consequently of the Church's involvement.

How could such an institution have been allowed to breed hatred in the name of Christ and get away with it for centuries? How could it preach humility when it was adorned with gold? How could it be allowed to give Christendom such an appalling reputation for so long? Jacob was confused.

He prayed that God would enlighten him. As he was trying to put his thoughts into perspective, he began to doze off. A dark cloak of morbid matter seemed to encroach upon his mind like a black eagle folding its wings over him. Then he heard the high screech of a gull, and a distant human voice.

'Land ahoy! Land ahoy!'

Jacob roused from his slumber amid the general agitation. He shielded his eyes from the light as the wooden flaps were pulled open. He then hoisted himself onto his feet and staggered to the porthole, where he set his sight upon a faraway lump on the horizon. He was looking at the New World for the first time. It was the afternoon of January 2, 1688.

THREE

BY MORNING, ONCE the mist had lifted, Jacob and a few other porthole viewers perceived not a clump of vegetation but a full-blown island densely clad in rainforest. Its sheer mountain cliffs fell abruptly into the sea. This was the most mountainous island of the Lesser Antilles. This was Dominica, home to the warrior tribes of the Caribs, who had lent their name to the Caribbean Sea.

This was the island the guards had referred to time and again. The place where they threatened to maroon the women who would not stop singing psalms, where the insolent young ladies would be tamed by the savage men, and the old maids gutted, grilled, and eaten.

But *La Marie* sailed on past the spectacular landscape of lush woodland and waterfalls where nature still ruled in all its primal glory. She headed northward on the leeward side of Marie-Galante, the French-occupied island, flat as the galette that the natives called cassava bread. It sat like an antithesis of Dominica. Even from the gun port, Delpech could easily spy the ox-powered mills dotted here and there among the patchwork of flat, laboured fields.

His thoughts turned to the fields of his native Tarn and Garonne: the waving wheat and the corn on the cob; the orchards of apples, pears, and plums; the peachy brick farm buildings that housed his farmhands; his ancestral home and his townhouse in Montauban. He wondered how the harvest had been over the past two years. Who was taking care of business now? Yet something told him he need not worry, that he would most likely never see his homeland again. But as long as he could recover his wife and his children, he knew he would still have the resilience and energy to build another patrimony, another home, wherever on earth that may be.

He had written to Jeanne when in Cadiz to inform her he ambitioned to escape from the Caribbean islands to London. He would send her word to join him when the time came. He had given one letter to a Dutchman and another to an Englishman to send on his behalf to the pastor in Geneva, where he knew his wife to have found refuge. By doing so he was increasing the odds twofold that his message would reach its destination.

Contrary winds made the going slow, though the many marvellous views at least broke the monotony—no more so than when a group of dolphins accompanied them a short distance by making arches over the clear, teal sea—and took their minds off their thirst.

By the twelfth of January, water was rationed to two cups per person. However, the following afternoon, even the guards thanked the Lord for the favourable wind that brought them relief, and pushed the pink into the bay of Guadeloupe for their first stop in the New World.

*

Guadeloupe is easily recognised on charts by its butterfly shape. The two wings were divided by a narrow channel that emerged on the south side into a large bay where French colonists from Saint Paul had established port villages.

The bay, consisting of a large south-facing inlet between these two areas of land, offered a natural harbour well sheltered from the easterlies, and well out of the way of the swell. From the gun ports on either side of the pink, Jacob could see that the shape is where all similitude to a butterfly ended, for the topographical features of the two wings were very different.

The land on the west side, Jacob was surprised to learn, was known as Basse-Terre, meaning lowlands. It actually offered splendid views of highlands covered in rainforest and gushing waterfalls. Delpech mused that given the clement climate and clear blue skies, the fresh water cascades and the luxuriant vegetation, it took no great leap of the mind to imagine this to be Paradise on earth.

Grande-Terre on the east side presented low rolling hills and flat land ideal for crop cultivation. Jacob remembered hearing this was the island where fortunes had been made cultivating sugar cane and distilling it into sugarloaves. He was curious to find out how the transformation was carried out.

But during the four-day stay, prisoners and slaves remained locked in their stifling cabins while cargos of pots, tools, and textiles were offloaded, and barrels of sugarloaves taken aboard. The captain may have been sozzled out of his mind on occasion during his forays on land, but he had certainly not lost his bearings when it came to trade, not by a long sea mile.

It was from their cabin in the natural harbour that many Huguenots saw black men for the first time. On Guadeloupe, the European colonists, many of whom were seeking a new life free from religious and political persecution, were building a tried and tested formula by which to make a fortune, and there were no scruples when it came to worldly wealth. Be you Protestant, Catholic, or a Jew, it was what made the world go round.

The men were rolling, humping, and hoisting barrels on the foreshore. One of them, a lad of seventeen—as black as a frigate bird—turned to an older man who was securing a load of sugarloaves onto a boat. It was to be transported the short distance to the ship where white faces peered out from the holes in the hull.

In his native tongue, the lad said, 'Who are they to keep staring at us working?'

The older man, who knew better than to stop for a natter under a slave driver's nose, continued securing the barrels as he said in a low voice, 'They are slaves.'

The answer came as no small surprise to the young man. His name was Imamba Kan, and he had once been a prince of the Akwamu tribe in West Africa. The bulldoggish slave driver gave the lad a stroke of his whip for daring to dawdle.

'Gimme that black look again, boy,' bellowed the slave driver, 'and I'll whip your black ass till it turns so red you'll be beggin' me not to make you sit on it, boy, let alone shit!'

The young prince turned back to his chore. 'I will get away from this wicked oppression,' he said to himself. 'I will get away from here.' But for the moment, Imamba had no choice but to hurry his movements or else receive another lash of the whip.

*

Four days later, *La Marie* was leaving the sugar cane fields, the African huts, and the ox-driven mills of Guadeloupe. A steady southerly wind allowed her to make good headway, and in just two days, on the eighteenth of January, she dropped anchor in the roadstead of Saint Paul.

Jacob knew from conversations with Professor Bourget that the first Frenchmen to set foot on this island were Huguenots back in the 1620s. They had long since moved on to the island northwest of Hispaniola called Tortuga, where they formed a small colony. But the island of Saint Paul had nonetheless come a long way in sixty years. For a start, the gentle slopes of the volcano, and the low-lying plain at its foot, had been cleared and given over to the lucrative sugar cane.

And, as a testimony to its newfound importance and the size of its population, Catholic Jesuits had even built a monastery here. Jacob knew as well as anyone that those of this order were not known to settle in places of little interest. Such was their grandeur that when two of them set foot aboard the pink, they were given full honours.

However, these reverent clerics did not deign to visit the Protestant heretics. There was, of course, no point. Besides, they only had time to inspect the casks of wine they had come to procure and to settle the sale of sugarloaves before it was time for vespers. They had two thousand African slaves to hammer the true faith into, which was no small task, especially when you considered that many scholars were still arguing whether or not the wretches had a soul at all.

While negotiations were under way, Jacob noticed a

cargo ship that flew the English flag. It was a normal occurrence in these waters, as the English occupied the central area of the island, and the two nationalities had found no better way to cohabit than by simply ignoring each other's company. It had been the modus vivendi ever since the French and English joined forces some decades back to wipe the rich, fertile island clean of its populations of trees and savages. Neither of these life forms was compatible with the white man's design. The vegetation was worthless, in spite of Carib complaints that replacing hundreds of healing plants with one crop was a senseless and disrespectful act against nature. But of course, these were savages who did not understand what made the world go round.

The Europeans' success had since enabled both nationalities to give themselves fervently to the intensive cultivation of their favourite crop, which the French called *white gold*.

The captain had manifestly found the discussions agreeable. On the departure of his venerable visitors, they were honoured with a three-gun salute, normally reserved for a governor.

On seeing the multitude of black slave workers going about their business on land, it suddenly occurred to Jacob that these islands that had once been the promised land for a few freedom seekers, had become a prison for so many. Surely this could not have been the intention of the first Huguenots, could it?

Nevertheless, the ease with which the English ship had come sailing past, without so much as a puff of animosity, bolstered his hopes that escape to an English territory was indeed a viable option.

29

*

After the nine-day stopover in the bay of Saint Paul, victualled and watered, *La Marie* continued her voyage towards the French territory on Hispaniola, the island of her destination.

The sea was dazzling and calm as they tacked north by northwest along the eastern side of Saint Eustache—a Dutch possession with lush volcanic slopes—and by the steep scarps of the little isle of Saba which belonged to the English. The Huguenots who were still eager and able took turns to huddle around the gun ports whenever they offered a new tableau of exotic vistas.

By the twenty-ninth of January, they were sailing eastward three sheets to the wind, past the even plains of the south coast of Saint Croix. The prevailing easterly kept the ship on a steady course, while giving her the advantage of manoeuvrability as she swept past the treacherous reefs of the southeast cape of Puerto Rico.

The south-facing coast of this island presented a profusion of settlements: more slave shacks and villages amid the fertile plains that sloped down from the timbered mountains. Jacob was becoming aware of the extent to which whole African populations had been transported to these new colonies. Be it Dutch, French, English, or Spanish, every island harboured settlements of African huts.

On rounding the southwest cape of Puerto Rico, they hit upon the tail end of a storm. The only safe place for non-crew members was lying flat on the floor on their canvas sacks. Even then Jacob and his eighty fellow inmates were often unable to keep themselves from rolling about like apples in a tub.

But the captain refused to tack back to the southern coastline that provided numerous anchorage points away from the swell. Even if they did manage to negotiate the dangerous reefs, putting into a southwest inlet would be as good as stepping out of the briny broth onto a Carib barbecue. At least, so thought Captain Reners. Besides, the captain had no trading partners on Puerto Rico, and the odd sprain and bruise would not devalue the chattel. So he held the ship's course, shortened her sails, and rode through the tail end of the gale to the northeast cape of Hispaniola.

*

At daybreak, the coast of Hispaniola came into view. Jacob was surprised to see they were barely half a league from the shoals where clumps of rock jutted treacherously here and there out of the water. During the night, the beacons that had appeared on shore had seemed to indicate that the island was much further away. However, upon examination, Delpech could see that the lights must have been lit on the far side of a bay which was protected by a spit of land. And this spit reached a good deal further into the sea.

The mist rose, revealing a verdant landscape of singular beauty, and a ship wrecked on the rocks. Her sails had been struck. Debris was still dotted around her, which told Jacob the catastrophe must have happened recently, probably during the storm which the pink had met rounding the southwest coast of Puerto Rico. It was impossible to make out the ship's colours from the gun port, let alone her name, although what was left of the three masts made some of his fellow Huguenots fear the worst.

'Lord, let it not be *La Concorde*!' said Marianne Duvivier, clasping her hands together. The whole congregation prayed for the lost souls and could only hope the ship they had seen was not the one with which they had sailed out of Cadiz.

Realising that the men above deck did not share their concern, Jacob sent a message to Captain Reners, asking for a boat to be sent to investigate the wreckage. The captain, who until now had refused any moral, physical, or verbal contact with the prisoners, thought it best this time to meet their demand head-on. The whole voyage had gone incredibly well so far. He had only lost five galley slaves—two of whom had come aboard half-dead anyway—and no heretics, which was by far his personal best. It would be a pity to suffer any moral blight on his reputation so close to his port of delivery. And as for that wretched Huguenot chief, Reners did not doubt the man would not hesitate to make a nuisance of himself before the governor.

So, flanked by two guards, the captain bravely entered the Huguenot cell like the top dog he was to deliver his answer, despite the stench and the risk of contagion. Though slightly smaller than most would have imagined, he stood as large as life before them in all his fine glory, which made the Huguenot leader and his band of bedraggled brethren look ragged and pale in comparison. It was the first time the Huguenots had seen the captain of their ship close up. They all stood silent at first. Some doffed their hats, speechless and in awe.

Delpech, who had no hat to doff, levelled his eyes at the captain's when he said: 'But, Sir, are you not bound by Christian values, if not common decency, to investigate the tragedy? There might be survivors, by God.'

The captain remained calm and firm. He said: 'We are

not a navy ship, and that wreck is in Spanish waters. My commission is to get you to port safe and sound, not for you to be captured by savages and Spaniards. I regret I cannot be held to account for other people's failures. You must realise this is a very dangerous coast.'

'But, Sir,' returned Jacob, 'have some humanity!'

'I have plenty of humanity within this ship,' said the captain, remaining the perfect master of himself. 'The place reeks of humanity, and I do not intend to lose any of it!' He thought that rather good and inwardly congratulated himself for his calmness and quick wit. Even his guards were infected by his superior reasoning and could not help their smug smiles. He continued, 'If there are survivors, they will have been picked up by Spaniards or savages by now, so there is nothing we can do anyway. Now, I suggest you bear up and examine your conscience in preparation for your new domicile.'

There, he thought, no one could accuse him of being dismissive or inhuman, or of failing to have a Christian heart. He was satisfied it would eventually sink into their scabby heads that he was acting for the good of all aboard. Moreover, he secretly looked forward to seeing the governor's face when he brought his pink to port ahead of *La Concorde*.

Despite Jacob's insistence, the captain stoically stepped out of the dank jail, and without so much as a glance towards the other unfortunate cabin, he made his way to his quarters for some fresh air.

Any captain ought to know to keep well away from that part of the island, he thought, not only because of the perilous rocks but because of Spanish wreckers who at night shone their lamps to provoke navigational errors. With a ship smashed and all aboard drowned or cut to shreds on the reef, they could tranquilly pick off the cargo that lay strewn along the shore. But Captain Joseph Reners, who well understood the practices and motivations of cruel people, never had trusted such lamps, even on his first voyage. He had always put double the usual distance between the shore and his ship.

The whingeing heretics should thank their Protestant God they had been transported under his command, he said to himself back in his cabin, as he poured himself another tot of rum to take away the foul taste of squalor.

*

A north-easterly wind filled the pink's sails as she bore westward along the north-facing coast of Hispaniola. This was the name Jacob knew Columbus had given to the island 196 years earlier. The French now occupied the western side which they called Saint-Domingue. Even a league from the shore, this, the longest Caribbean island Jacob had seen so far, was a spectacle of beauty. Dense forests of broadleaved trees that covered the foothills, palm trees that fringed the tracts of golden sand, and conifers that reached up the mountain sides gave it an aura of Eden.

The island's mountain ranges were some of the highest in the whole of the Spanish Main. Consequently, there were quick variations in climate. Sometimes a leaden mass of cloud would darken the horizon to such an extent that it seemed inevitable that the ship would be in for a deluge. But the threatening clouds yonder that flared up with great flashes of lightning invariably dissipated come nightfall, and more often than not, the waxing moon shone large and bright.

The wind direction was not always constant and sometimes followed the morning sun, then blew westward again. But come midday the sea often became very calm, and progress was slow. Thankfully, this was not the hurricane season, and the last leg of the voyage passed by without further incident.

On the eleventh of February, they dropped anchor between Saint-Domingue and Tortuga Island, where a contrary current and lack of wind obliged them to wait.

The following morning, the pink weighed anchor for the last time with the Huguenots aboard. She anchored at midnight off Port-de-Paix, where the governor of Saint-Domingue had his residence.

*

Jacob had lost weight, his body was drained, and his joints were stiff, but his chances of escape were better than ever. He was looking forward to standing with solid earth beneath his feet after five long months aboard the ship in abominable conditions.

However, the governor, Monsieur Tarin de Cussy, an orderly man of principle, only allowed sick Protestants and the galley slaves to disembark, the latter to be sold.

It was not until three days after their arrival in the roadstead of Port-de-Paix that the rest of the Huguenots were able to leave the detestable pink, but only to embark on another vessel, coincidentally called *La Maria*, which had not long dropped anchor. She was under the command of Monsieur de Beauguy, a newly converted Catholic and captain of the king's navy.

The governor gave the order to assign the Huguenots to

Leogane, a port village sixty leagues from Port-de-Paix, which lay along the west coast in Gonâve bay. From experience, the governor knew it was wise to mix slaves, indentured workers, and prisoners throughout the territory rather than congregate them in tightly knit communities. A concentration of one type would only lead to friction and the need for rigorous repression, which was good for no one. The idea then was to build communities with a mixed bag of subjugated subjects. "Divide and rule" was the governor's motto. De Cussy was indeed a clever man, and what is more, well born. His excellent breeding and fine manners meant that his word was taken with solemnity, and it was so eloquently delivered that it was difficult for the commoner to contest his reasoning without seeming uncouth and coarse.

With simple elegance he stood on the middeck steps before the group of bedraggled Huguenots and said: 'This little voyage will last three or four days. I pray you will find some comfort at your port of destination, where you will live among many former Protestants who came here to start a new life. It is our hope that you will understand why they became Catholic, and that you too will become royal subjects once again.'

Jacob had heard it all before, but before the governor returned above deck, he raised his finger and asked: 'Sir, if I may. We are without news of *La Concorde*, which transported many of our brethren from Marseille. Would you be so kind as to light our lantern?'

'I am sorry, my good man,' said the governor, tactfully feigning to ignore the grubbiness of the well-spoken gentleman in front of him. How easily an individual could lose all trace of decorum and respectability, it was frightening, he thought to himself. Instinctively slipping a hand beneath the gold-braided edge of his red satin waistcoat, he continued: 'I am unable to divulge information of the whereabouts of your co-religionists, or any of the king's adversaries for that matter. I trust you will understand that I am under oath.'

'But, Sir, please,' said Mademoiselle Duvivier, taking a resolute step forward. She had more important things on her mind than the shame of her appearance. Besides, if she could face the embarrassment and humiliation of crossing the ocean with no privacy at all, she could jolly well stand up, albeit in rags, to a frilly-sleeved middle-aged nobleman. She said, 'We saw a ship wrecked on the rocks last week as we came into sight of this island. Our captain said it was too dangerous for him to investigate. We should very much like to know whether or not *La Concorde* has come safely to port, Sir.'

'I am sorry, Mademoiselle,' said the governor, with a pinch of impatience, 'I have no such information to impart to prisoners of His Highness.'

'But, Sir, please,' insisted the girl. 'My grandmother was on le Concorde!'

The governor calmly and in a lordly manner held up a hand, as one who was used to wielding authority and negotiating with rebels, slaves, and savages. 'If you desire the assistance of a king's officer,' he said with an indulgent, almost paternal smile, 'it goes without saying you must be a friend of the French state.'

The governor's time was counted, his mind crowded by a multitude of other concerns. The interview was thus curtailed with elegance, but curtailed all the same. He nodded to Captain de Beauguy, standing at the capstan for him to give the order to weigh anchor. Then he retired to his cabin.

FOUR

'DON'T THANK ME, Madame Fleuret,' said Jeanne Delpech, handing the roll of fabric to the carpenter's wife. 'The loom does all the clever work!'

'True enough, but it wouldn't work at all without Madame's deft fingers and keen eye, and a good head on her shoulders, would it? my word!'

Jeanne smiled without reserve at Ginette Fleuret's way with words, typical of southern French folk and reminiscent of her own hometown. She was nonetheless glad that Madame Fleuret had learnt to lower the volume to a level more suited to Genevan manners—more restrained, more concise, and less exuberant than in the Mediterranean walled city of Aigues-Mortes. That being said, given her talent for dressmaking, few minded her Mediterranean vociferations, for Ginette would willingly fit out woman and child without taking a single *kreutzer* piece for her toil, provided she was given the fabric. And together, Jeanne and Ginette had made an unlikely match.

They were standing in Saint-Germain's church under the fine carved pulpit which, true to Calvinist tradition, was situated midway down the nave on one side. The church—whose interior walls presented remnants of colour and empty statuette niches that bore witness to its Catholic past—was peopled mostly with women of all ages and rank, some chatting in clusters, some sipping hot soup around trestle tables. This was the midweek get-together where Huguenot refugees and local parishioners could exchange news and views, offer mutual assistance, and sing psalms together. Numbers had swollen since Jeanne's first visit in October, and these days French Protestants by far outnumbered Genevans.

The church had become an assembly point as much for establishing contacts as for bolstering faith. It was a favourite place for Jeanne where she could encounter God, refugees, and her customers all under the same roof. Here she could distribute her rolls of fabric to French fugitives who were able to pay, and to the needy who could not. People travelled great distances in harsh conditions to reach the walled city of Geneva, and more often than not, their first requirement, after food and lodging, was a new set of clothes. Ginette had unreservedly volunteered to help those without dressmaking skills. In this way, the mutual aid had brought people closer together, and their church had become a happy sanctuary—the ringing of laughter during such meetings bore testimony—despite its austere interior.

'How is your husband faring now?' said Jeanne, placing her empty earthenware beaker on the trestle table.

'He says he misses his bouillabaisse, which means he's recovered his appetite. Otherwise he's happy as a clam at high water now that he's helping down at the sawmill.'

Ginette Fleuret lived down near the river with her

husband and three children. It was damp and penetratingly cold, but they had all recovered from their winter fevers, and they were not unhappy. Their lives might have radically changed in this colder climate, but now at least they were at one with their conscience. Wasn't that worth all the sun in the French Midi?

'Good. But we'll have to find you somewhere away from the damp.'

'Couldn't do that, Madame Delpech. We'd be all at sea if we didn't at least have a view over the water, my word; never lived without it. Anyway, I shall crack on with this little lot with Madame Lachaume.'

'I am so glad you were able to make space for her little family. It is becoming increasingly difficult to find accommodation within the city walls.'

'Difficult? Ironic, I'd say. Ironic, my word! My Jeannot volunteered to help build up the new floors on Taconnerie Square, but the guild won't have it, not without a work permit. Result, they've got too much on their hands, and my Jeannot ain't got enough. I don't know what we'd live on without the relief fund, I'm sure. So I'm only too glad to pay something back, Madame Delpech. Puts me on a level pegging, see? But if things don't move forward by the time the warm weather comes along, then we'll have to be moving on to pastures greener, where we are wanted!'

'You might have to be patient, dear Madame Fleuret. The Genevans do have a penchant for things done well, and unfortunately, that takes time . . .'

'Well, I call it stalling. Most of us would be working by now if it weren't for their licences for this and their permits for that.'

Jeanne had grown used to Ginette's little rants and was not offended by what could have been taken as blatant ingratitude. After all, it wasn't the fault of Genevans if they were on the French king's doorstep. But there again, Ginette was only voicing what everyone else thought deep down. This was the centre of Protestantism, after all, and they deserved to be treated as all God's children, did they not?

'I'll leave you to your ponderings, Madame Fleuret, I am expected at the tailor's,' said Jeanne. 'Which reminds me, my coat. Where's my coat?' Jeanne stared blankly at the empty pew in front of her, where she had been sitting during the service. Her coat was there a minute earlier. For the first time, Ginette read anxiety in Jeanne's eyes. However, looking past Jeanne's shoulder, she saw the ragged-looking man whom she secretly called the pauper, walking up behind her.

'Madame Delpech, I believe this is yours,' said the ragged-looking man.

His name was Cephas Crespin. Of average height, in his mid-thirties, he usually helped the vicar out with putting away tables and chairs and such like. His distinguishing feature was mutilated thumbs, which he claimed had been placed in thumbscrews to persuade him to abjure.

Every time he went to a church service, Cephas Crespin felt amusement mixed with anger, but he kept it to himself. There he was amidst the niceties, trying to start over again, on par with everyone else, but try as he would, he could not get the coarseness out of his voice. It was just unfair. Any attempt at fancy language and fine manners just made him stick out, and whose fault was it if he had been earmarked from birth? Didn't God put paupers on the earth to test rich people's conscience? He never wanted to be a Lazarus, though, made to feed on leftovers. Yet when you were born as common as muck, that was all you could expect. However, at least the after-service soup made him feel better again. There was nothing better than a hot bowl of soup for spiritual comfort and peace within.

'Thank you, Monsieur Crespin,' said Jeanne, relieved to find her coat folded over the pauper's arm, though she tried not to show it.

'Let me hold it for you, Madame Delpech,' said Cephas, 'so you can put it on.' Cephas liked to hold coats for the ladies; the clumsiness caused by his disability always brought a smile of pity. As the pauper held out Jeanne's coat, his expression changed from one of polite obedience to one indicating an alarming realisation.

'Feels like you've got the family jewels in there, Madame Delpech, ha ha,' he joked.

'Ha ha, no, no,' said Jeanne with a level smile. 'I've weighted the hem with pebbles, Monsieur Crespin, that is all. It helps keep it from flapping in the wind, and I like to feel the benefit of the weight on my shoulders.' She remained high-minded, unflappable. But the pauper could have sworn it was a different kind of stone she had sewn inside the lining. He said no more about it as Jeanne's gaze turned to her nine-year-old son, running up to her with another boy, slightly older, southern-skinned with a forthright smile. Young Pierre, who most people called Pierrot, was a practical lad and clever with his hands.

'Mama,' said Paul, 'can I stay with Pierrot till lunchtime?'

'I am sure his mother has enough on her plate,' said Jeanne, who hated to see her son leave her side for five minutes, let alone a few hours.

43

'Get away, woman, he'll be no trouble,' said Ginette. 'They can help gather offcuts down at the mill for our fire!'

'Please, I never go anywhere,' said the boy. Jeanne could not dismiss the fact that he needed some leash after being cooped up in a room all winter long. Besides going to church, his only outings without her had been to fetch up water from the Molard Square fountain below their rooms, and even that he accomplished under her watchful eye.

'Youngsters do need their running-around time,' said Ginette, with a wink to the lads.

'I'll look after him, Madame, promise,' said Pierrot, who was a head taller than Paul.

'And I'll get Jeannot to walk him home safe and sound in time for his lunch.'

'Fair enough,' said Jeanne, trying her best not to sound too put out. 'I shall be off to the tailor's on my own then.' She could not resist the impulse of trying to make her son feel guilty for his momentary freedom. It was not envy but fear that put the words into her mouth. She had lost him once. She was petrified of losing him again.

'Then I shall accompany you!' said a mirthful voice.

Jeanne twisted her torso. 'Claire! I thought it was you I saw earlier,' she said as Ginette's boy tugged Paul's sleeve with a wink, and the lads shot off across the crowded church before Paul's mother could change her mind.

*

Wrapped up in woollen layers, booted and shawled for the season, the two ladies stepped into the sharp March morning from the vestry door. Despite the jaw-trembling cold, the sky seemed to be lifting, and patches of clear icy blue were

44

widening. They walked briskly at first, to distance themselves from the stench of the noblemen's stables that stood opposite the church building.

Jeanne knew that Claire had some trouble on her mind, that she wanted a word in private. Why else would she have turned up late at church in her condition, only to leave ten minutes later? The young lady with whom Jeanne had escaped out of France now had a double hoop ring on her finger and a baby in her belly, having been sworn into wedlock shortly after her arrival in Geneva. Her cheeks were already fuller and her bump, despite the amplitude of her robes, was becoming visible. And she needed her mother. In her absence, Claire often sought guidance from Jeanne, who tacitly complied.

'Has the sickness passed at all?' she said as they emerged from the narrow passage that led into the busy Grand-Rue, lined with boutiques. The puddles that only yesterday crunched under foot now splashed muddy slurry which speckled ladies' hems and gentlemen's stockings.

'Yes. No, not quite, but I do feel less queasy,' said Claire, with an anxious but brave smile. 'I do not mind the sickness so much. It is the salivating I cannot abide. I keep wanting to empty my mouth. Now I know why a pregnant market woman I once saw kept spitting all the time like a trooper; I well recall how it verily put me off my purchases. I understand now how she must have felt. I cannot go anywhere without a pile of handkerchiefs.'

'It will pass, my dear Claire, or you will have to get Etienne to follow you about with a pillowcase!' Claire let out a jovial laugh and swiped her mouth with her handkerchief again. Jeanne continued. 'Unless you learn to spit like your market lady!'

'Oh, no, I could not do that,' said Claire, laughing mirthfully and momentarily losing her look of anxiety.

'How is Etienne progressing with his plans?'

'He is not,' said Claire, her face now etched anew with lines of worry. 'Formalities, endless formalities.'

'For a man of means, it is surely only a question of time,' said Jeanne, thinking to herself how impatient and demanding the younger generation were becoming. 'Once he has his licence and has been admitted into the guild, he will be settled for many years to come. For from what I gather, decisions made here are meant to last. It is why they take so long in making them.'

'But what about the resident?'

'Monsieur Dupré thankfully has no executive power here. This is not France.'

'Yet.'

'They cannot invade. If they try, the northern cantons will declare war.'

'The mere thought makes me shudder.'

'And Geneva is a republic. Besides that, the king's resident is not loved in Genevan circles, I can assure you.'

'Perhaps, but he can keep up the pressure to prevent us from being able to earn a livelihood.'

'Fear not, my dear Claire. You have enough to worry about with your baby.'

'That is the problem. I do wonder where I am going to have it, and who will be with me.'

'I shall, of course.'

In a more sombre tone, Claire said, 'Etienne is worried that he will not be allowed a permit to work. He wonders if we are wasting our time here.'

'He wants to move on?'

'Further away from France. We are seriously considering leaving next week, Jeanne.'

'I see.'

They turned right onto Rue du Soleil-Levant, a wide, well-to-do cobbled street of the upper town, where well-heeled ladies and gentlemen purchased their provisions and clothing. The tailor's boutique was at the top of the street. Remaining on the sunny side, they mutually slowed their pace to time their arrival with the end of their conversation.

Claire's announcement had roused Jeanne's own fears. In truth, she too had been anxious about residing in Geneva ever since she learnt about the French king's attempts, through the resident, to oblige Geneva magistrates to expel Huguenots from the republic, and send them packing back to their Catholic sovereign. Thankfully, the Swiss cantons of Bern and Zurich had responded by offering military support in case of imminent hostilities. And Geneva authorities had found pretext to reinforce the city's medieval fortifications. Consequently, Louis had tempered his tone, although his intentions towards fleeing French Protestants remained unchanged.

Prompted by false rumours—rumours spread by malevolent souls—tension in the crowded walled city was growing of late. More and more, Jeanne noticed hard stares from market wives, and ladies pursing their lips and flaring their nostrils as she passed them by. She overheard quips about Huguenots bringing the menace of war, complaints about the rise of the cost of living, and protests of the price of building more living space within the city walls by adding extra floors to the tall buildings of entire districts. The resident's strategy was worming its way slowly but surely into the thoughts of the population of the republican city. His informants and agents were doing a good job.

Jeanne's greater burden, however, was knowingly working illegally, even though half of her weaving was destined for the poor. The other half, which went to the moneyed church acquaintances, allowed her to pay her own way. She was not wronging local weavers, though; she did not poach on their clientele. And if she ceased to operate her loom, she would only constitute another strain on the already stretched Bourse Française, the Geneva refugee relief fund, which granted the poor two *batzen* a day to live on.

No, until she knew where in the world Jacob was, she would have to keep quashing her fears and stay put. Moreover, every step further north would be another step away from her children, taken away from her and now living in Montauban. Here, at least, she could receive news from her sister who, having converted to Catholicism, had been able to take them into her care.

'Etienne is keen to leave before the spring rush,' said Claire.

'Does he really think, despite having means, he would fail to secure a permit?'

'He is not sure, but both he and my uncle agree that the king has too strong a hold over Geneva. They believe the magistrates will not be able to stave off his demands forever. Then what would become of us? Etienne feels we would be safer and better off in the Duchy of Prussia where the grand elector is calling for Huguenot tradesmen to settle in Brandenburg.'

'But should you not wait till the baby is born?' said Jeanne.

'If the baby is born in October, we should not be able to leave until next spring. That means another year's wait,' said Claire, catching saliva from her mouth again with her handkerchief.

'I see.'

'Etienne says he does not mind going ahead without me first, and then fetching me once he is settled. I know not what to do, Jeanne.'

The two ladies were now standing at the roadside, letting an elegant carriage rattle by. Jeanne placed a gloved hand on the younger woman's forearm and said, 'He is a kind and considerate young man. But no, my dear Claire, you must not let him go without you. You must stay together for better and for worse. He will love you all the more for it.'

Claire laid her free mittened hand upon Jeanne's, and the two ladies crossed over the Rue du Soleil-Levant.

*

It was not yet eleven o'clock when Jeanne pushed the glass door and sailed into the spacious room of the master tailor's workshop. The conversation with Claire had allowed her not to dwell on the meeting with Maître Bordarier. But now, inside the muted room where cut cloth and an assortment of garments were hung up on rails, she suddenly became conscious of her nervousness. Claire followed her to the light-wood counter that stood eight yards into the boutique.

On the other side of it, three young seamstresses, who had glanced up at the pleasant ping of the doorbell, again buried their heads in their needlework. They were seated cross-legged on cushions, darning and sewing, on a very large table in front of the rear window that faced them. A well-endowed lady approaching middle-age, sitting on a stool by the stove, put down her work. Getting to her feet, she gave a professional smile and approached the counter. While passing her eyes from Jeanne's waist, up her shawl that had seen better days, and to her simple coif, in a superior voice she said, 'Madame?'

Jeanne knew full well the woman recognised her from a previous visit. Nothing put fire in her veins like being treated with scorn, and her apprehension quickly turned to steely determination. Holding her head high, she said, 'Madame. I have an appointment with Maître Bordarier.'

Jeanne had become acquainted with the master tailor after delivering fabric, made for a gentleman churchgoer for the master tailor to turn into a long coat and breeches to match. One thing leading to another, Bordarier, who appreciated the quality of Jeanne's weaving, asked her if she would care to produce the cotton fabric that was all the rage in Europe, including France, where it had been forbidden by French customs. This meant that there was a fortune to be made there with the right network.

Bordarier, a spindly, clean-shaven fifty-year-old, was busy measuring a gentleman from shoulder to thigh with the aid of his assistant, a certain Michel Chaulet. Chaulet, in his early thirties, stole a sly glance at the French ladies as Jeanne turned to face the tailor. She had noticed the young man's hard stare before when she once dropped off a roll of caddis, a coarse but robust fabric, from which the tailor had agreed to make capes for the poor. But this time she thought she saw the young man almost gloating, which sent a shudder down her spine. She knew full well from her church client that Chaulet's brother-in-law was also a weaver. But Jeanne had no intention of pinching someone else's work. She had agreed to produce the sample as a thank-you gift for the tailor's help with producing clothes for poor Huguenots at a discount which, nonetheless, also gave him access to their wealthier co-religionists.

On hearing Jeanne's voice, Maître Bordarier looked over his shoulder. Peering over his pince-nez, he called out, 'Ah, Madame Delpech.' He then left his customer in the hands of Chaulet so he could join her at the counter. 'Thank you, Madame Laborde.' The big-bosomed lady waddled back to her stool near the stove.

'This is what I came up with, Monsieur,' said Jeanne, spreading the square piece of fabric over the smooth surface of the counter, while trying not to let her words slip into her throat. She had spent hours threading the loom. But that was no reason to be nervous about the tailor's judgement, she told herself. It wasn't as if she owed him anything.

Perhaps it was not the thought of his judgement but the prospect of his approbation that made her nervous. And perhaps, though she expected nothing in return, she nurtured a secret hope—the hope of a woman bordering on poverty.

Claire, standing beside her, let out a gasp of admiration at the shimmering blue fabric. The tailor adjusted his pince-nez on the bridge of his nose, then touched the fabric with his open palm, spreading out his fingers wide to fully appreciate the texture. Jeanne was suddenly anxious about being found out that she was no more a weaver than Claire was a fishwife, or Ginette a countess.

She was suddenly fearful of being found out, of being labelled an impostor. How could she for one second dare to consider herself as good as a trained weaver, a seamstress, or even a spinner? The tailor glanced up with a raised eyebrow. She was regretting having accepted the offer to show off her handicraft. Surely any master tailor would see straight through her, she thought, as he now held up the cloth to the light to see how the threads interwove, and how evenly they were beaten.

He placed the cloth back down on the table, whipped off his pince-nez, and blinked at the French lady standing before him, oblivious to the turmoil going on inside her. He said, 'You are gifted, Madame.' Jeanne said nothing, instead emptied her mind of any thought that would cause her eyes to fill up. 'I should like to place an order, for twelve yards to begin with. Then we shall see how we can proceed.'

The woman on the stool, who had pricked up her ears, could not resist a secret smile from pleating the corners of her mouth. For a moment Jeanne thought she had maybe misread the woman's jealousy. Yet, it seemed so out of character.

*

'Why did you say you would think about it?' said Claire once they were back in the street, and had walked out of earshot from the boutique.

'Don't get me wrong, I am very flattered, but it puts me in a predicament. You see, if I refuse, the tailor might be offended. He might accuse me of only wanting to work with French Huguenots, and of remaining in my clan. And that is precisely what we do not want.'

'All the more reason to accept, then. It will put an end to your money worries. It might even be the debut of a successful business. That is how the Turrettinis made their fortune, you know.'

'Don't tease. Besides, if I accept, I will have the whole guild of weavers upon me.'

'Not if you don't tell them.'

'They are bound to find out sooner than later, especially in the present climate.'

'I know. Why don't you make a deal with a local weaver?'

'Actually, that is what I was thinking. But I do not know whether a weaver would take on a woman. I have to find out how to go about it first.'

'I dare say, if you bring profit . . .' said Claire, clapping her hands. 'Oh, Jeanne, how exciting for you!' They made their way across the cathedral square towards the Madeleine district, where Claire resided with Etienne and her great uncle. In her enthusiasm, she must have dropped her handkerchief along the way, and with nothing to hand, she now had the choice of either swallowing a mouthful of frothy saliva or discreetly spitting it out. 'Oh, my gosh, look away!'

'Claire!' said Jeanne with mirth in her eyes as the young woman spat out a blob of spittle onto the cobbles like a trooper.

'I am sorry,' she said in guilty giggles, and she brought out a spare white-lace handkerchief with which she wiped strands of drool from her mouth. 'I didn't see that coming.'

The ladies hurried along arm in arm into Rue de L'Eveché, cheerfully leaving their improper conduct behind.

'But wouldn't it be formidable?' said Claire.

'It is true, I would be able to put some money aside for when I recover my other children,' said Jeanne. Then in a lower voice, she said, 'Keep this under your bonnet, but my sister plans to leave France with her husband at the end of spring.' The instant her secret was out, she almost regretted divulging it. But she was glad to tell someone about the long-awaited letter she had received the day before, which Pastor Duveau had passed on to her. Besides, she knew Claire would keep the news to herself. The two women had developed a trusting relationship, and Jeanne would be sorry to see her go.

'Jeanne, how doubly wonderful!' said Claire, who did not need to be told that it meant they would bring Jeanne's children with them.

'Shh.'

'So you must accept the tailor's offer. He did say you were gifted.'

'I had good teachers,' said Jeanne.

Claire knew from previous confidences that Jeanne was referring to her maid and a weaver in whose workshop she had hidden for a year and a half in France to escape imprisonment. 'I foresee a bright future for you.'

'I am not sure about that, but the extra will definitely not do any harm.'

'It is surely a godsend, Jeanne.'

'Is it, though? For I shall nonetheless be an illegal worker. Sometimes the difficulty is in knowing whether a thing is a godsend or a lure of the devil, is it not?'

'I do know what you mean,' said Claire with a sigh. 'Choices.' They had stopped before the large door of a tall, elegant building made of fine masonry.

Jeanne touched the younger woman's arm and said, 'Listen, Claire, as long as you do not overstretch yourself, there is no reason why you should not go on that journey. You are not ill.'

'Yes,' said Claire, emptying her mouth again into her damp handkerchief, 'you are right.'

'He will need your support; they all do. Our position, my dear, is to endear them to common sense. Otherwise there would be even less of it in this mad world, would there not!'

Jeanne declined Claire's offer to ask Etienne to accompany her back to her rooms. 'As I told Pastor Duveau, I am perfectly capable of walking the streets on my own,' she said with a smile. 'And I want to stop off at the butcher's for a surprise lunch for Paul,' she said, hinting at the money the tailor had given her for her sample.

Jeanne left Claire to pass through the tall door and then wended her way back to Rue du Perron. She liked taking this route which sloped down steeply from Saint Pierre's hill into the lower town. From the top she could see the blue, shimmering water of Lake Geneva. Its proximity gave her comfort. For in the event of hostilities, she would only have to board a boat to flee to the northern Swiss cantons.

She was glad to be able to walk on her own and think everything through. How could she turn down such a lucrative offer? Could it really be pennies from heaven? However, her mind would soon be made up for her.

FIVE

'THE KING OF FRANCE sees no harm in your reinforcing your fortifications, as long as you do not employ Swiss soldiers to do so,' said Monsieur Roman Dupré in his usual courteous, albeit condescending manner.

The French resident was sitting in his sumptuous office with the fat syndic, Monsieur Ezéchiel Gallatin, whose large buttocks comfortably filled the low, wide armchair on the other side of the ministerial desk.

Monsieur Dupré continued. 'Why, it would be defeating the object, for you would have your potential enemy inside the city walls even before hostilities began!'

'With all due respect, my Lord,' said Gallatin, 'our Swiss allies offered their support because they were afraid that His Majesty would invade Geneva and the republic.'

'Nonsense,' said Dupré with a dry laugh, 'mere fabricated rumours!'

Gently patting the edge of the polished desktop with his large, chubby fingers, the syndic said, 'Monsieur de Croissy did warn he would take action if we continued to harbour Huguenots, did he not?'

'A reaction of the moment, and I might add, only to be expected. They are, after all, the king's subjects, are they not?' said the resident with a courteous, thin smile—a facial technique honed in Versailles which subtly suggested he had urgent business to attend to and had no time for pettiness.

However, the seasoned syndic, having often rubbed shoulders with the elite on missions to Paris, was not to be intimidated. For sure, his rotund appearance lacked the physical elegance of his French counterpart, but he had personality, patience, and a deceivingly smart sense of business—and what is more, any verbal blows seemed to bounce off him like little cherub fists punching into a bloated pig's bladder. So, remaining solidly seated, he said, 'We could hardly throw them out in the middle of winter, my Lord. As you are well aware, we make a point in Geneva of putting up any subjects of His Gracious Majesty, in spite of the cost.'

'I assure you we do understand the predicament, Monsieur the Syndic. And I am all the more pleased to inform you that His Majesty has found a means of dropping the tithe case lodged against you.' Gallatin gave a slow nod of his large head as a sign of deep gratitude. Dupré continued. 'It is thus hoped that our mutual understanding shall be rewarded, and that the tithes from the region of Gex will serve to replenish your coffers, emptied by the king's subjects who are outstaying their welcome.'

'Yes, my Lord. My colleagues, indeed the population of Geneva, are most grateful for your intervention in the matter.' He was referring to an attempt by the authorities of Gex to recover a tithe which was customarily paid to Geneva.

'What is more, His Majesty extends his affection to the people of Geneva and promises to provide continued protection against enemy invasion. And he insists, my dear Sir, that he had no intention of invading. Fabricated rumours, that is all.'

'I am sure, my Lord.'

'However, he does advise you to be henceforth more cautious regarding the *good intentions* of your Swiss neighbours. For it is evident that Bern and Zurich are trying to lull you into letting their soldiers enter the city without any resistance at all, God forbid. His Majesty therefore warns you, with love and fervour, not to fall victim to their malicious ploy.'

'Yes, my Lord.'

'Otherwise he will have no choice but to take action in your defence. I am sure you will understand, Sir.'

'Yes, my Lord. Rest assured, as I said, the Council of Geneva are most grateful for our illustrious ally's continued support and protection.'

The resident gave another thin smile and got to his feet, which this time obliged the syndic to do likewise. The resident grinned condescendingly at Gallatin who, because of his cumbersome weight, did not wear heels, unlike Dupré, who was consequently able to tower over the fat syndic as he said, 'And you must keep your word regarding the Huguenots! And this time please remember to send them south, not north.'

'My Lord,' said Gallatin, bowing on the other side of the desk, 'you have our reassurances that they will be asked to leave come spring, as agreed. Moreover, it will ease our relief fund, which has been a bit stretched lately, as you well know.'

The resident showed the syndic to his door, both men satisfied with what they had achieved. The Genevans had gained the king's assurance his army would not invade, plus the unhoped-for tithes of Gex; they had also gained precious time, something the Genevans were inherently good at. The French had gained the imminent banishment of Huguenots from Geneva.

*

Five minutes later, the resident was standing in his private chamber, accessed by a door set in the panelling of his vast study. He was gloating over the mahogany serving table stacked with savoury dossiers, each contributing to his grand project—the exclusion of Huguenots from Geneva, thus removing one major route into Germany and Holland.

Roland Dupré had built his reputation on his diplomatic ability, and also on his methodical mindset that gave him the intellectual agility to pursue several channels of intelligence simultaneously. He had learnt from experience that it would be unwise, indeed counterproductive, to bank solely on the action of the magistrates for the success of his project. For magistrates in a republic required the driving voice of the people—in other words, bourgeois, merchants, and guilds. So he had been painstakingly building up a network of agents to fan the fire of discontent among the population.

It is something His Excellence, the Minister of Foreign Affairs, Monsieur Colbert de Croissy, surely failed to fully grasp, keen as he was to please the king. One had to coax the Genevans into submission on their own terms; any precipitation would inevitably backfire. And what in God's name had got into the minister to wave the threat of invasion? wondered Dupré. Now they were capable of bringing Bern and Zurich soldiers inside the very city, which would be awkward, to say the least, what with the Dutch crisis. No, he thought, gently does it with the Genevans, and that takes time, a good network, and a table full of dossiers.

He picked up the one concerning the trade guild which was slowly but surely being fired up against refugee carpenters taking work from the tax-paying native. Then there was the housing dossier which was coming along nicely, what with refugees pushing up the prices, which was a paradox because the weavers were complaining about illegal cheap labour driving the prices down. He had the situation in hand. All he had to do was to keep gently pushing, and the magistrates would have no choice but to carry out the terms of their agreement.

A scratching at the door brought Roland Dupré out of his projections. Without looking up from his desk, 'Entrez!' he said.

'My Lord, a message,' said the valet. Dupré held out his hand, eyes still glued to his table of dossiers. He brought the sealed letter into his field of view. He would normally lay it down at this point, but this one rumpled his brow.

'That will be all,' he said, taking a cutter to the seal.

He opened the message and read: *Job done, lady in for a surprise*.

With a smile of satisfaction, Roland Dupré placed the message in the dossier titled "Weavers."

*

Today, more than any other day, Jeanne Delpech enjoyed descending into the Rues Basses of the lower town. She now felt that she knew them as well as the alleyways of her natal Montauban. She admired the Genevan love for things well made, and their practical approach borne of necessity: the sheltered stalls on one side of the thoroughfare, the central carriageway for horse-drawn traffic, and the convenient *dômes*—protruding roofs or upper floors that advanced over the street, providing shelter to pedestrians come rain, shine, or snow.

The blue patches of sky put smiles on faces and joviality into banter despite the nip in the air. Jeanne too felt that a cloud was being lifted from over her. She had received professional approbation of her work; she would no longer feel embarrassed or unqualified about asking the small price she charged for her cloth. It even occurred to her that she could increase it in par with market rates. If Maître Bordarier thought her good enough to provide him with cloth, there was no reason why she could not aspire to become a fully-fledged weaver in the eyes of the guild, even if it meant working for a master weaver. Pity the council still would not authorise Huguenots to work for a living, she thought to herself with an inward sigh.

For now, though, she put the thought to one side as she purchased a choice piece of tournedos and a cabbage on Molard Square, where the vendors were beginning to pack away their wares. Dockers on the far end were stacking articles and merchandise from France by the lake harbour. The bakery below Jeanne's third-floor rooms was animated with late-morning customers. Commis were tidying up after the morning bake, and Madame Poulain was serving an old lady behind the large counter where wooden racks contained the last of the day's round loaves. As the baker's wife took the change, she lifted her head to see who had just walked in. Her commercial smile vanished, and her chubby jowls sagged as her eyes met Jeanne's.

'Whatever is the matter, Madame Poulain?' said Jeanne, taken aback by the woman's visible anguish.

'There's been an incident, Madame Delpech,' said the woman.

Jeanne felt weak in the stomach as she raised her free hand to her mouth. 'Lord, no, please, not my Paul,' she said, suddenly hot, pallid, and trembling.

'No, Madame, not Paul, not your family either.'

Jeanne nearly passed out with relief. Then, realising what could be the only other cause for such concern, she dumped her provisions on the counter, lifted her skirts, and hurried out to the stairway entrance before Madame Poulain could utter further explanation.

On the third-floor landing, she encountered Monsieur Poulain fixing a forced door, her door.

'We heard a banging noise and thought for a minute someone was moving furniture,' he said, standing aside to let her into the room. 'Then, before we realised what was up, a couple of blokes came bolting down the stairs, and off they went.'

Even before setting her eyes on the shambles inside, she knew it was her livelihood they had come to wreck. The frame of her loom was shattered—beaten by sledgehammers by the looks of the dents in the wood—smashed and rendered unusable.

Across the wall, an untutored hand had painted in red the words: 'Geneva For Genevans. Huguenots Get Out!'

SIX

'SO YOU SEE, my dear Delpech,' said Monsieur Verbizier, in whose home Jacob had taken quarters. 'Be you Protestant or Catholic, you're better off here than in the Old World, are you not? For there, as you well know, your livelihood can be taken away on the whim of a king!'

Monsieur Elias Verbizier was a self-taught, free-thinking convert whose heart swayed more to the balance of power than with religious fervour. But if one thing made him angry, it was a state-run monopoly, and he secretly hoped the French king would get his comeuppance for all the monies he had been made to pay in tobacco taxes.

Born into a Protestant family of rope makers, he had left his native La Rochelle as a young man in search of his fortune. He had been a planter in the early days of the buccaneers on Tortuga Island. Now in the force of age, he owned one of the largest plantations in Leogane.

Delpech had been listening to his host's update of events in Europe with one ear. The planter had been relating that a league of states neighbouring France had been set up on the suggestion of William of Orange—the champion of

Protestantism and sworn enemy of Louis XIV—to counter potential French aggression. They called it the League of Augsburg. But even this might not suffice to contain the French king, as events in England were taking a surprising turn. William's father-in-law, James II, who was also Louis's cousin, had refused to join the league and was attempting to catholicise his country. Indeed, should James's pregnant Italian-born wife give birth to a boy, a Catholic dynasty would be established again in England.

However, neither Louis nor William nor James was among Jacob's concerns—that is to say, not yet. He said, 'I grant you that starting a life afresh in such a new world certainly has its advantages.' He took another sip of coffee and then continued, 'But as for myself, there is no place better on earth than with one's family. In a Christian home, which, I might add, is a home without slaves.'

They were sitting on the ground-floor balcony, finishing their breakfast of exotic fruits, dried sausage, bread, jam, and coffee. The planter's residence, one of a few made of stone, was built near a vigorous stream that ran down from the densely wooded mountain. It offered a splendid view over the township of Leogane on the backdrop of the beautiful teal-blue anchorage.

The large tract of land that stretched out before them was divided into fields of indigo, cotton, tobacco, and sugar cane. Especially sugar cane.

The present harvesting period was proving successful, and there was still a good month left of cutting cane and distilling the juices into sugarloaves. On a normal day, Negro slaves would have long since been hard at work. But today was Sunday. Instead of the usual animation of hacking, hauling, thrashing, grinding, and digging, the air was filled with blithe indolence and the laughter of children.

Jacob cast his eyes a hundred and fifty yards down the slope to the left, where trees screened the slave shacks. A headless chicken was running round with a bunch of slave sprogs dancing along after it.

Elias Verbizier contentedly scanned his possessions. He was at peace with the world, more so than ever before, now that the Black Code decreed by King Louis gave him an official framework by which to properly administer his black population. His conscience was clear. And now, with these free Sundays, the death rate had fallen, which meant fewer trips to the slave market, and the yield so far had made an extraordinary profit. He was so glad he had made the switch from tobacco to sugar cane. This is the life, this is how it should be, he thought. How could the gentleman sitting next to him want to go back to the Old World?

But there again, once the Huguenot had settled into the benefits of the Indies, Elias felt sure the man would come to his senses. Not only that, it did not sit well with the planter to see such a qualified gentleman having a social status hardly higher than that of a mere slave. It did not fit into his notion of social order. At least being allowed to pay Delpech for his expertise would enable him to properly establish his ascendance. But for that, the man would have to fall into step with current standards.

Verbizier gave another puff of his pipe, then turned back to Jacob. He said: 'You've seen for yourself, farming would not be viable without good slaves. All this wouldn't exist. What do you think the Code Noir is for?'

'It is unchristian, Sir,' said Jacob.

'It is in the Bible, Sir,' said the planter. 'Slavery has been around since man first walked the earth.' Here he held up his right hand solemnly and rolled off the cuff a quote he had learnt by heart. He said: 'Your male and female slaves are to come from the nations around you; from them, you may buy slaves. They will become your property!'

Jacob had never confronted slavery and at first was disconcerted by its overwhelming acceptance. He could not help feeling uncomfortable about it. He had prayed for enlightenment and had come upon a passage in the New Testament which he now used to respond to the planter's argument. He said, 'The teachings of Christ are thus: there is neither Jew nor Greek, there is neither bond nor free, there is neither male nor female, for ye are all one in Christ Jesus!'

'Hah, tit for tat, fair dos,' said Monsieur Verbizier, who was always game for a battle of wits. He lifted himself lithely out of his rattan chair. 'But come with me, Delpech,' he said. 'I have something to show you that might make you think twice about your movements of the soul.'

Verbizier had decided the time was right. He was ready to give Delpech some enlightenment, the same that had freed him from religious foreboding and such like so many years ago. Since that fateful day, he had been able to adapt his opinion and behaviour according to his own advantage. And today he was a successful man. As for Delpech, he was still imprisoned by his hopes of heaven which had made him so miserably poor. So Verbizier took it upon himself to free this poor man who deserved much more for his talents.

Jacob now found he could get up from his chair with hardly a crick or a crack. And he definitely felt that he had put on a bit of flesh. He no longer felt the sharpness of his bones on the seat. Life, it was true, was not so bad on the island. Small, perhaps. Remote, certainly. Impenetrable, without doubt. But apart from the wretched insect bites, he had become accustomed to its climate. And he had been working on Monsieur Verbizier, trying to make him realise the true Christian path. For in the short time he had been there, he had sensed the planter's want of spiritual direction.

Jacob followed into the cool and comfortable study where leather-bound books were displayed in a bookcase, and a series of sketches and paintings of Caribbean landscapes adorned the walls. A two-branched candelabrum was already lit on the acajou writing desk. Verbizier had displaced a brass telescope on a tripod and was pulling the shutters tight to completely shut out the morning sunlight.

'Do not fret, Delpech. I would just like to show you a little experiment of my own fabrication which I stumbled upon some time ago. I pray it will enable you to see some sense and help you out of your needless quandary. Now come, please.'

The planter closed the door and invited Jacob to the desk. He then pulled up a comfortable armchair and asked Jacob to take a pew on the one that was already positioned. Jacob sat down.

'Now, watch this,' said the planter, who brought out a three-sided mirror from a cabinet and placed it behind the candelabrum on the desk.

'There,' he said. 'What do you see?'

'I see a man who could do with a shave and a haircut,' said Jacob, trying to make a jest of the situation which was becoming a little strange.

'But how many faces can you see?'

'A great many, I suppose. Depending on how I sit and face the mirror.'

'I would venture to say that there is an incalculable number of faces. In fact, I would go as far as to say that it would prove that your theory of infinity really does exist, would it not?'

Verbizier was referring to a conversation they often had about the immortality of the soul and the infinity of heaven.

The planter had maintained that life is not infinite in any shape or form, neither in one's life nor in one's death. Once you are gone, you are gone. That was all there was to it, he had said. This was shocking to hear and something that was hardly ever even whispered. But the planter was a plain-speaking fellow who had seen life and death. And he knew one thing for sure: a dead man does not come back! Though of course, he also knew when and when not to share his private thoughts, as well as with whom, or else he could end up being roasted at the stake like a soulless savage.

'An astonishing observation, I grant you,' said Jacob, peering into the mirror so that his reflection appeared to recede in an endless stream of faces.

'Now, watch this,' said the planter, whose mischievous little chuckle announced one of his tricks. He then licked his thumbs, leant over the acajou desk, and snuffed the candle flames out simultaneously.

'And there is your proof of nothingness. No infinity, just plain nothing!' said the victorious voice of the planter from out of the darkness.

There was a moment's silence as Jacob, stumped for words, took in the abominable notion.

Then he said, 'But, Sir, I ask you. Who created this nothingness? What is this blackness in which we hear ourselves speak? It is part of God's creation! For if there were no darkness, how would we recognise the light? In the same way, if there were no sorrow, how could we appreciate happiness?'

'Hah, damn you! When a man don't want to learn, he won't learn!' said Verbizier, pushing away his chair with a forced chuckle. He then charged across the room to open the door as the Sunday mass bells began to chime. But his cordiality had returned by the time he turned back to Jacob.

'Will you come to church?' he said.

'As I have told you every Sunday since I came here, I do not need to visit a Catholic building to go to church.'

'A more stubborn one there never was. But even if you keep your infinity, and your heaven and hell, think over what I say. You only have to join in the ceremony to be a wealthy man again, Delpech.'

'That may be, but certainly not a happy one!'

This Huguenot was decidedly Protestant to the marrow.

'That is why, Sir, it is important to live for the day!' said the planter, who always liked to have the last word. He took his leave and met his wife with their children and her pretty slave girl, at the front of the grand house where a coach was waiting to take them to church.

*

Strolling down towards the village, Jacob contemplated the view over the bay. If only he could find a way to cut and run. However, the forest around was impenetrable, the mountain behind impassable. And as yet he had not seen a single foreign vessel come to anchor in the roadstead.

Upon arrival at Leogane, the governor had handed the

Huguenots over to the lieutenant governor, Monsieur Dumas, who had advised them to find lodgings among the inhabitants. They were assisted in this delicate undertaking by Catholic priests who acted as go-betweens. But the Protestants did not come without resources. Most of them had skills and expertise to offer in exchange for board and lodging.

Given his knowledge of farming and irrigation, Delpech was offered the room at the plantation, where Verbizier was glad to have a gentleman of quality with whom to converse, and who knew about farm management.

Jacob had been at Leogane for over a month already. He had established a cordial relationship with the Catholic clergy who, despite their numbers, had failed to convert him. On the contrary, he had become a popular speaker and defender of the Protestant contingent, one that the priests would rather have been without.

He rejected the Catholic Eucharist, impertinently questioning how the act of taking bread and wine could make you more righteous.

He asserted that praying to God through saints was another invention of the Catholic Church which had made it rich.

And he even went as far as insinuating that the Roman Catholic doctrine of the celibacy of the clergy was unwritten, unnatural, and misleading for its ministers.

Such was his heretic verve and foolhardy conviction that the poor priests ended up complaining to the lieutenant governor, a former Protestant himself, that Delpech was impeding them in their mission of conversion.

And as if all that were not bad enough, now he was teaching African slaves who—since the Code Noir had granted them a human soul—were supposed to receive instruction in the Christian faith by their master. And there was no point counting on the likes of Verbizier to set his man on the right course. A moral compass he was not, more a weathervane. Everyone knew what he got up to when away buying slaves.

Even the other indentured workers were turning to Delpech for spiritual guidance, which he had the cheek to dispense in French instead of Latin. For the love of God, had the man really no sense of tradition?

Apart from the Huguenots themselves, many of these indentured workers had also been Protestant. Labourers for the most part, they had to give three years of their lives to a master for the right to a plot of land, a little cash, and their freedom at the end of their term. And they were the fortunate ones compared to the African slaves whose term only ended on the day they drew their last breath.

It is written in the Bible, the likes of Verbizier would say, then quote a learnt-by-heart extract such as: '*And ye shall take them as an inheritance for your children after you, to inherit them for a possession; they shall be your bondmen for ever.*'

But Jacob found the Bible also warned: *Masters, give unto your servants that which is just and equal; knowing that ye also have a Master in heaven.*

Treating someone *just* and *equal* is certainly not to whip and beat them like stubborn beasts, thought Delpech. Yet, for all his research and reasoning, he had to admit that slavery was the way of the world here, and perhaps something he might have to get used to.

*

An hour later, he was standing with Mademoiselle Duvivier. She had taken a room at the house of an old lady, Madame Grosjean, whom she had agreed to care for. Marianne had blossomed in the time Jacob had known her, which equated to eight months, and which seemed like half a lifetime. His paternal presence still bolstered her confidence, especially since he had asked her to organise their secret assemblies, which she did with relish and gusto.

They were at present quietly singing a psalm with as many Huguenots as could fit into Madame Grosjean's small downstairs parlour. It turned out that the old lady had only converted to Catholicism to be left in peace, but her heart was firmly Protestant. And the house was conveniently located at the opposite end of the village from the church. Secret assemblies like these took place throughout the township. In fact, Jacob was finding out that every other white person he met was of Protestant stock. Like Madame Grosjean, they had many a tale to tell of the days of the first buccaneers, who were not filibusters at all, but Protestant planters and hunters who initially settled on the northwest coast of Hispaniola, and on the island of Tortuga.

After the clandestine service, Delpech led a small party around the sugar works on the pretext of assessing the advancement of the new mill that he had been commandeered to oversee, along with the construction of wells. The works was located at a five-minute walk along the palm-lined track from the township, and gave a legitimate reason for them to meet in plain view.

The mill, the boiling area, and the drying room were situated near the river at the bottom of the plantation, where the first fields of sugar cane had been planted. A water-powered mill, like the ones made by the Dutch, was under construction to cope with the extra land to be freed up for the lucrative crop.

The party were at present speaking around the old ox-powered mill. Here, only last week, a slave had caught his hand in the vertical rollers that normally mangled the sugar cane. It only took a couple of ox strides for the columns to travel the equivalent of a yard, and before the ox driver could bring his animal to a halt, before Jacob could process the screams, the poor man's body had been drawn in and his head crushed like a pineapple.

Six days out of seven, from daybreak to dusk, the plant was busy with crushing cane, boiling juice, clarifying, thickening and crystallising the sugar, and drying it in sugar cones. But today the place was empty, except for the party of Huguenots. From afar, going by their gesticulating, it looked like they were discussing a feature of the mill construction. But they were not. Their conversation had turned, as always, to their favourite subject.

'I say we just take a rowboat,' said Monsieur Coulin, a master carpenter, while inspecting the wedge of a mortise and tenon joint.

'The problem,' said Professor Bourget, the surgeon, 'is what to do with it.'

'We hug the shoreline until we reach the south coast,' said Monsieur Roche, a stocky mason who spoke in a tenor voice.

'We would risk getting caught by Spaniards,' said a lanky solicitor by the name of Lautre.

'Then it's out of the rowboat and into the whale's mouth!' said the professor.

'No, no,' said Coulin, 'I've heard that English vessels water there on their way to Jamaica.'

'Madame Grosjean told me they like to put in at a place called Cow Island,' said Mademoiselle Duvivier, who was not too shy to add to a predominantly male conversation. In fact, despite her prisoner status, ironically she had never experienced such freedom. She even enjoyed walking among Huguenot men without a chaperone. She continued. 'It is not far from the south coast, I am told.'

'That may well be, Mademoiselle,' said Monsieur Lautre. 'Nonetheless, I still think it safer and wiser to bide our time a while longer until a Dutch *fluyt* puts into the bay.'

'With all due respect,' said Monsieur Roche, 'we've been saying that for the past three weeks, and we've still seen neither yards nor prow of a cargo ship, have we?'

'I fear we are not likely to either,' said Jacob, 'given the current state of affairs back in Europe.'

'To look on the bright side,' said Monsieur Lautre, 'at least we have been able to send word home.'

'Did they go?' asked Jacob to Marianne.

'Yes, my uncle,' she said, 'they went this morning with the store keeper to Le Cap Français.'

The church bells began to chime, announcing the end of the long Catholic mass. The company instinctively took their leave from each other in twos and threes to avoid any risk of being accused of congregating, which was punishable by imprisonment.

'My dear niece,' said Jacob, 'will you walk with me a while?'

Marianne and Jacob had kept up their little ruse of being related to avoid rousing suspicions whenever they met to organise the assemblies, which they did often. It also let everyone know that the young lady was not alone in this strange, torrid, and colourful world. Even Huguenots, as she passed by alone in the street, would give their regards to her uncle.

*

The two of them headed in the direction of a newly dug well which was on the opposite side of the plantation, and barely a hundred yards from the slave shacks under the trees. Delpech had positioned it so that it would provide the most efficient water supply for Monsieur Verbizier's new fields of sugarcane.

'We must find another place to assemble,' said Jacob. 'I fear we are watched, and I suspect it is only a matter of time before Madame Grosjean's house is closed, and then where will the poor woman go?'

'She says she is fully aware of the risks,' said Marianne. 'But she says that it uplifts her to no end to feel the grace of God in her home again. And she says it will not be long now before she is taken to her husband and her son.'

'But I fear they could send you away too, Marianne. I promised your grandmother I would look after you.'

'You need not fret, I can look after myself,' said the young woman with an endearing laugh. 'Now, you said you would teach me how to find fresh water, do you remember?'

'Indeed, I do.'

'Heaven knows, I might need to know one day if I become marooned on an island.'

'We are marooned on an island, my dear,' said Delpech, with a chuckle which allowed him to disguise his smile at seeing her so grown up, and a fine figure of a woman at that.

Marianne, who had come to understand his moods, knew at that instant his mind was not preoccupied as it usually was by his family and the grief of losing Louise, his three-year-old daughter. It was one of those rare moments that relaxed his rather handsome features.

He opened his jacket and brought out the Y-shaped slender branch he used for locating water veins, a method dowsers used on his farms in Montauban.

'Oh, wonderful,' she said, clasping her hands together.

He handed her the foot-long dowsing stick as they approached the well.

Looking over her shoulder, she said: 'You are sure this is not witchery?'

'Bah, no,' said Jacob. 'Even Father Jeremy uses one. We had a good chuckle together when he saw me locating the other wells. Now, let us see if you have the gift.'

Black slaves were now walking, some running, back to their quarters in the Caribbean sunshine. They had been locked up inside the church for three long hours and were eager to spend what was left of their free day as they pleased.

A band of barefooted youngsters skipped past them.

'M'sieur, M'dame,' they hurled out as they ran excitedly towards their usual play area beneath the leafy trees.

To think that these young wretches would live their whole lives in servitude brought a frown to Jacob's brow. Then again, perhaps they would not be unhappy after all. Perhaps they would find comfort in God's grace, he thought. At least, this way, their daily objectives in life would be clear. They would not become beggars, and they would not be hindered by ambition. Moreover, their own civilisation was very rudimentary, was it not? So perhaps this was the life that was meant for them. Was it not a lesser evil than remaining in ignorance of the Lord?

'Forgive them. They are excited,' said Marianne, sensitive to his fleeting change of mood.

'Oh, it is not that,' he said, waving the thought away like a fly. 'Right, hold the forked end lightly at the extremities. That's it. Now walk slowly towards the well.'

After a few slow strides, she said, 'My word, I can feel it moving.'

'Keep walking slowly.'

'Oh, look, my uncle—incredible. It is working—it is dipping.'

'The water vein is right under your feet then, my niece!' laughed Jacob, both proud and touched by her wonderment. There was still the little girl beneath the veil of budding womanhood. 'Now you know what to do if you get marooned on a desert island!'

By now a little group of slave women and their children had gathered around them to marvel at the magic, which always gave cause for wonderment.

A child of three or four wriggled down the hips of its young mother. The young woman was engrossed in the spectacle of the white girl learning magic—the same magic performed by the elders of her village in west Africa, just half a day's walk from the Youbou River. The little girl tugged at her mother's dress and pointed towards the slave shacks near the trees. She was thirsty.

Marianne walked in zigzags, experimenting with her amazing new power.

Two minutes later, Jacob looked up to see how far they

77

were from the well, so that he could trace the trajectory of the underground water vein with his eye. Then he saw a little girl in a short-sleeved dress, running barefoot towards the well. It should have been covered over. But Jacob could see that it was not.

'My God, no! Stop the child!' he cried out. The little girl gave a glance over her shoulder as she toddled on; the next instant, she was gone. There was a short scream. The mother, seeing her daughter disappear into the ground, let out an agonising cry as she sank to her knees, clasping her face in despair. Jacob wasted no time in dashing to the gaping hole in the ground, thirty yards ahead. It was a fourteen-foot drop to the bottom, which was still plugged for the interior walls to be sealed, so it contained no water.

He braced himself, then looked over the rim.

The child let out a wail of shock, fear, and pain on seeing the face of the white man looking down from above. But at least she had survived the fall.

Without a second thought, Jacob ripped off his jacket, stepped into the well, and descended the wooden ladder.

As he approached the bottom, he saw the whites of the child's large eyes, staring fearfully up at him. 'Don't be afraid, my girl,' he said in the same soft voice he used when his own children had hurt themselves. 'Good girl, there's my sweet,' he said as he managed to squat astride her.

She was sobbing. 'Legs,' she said. 'Legs hurtin'.'

In the dimness of the well, Jacob felt her legs. Her scream of pain when he touched the limp right foot told him the lower right leg was probably fractured. He only hoped that was all the poor child had broken. He felt the rest of her tiny body, her pelvis, her ribcage, her arms.

'I'm going to take you to your mama, my girl. To Mama,' he said.

'Mama,' said the child. 'Wanna go home,' she sobbed.

'Yes, Mama's waiting. Now, tell me your name, my sweet.'

'Lulu,' said the girl, bravely swallowing another sob.

It was the pet name of his daughter, his darling little Louise, who died while he was incarcerated in France for his faith.

Was it the words, the emotion, the adrenaline? Or was it something else that made him suddenly feel ashamed? Down in that dark pit, he now saw through the fallacy of the slaveholder society. How could he, even for a single instant, have fallen for the false normality of servitude?

'My God, I have been blind!' he said to himself as he ripped off his belt and, looking up, cupped his hand to his mouth. 'Marianne!' he called. 'Marianne, throw me something I can wrap around her legs. A belt, some string, whatever is closest to hand.'

Two seconds later, a white woman's shawl was falling towards him. He fastened the belt around the child's legs below the knee amid little yelps of pain. But Lulu was very brave. He tied the shawl around her calves just above her feet, so that the wounded leg was fastened to the good one. Then he scooped up her crumpled body in his big hands.

'Good girl, Lulu,' he said, trying to reassure her. 'Such a brave girl. Now hold on tight, there's a good girl. And don't let go.' The child held onto his neck as if for dear life. He could feel her shivering, her soft skin against his neck, her woolly hair on his cheek. How brave she was for such a mite.

It was a changed man that Mademoiselle Duvivier saw

climb out of the well. The anguish etched on his face was the anguish of a father.

'Marianne,' he said, panting from the ascent, 'I want . . . you to fetch Monsieur Bourget . . . fast as you can. Tell him a child has broken her leg.' He then looked at the nearest slave and said, 'Bono, you go with her and bring back anything the doctor needs.'

'But, M'sser . . .'

'Don't stand there, man, run!'

The mother's relief was palpable as she put her hand on her child's head and mumbled reassurances in her native tongue. But the child kept hold of the white man who had told her not to let go, and he was already striding in the direction of the slave quarters.

'Come, Madame, take me to your hut,' he said to the mother.

Five minutes later, he was standing in a windowless hut. Its roof was covered in palm leaves, its walls made of wattle. He lay the child down on a wooden board where the mother had laid a woven palm-leaf mat. The bone had not broken through the skin, but the fracture was evident from the swelling. The child looked alert while her mother bathed her grazed face; she must have hit the wooden ladder, which must have broken her fall.

Jacob was examining the splinter in her hand where she must have grabbed the ladder rung, when there came a sudden commotion from the gathering crowd outside, and a raised voice.

'What in God's name is going on here!' thundered Monsieur Verbizier, lowering his head through the doorway.

Jacob, who had never seen the man in such a wicked

mood, told him what had happened. The planter said he would have the bastard who left the well uncovered stripped and whipped.

'There is really no need,' said Jacob. 'She will be all right . . .'

'I'm not talking about the brat. I am talking about discipline, Sir! Give them a loose rein, and the place will be like a savage village in no time!'

Verbizier looked about him in disgust at the shack, where small dead birds were strung up to be roasted on the spit that evening. Jacob continued his examination, but the child began to tremble with a new fear and reached for her mother.

The planter continued: 'And what if a mill worker had fallen in? Then what, eh? We are hard put to finish the harvest as it is!' Turning to the doorway, where a crowd stood at a respectful distance, he hurled: 'If no one owns up, I'll have the lot of you thrashed!'

Jacob got to his feet. 'It was me,' he said. 'I was showing the well to my niece. You will have to flog me instead! Now leave us, I beg you, you are frightening the child!'

'What?' said Verbizier, who stood as stunned as if he had received a slap on the face.

'You are frightening the child! Now leave us, I pray,' said Jacob, seething now, though keeping his voice down so as not to scare the patient further.

Verbizier knew when a man was beside himself. He knew too when to retreat in order to get what he could out of a person before the relationship ended. Pity, he thought. Delpech would have made an excellent plant manager.

He gave the Huguenot a stern once-over, turned, booted

a chicken out of the doorway, and stomped out with orders to cover the well before someone else fell down it.

Professor Bourget arrived seconds later, followed by Mademoiselle Duvivier, who was carrying a leather bag. The slave named Bono was behind her, carrying a chest which he put down inside the hut. It had been presented to the doctor to enable him to carry out chirurgical and medicinal work in the colony. Given his past career as a surgeon in the king's army, Bourget had acquired vast experience and had quickly become a respected figure in Leogane.

It was a clean fracture. But the surgeon had to open the area to remove bone debris. He then set the fractured ends of the bone in place so that it could properly mend. Next, asking Jacob to hold the lower leg firmly, he wrapped it in a bandage, placed a wooden splint beneath it, and bound everything together with tape ligatures. Lastly, he thrust other splints beneath the tapes all the way around the dressing, and then made sure they were tightly in place. Throughout the operation, the mother, whose name was Monifa, tried to comfort her daughter while Mademoiselle Duvivier held the child's arms. She writhed in pain before falling unconscious.

At the end of two hours, Jacob stepped outside into the bright afternoon light. He reflected on the fascinating view into the world of medicine, and the powers of knowledge the Almighty had given to man. He was sitting in the shade of a tree when the young black man named Bono came up to him. Jacob knew his name because he was one of the well diggers. The man gave a bow. Jacob rose to his feet as Bono said, 'Thank you, M'sser.'

Jacob, seeing the young man had tears welling in his eyes,

realised with mortification his blunder. He said, 'You are the child's father.'

The man nodded.

'I am sorry,' said Jacob, touching the man's shoulder. 'I should have asked and sent someone else with Mademoiselle Duvivier. You should have gone with your daughter. Please forgive me.'

Bono gave a brief nod, and with dignity, he said, 'I forgive you, M'sser, and I thank you.' Then he went back into the hut.

Jacob reeled the sequence of events through his mind like a magic lantern. The child's fall—the mother's collapse—the child's fear—the father's gratitude. How could he have been tricked into believing, even for a wicked second, that these people were any less human in any way, shape, or form than the white man? How dare he have doubted, even for an instant. He would never let himself become so base again.

He let himself slump against the tree and soon found himself pondering the Code Noir that Verbizier had spoken of. There was one article which he was glad of, article 47. It forbade husbands and wives from being separated from each other and their offspring. Delpech saw this as a fundamental right for all men and women of honourable intent.

'Monsieur Delpech, are you all right?' said a soft and spirited voice. It was the voice of Mademoiselle Duvivier. Jacob looked up and felt tears water his eyes.

He was grieving not only over his shame, but for his own child who had died without him, for his destitute wife who was now a refugee in a foreign land, and for his other children abducted in France. Who was watching over them now? he wondered.

SEVEN

THE ELEGANT FRENCH resident had summoned the fat syndic to his study. They were sitting on either side of the deep walnut desk that stood delicately and with solidity on scrolled feet in front of the bookcase crowded with leather-bound works of law.

'Ever since the council ordered the deacons to remove the wretched fugitives, there have never been so many of them in Geneva, Sir,' said the resident. 'How do you account for that?'

'It is as I said, my Lord,' returned Monsieur Gallatin. 'Now that April is upon us and the winter eviction truce is over, there are more departures than ever before. But there are also even more refugees entering through the city gates.'

'What am I to tell the king?' said the resident, leaning forward and pressing his fingers upon his desk.

Sinking his chin into his collar, the fat syndic said: 'With all due respect, my Lord, you might tell him to stop sending imprisoned Huguenot nobles from his kingdom so that he may confiscate their fortunes.'

'It is not to confiscate their fortunes, Sir!' said the

resident, holding up a correcting finger. He got to his feet, gesticulating as he spoke. 'It is so that their fortunes, or want of, may bring them round to their senses.'

'But for the vast majority it does not seem to be working, my Lord,' said the syndic, remaining wedged in his armchair.

'That is beside the point,' said the resident, pouting his lips and striding away from the desk toward the tall window draped in blue velvet curtains, neatly retained either side by braided tie-backs with golden tassels. 'They have been banished as enemies of the state, a punishment which, I might add, they have brought upon themselves. And I may add that it is working . . . to a certain extent.'

'Yes, my Lord,' said the syndic, whose heavy jowls drooped with his doleful smile, 'but the extent to which it is not working far outweighs the extent to which it is.'

'Some have abjured,' said the resident, turning in defence. 'I receive demands every day from people desirous to return to France. And indeed, the king has generously welcomed them back into his fold. What is more, they have even recovered their fortunes and estates without incurring any penalty.'

'And yet there are tens, hundreds of incoming fugitives, my Lord.'

'And you have been invited time again to rid this city of the king's disloyal subjects, especially those who have been here for many months.'

'I take it you are referring to the poor who have nowhere else to go.'

'Yes. Along with the profiteers and the beggars who have taken advantage of your bourse to obtain free meals and money on a daily basis.'

'If you could provide us with a list, my Lord, of those who have wintered here along with their address, then we shall be able to cooperate as we have always done.'

'I gave you a list the other day.'

'We expelled every one of them, my Lord.'

'Then why am I told they are back again?'

'Are you certain it is the same people, my Lord?'

'Why, yes, my people tell me so.'

'Then we shall act again. However, as you well know, we have not the resources to check every person who walks through the city gates; it would hinder trade. And if that happened, we would have a revolution on our hands!'

'I could ask the king to send a battalion of soldiers,' said the resident eagerly.

'I would rather not, my Lord. If we did, the gentlemen of Bern would not be amused. They would certainly attack our city, or defend it, depending on how you stand. It would lead to war, which would not sit well with the king, I am sure, what with the Dutch threat on his northern borders, you know.'

The resident found himself at an impasse, and it was all the king's fault. It now struck him how much he hated his royal posting, and the wretched city with all the harassment and jeering behind his back, especially from the in-laws. With searching eyes, he said: 'Then, I repeat, what am I supposed to tell the king?'

The syndic had seen it happen before to other men. Roland Dupré had put up a good fight, but Gallatin could now clearly see the resident was near his wit's end. With a reassuring smile, and in his deep voice of reason, he said, 'That we are doing everything we can to oblige his subjects to leave Geneva, except, of course, those of noble birth he has expelled, who might want time to ponder whether they should return to their homeland.'

'Good Lord, I shall be glad to see the back of this place of perdition!'

'We are doing our best, my Lord,' said the syndic contritely.

A quarter of an hour later, alone in his study, Roland Dupré poured himself a strong cordial. Blasted Genevans, he thought to himself, blasted king, blasted de Croissy. It was like being caught between a rock and a hard place. He had had enough of this farce; the whole matter was becoming like a scene in a play from that Moliere fellow. And whatever had gotten into him, he, the king's representative, marrying a local Protestant girl? She had converted, yes, and he still did love her, but you could not convert the in-laws, could you? It was the king's fault for sending him to such a hapless place in the first place, where there were no Catholic ladies.

He had tried so very hard to play the tyrant, firm against adversity, but how long was one person able to row against the current? More and more, he found himself longing to flee, as much from his in-laws as from the city itself. The floorboards creaked under foot as he advanced to the tall window. To think, he had been a young man insouciant, full of spirit and ambition, and with a full head of hair, when he first entered that great courtyard door all those years ago. His stance had since acquired a slight stoop, his clothing had become heavier, and his periwig had grown higher and thicker, as like his king, he had moved into middle age. As he watched the fat syndic ambling towards the great wooden door, he hoped to God, for the sake of his sanity and his half Protestant children, that he would not be refused the commission in Florence.

EIGHT

'WHERE ARE THEY all headed?' said Paul, standing with his mother at the open window of their first-floor accommodation on Molard Square. Behind them, Jean Fleuret, Ginette's husband, was fitting a new beater to Jeanne's loom.

She was gazing at the crowd waiting at the port quayside, at the far end of the square. Judging by the agitation, the flat-bottomed ship was now ready to take on board another load of fugitives, mostly country folk by the look of their garb and their stance, and a few ladies and gentlemen of quality.

These first days of April sunshine had prompted a new surge of mass departures, and for the past week passenger numbers had swollen, which in turn had increased the morning hullabaloo rising from the market below Jeanne's window. She did not mind the noise. On the contrary, the proximity of her lodgings to the port never ceased to give her reassurance. The hundred or so refugees began to board with their bundles and baskets, bags and pouches, but no heavy chests. Jeanne wondered how they would all fit aboard.

'Further north,' she said to her son at last, 'Lausanne, Bern, perhaps as far as Berlin.'

'There's some that goes as far as Holland too,' said Jean Fleuret, punctuating his words with another tap of the mallet. 'There,' he said, 'that should hold good and proper this time, Madame Delpech.'

Pulling herself back from her window view, Jeanne thanked him and moved back to her loom.

He said, 'I've replaced the whole beam part this time, good as new now.'

Jean Fleuret had kept his word which he had given when he, his son Pierre, and Paul found Jeanne depleted in a chair in her room with her loom in pieces. He had made makeshift repairs at first and then replaced each splintered part over the ensuing weeks.

'I can't wait to try it,' said Jeanne, pulling up her stool. 'And how is your work at the Bourse?' She had put in a word for him when the deacon had mentioned they were lacking a woodworker.

'What with the spring and more and more people flooding through the city gates, there's every day more deceased to bury. Be they dead from accident or disease, their next of kin bring 'em here, see? I s'pose they can't very well bury 'em along the wayside, can they? Consequently, I spend a good deal of my time putting coffins together. That's where the wood for the beam came from. And at this rate there'll be hardly any room left in the cemetery for the residents, let alone fleeing Huguenots!'

'Have you decided upon your plans?'

'Aye, we reckon we don't wanna be outstaying our welcome now that spring is well in full bloom. And what with the king's resident, I doubt very much I'll be able to get a proper job of my trade here anyway. So we're definitely planning on pushing north.'

'Yes, I see.'

'Will you and Paul be coming, Madame?' said young Pierre, who liked to talk as an adult now that he was on the cusp of adolescence.

'I cannot say yet, dear Pierre,' said Jeanne, with a motherly smile.

'Any news of your husband?' continued Jeannot Fleuret.

'Alas, none.'

'Your sister?'

'Neither. But I shall wait here if I am able to.'

'You do so much, you deserve something back. Let us pray good news is on its way, Madame Jeanne. As for us lot, I reckon we'll be leaving in a few weeks, soon as the nights become less chilly. My Ginette does hate the cold, she does. And I've said it before, you and the boy are more than welcome to join us. The more the merrier, that's what we say, don't we Pierrot, me boy?' The boy gave a resolute nod.

Jeanne did not want to go further north; it would mean moving further away from her children who were taken from her in France. But deep inside, she knew she might soon have no choice, whether her sister had arrived or not, for the authorities were becoming more insistent for refugees who had wintered in Geneva to move on. And if it came to it, she would rather go with humble people she knew, people who had been of mutual support, than with a crowd of passing strangers, even those pertaining to her former social rank. How she had changed, she thought. So she was glad to hear that the Fleurets would not be leaving just yet. It would give her time, time to receive news from Jacob, time, she hoped, for her sister, her brother-in-law, and her children to join her in Geneva. However, for them to arrive in May would mean they would have left in late March, early April latest, which was probably hoping for the impossible. Then again, Robert had means. They would be travelling by carriage, stopping at inns.

'Thank you,' she said.

'I reckon it'll be hard going, mind.'

'I know. Some people prefer to return to France, even if it means abjuring.'

'How I see it is as soon as folk see that Geneva i'nt so much a haven as a stopover, they realise life ain't so easy in exile, and travelling ain't gonna be no Sunday stroll neither!'

Jeanne knew full well what the carpenter meant. Though a welcome refuge, Geneva was not a viable place to settle, not without guild approbation—unlikely for a Huguenot, let alone a woman. She herself had already paid the price for stepping over the line. Since the incident of her loom, she had not returned to the master tailor's boutique. She did not want to see the employees gloat; it would only make her mad, and she would not be able to hold her tongue. So, she had not started a successful enterprise. No, instead, she had kept to making fabric exclusively for fellow Huguenots and poor fugitives—fabric which she either delivered to Ginette or to Monsieur Binet, the official relief fund tailor.

Jeannot Fleuret gathered his tools into a leather shoulder pouch, and under his arm he tucked a roll of Montauban cloth which Jeanne had handed him for his wife to perform her magic on. He then took his leave with Pierre. She told Paul he could go with them as far as the fountain on the square in order to fill the leather water bottle, but then he must come straight back up without dawdling with the venders' children.

'Don't worry, Madame Delpech, I'll see him back,' said Pierre as the three passed through to the landing.

Jeanne returned to the window to view her son, Pierre, and Jean Fleuret emerging from the street door by the bakery, and heading for the fountain among the market crowd. She glanced to her left, where the last migrants were boarding the ship, and where a family was scurrying, each with a sack, to join the end of the queue. In all the months she had been residing above the bakery on Molard Square, she had never seen a vessel loaded with so many people. Hardly could she see a flat surface unoccupied. It was quite frightening, and to think that this was just the beginning of the season.

A good thing the wind is soft and the weather clement, she thought to herself as she recovered her seat at her loom. To think of all those people in the same boat, courageously moving to a new life, carrying the same grief of never seeing their hometown again, put her own remorse into perspective. Images came of the peachy brick buildings of Montauban, the clear view from the Quercy ridge over the flat, fertile plain that reached all the way to the foothills of the Pyrenees. Then she pictured her children playing at their country house in summer. But she pinched the bridge of her nose to halt the subsequent flood of misgivings, then began threading to give herself something tangible to focus on.

A short while later, she found herself hoping again that Jacob would be among the released Huguenots from the king's prisons, and wondered with excitement what life would be like in London, Brandenburg, or Amsterdam. In this way, she was able to weave her sorrows and joys together, and alleviate the ache in her heart.

A familiar knock at the door interrupted her escapade into the future. She pulled down the beater of the loom and went to the door.

'Pastor Duveau. I was lost in my thoughts; I didn't hear you coming,' she said after opening the door.

'I have a letter for you, Madame Delpech.'

Jeanne let him into the room and offered him a seat at the small wooden table. She knew he was as eager as she was to know the contents of the letter, and he did not look as though he was ready to let her open it in her own time. But it was only fair, she conceded. He deserved as much as anyone to know her fate, after all he had done to make her comfortable, and the lengths to which he had gone to integrate her into Genevan society, insisting every Sunday that she join him with his Sunday guests at his table. And they had after all formed quite a robust partnership, organising accommodation, food, and clothing for the newly arrived and the needy. He was entitled to sit down at her table now, as a partner, a friend, and her pastor.

She sat down on the other side of the table where he had placed the letter. She briefly examined the handwriting and opened the folded sheet of paper.

'I was hoping it would be from Jacob,' she said out loud. The pastor kept his silence as she proceeded in reading her sister's note to herself.

My dear sister,

I send you news which I will develop further in a subsequent letter, but I want to get this off to you as quickly as I can, for I am told the messenger is shortly to take to the saddle. R has been taken ill. I know this will come as a terrible blow to you, but I cannot express it any other way: I fear we will not be able to travel. I cannot leave him on his own. I am so very sorry, my dear sister.

It will bring you no solace to know that Lizzy still refuses to leave Montauban. She says she will not leave her sister's grave unattended, so it may be just as well we cannot travel.

Before becoming bed-ridden, R found out that J did embark for the Americas, either for the Martinique or Saint-Domingue, we believe.

My darling sister, I will write with details of R's ailment later, but I do fear for his life. I pray to God every day that you and my nephew have found a safe haven. Your darling baby brings us much joy; the first thing she does in the morning is go to your portrait. My dear sister, you will not be forgotten.

Remember me to the pastor.

Your loving sister

Jeanne sat gazing into mid-distance, her eyes glazed over. She was not conscious of how long she was staring like this and was only brought out of it by the pastor's gentle insistence.

'Madame Delpech, Madame Delpech . . .' She felt a hand touch her forearm, and at last she acknowledged his presence. He was standing, pouring out a glass of *fine* from a bottle he had brought with him. 'Drink this,' he said, handing her the drink. 'It will bring you back to yourself.'

She raised the earthen beaker to her lips and took a sip of the liquid, which stung her tongue and then her eyes, but then left a warming glow in the region of her chest.

'Madame Delpech,' said the pastor, sitting back down opposite her. He wanted to reach out to the lady, but he could only touch her with his words. She looked suddenly frail, her brow pleated, her eyes searching. What did she see when she looked back at him? he wondered. He continued. 'Madame Delpech, whatever your troubles, please know you will not be alone here in Geneva. There is a way for you to remain here.'

She read the discomfort in his expression, and she saw he knew full well she had understood the meaning between his words. She gave a short nod, her eyes expressing gratitude for his caring. She knew too that his heart was sincere. The implicit insistence to remain in Geneva did not shock her either. In fact, it gave her some comfort. Her mouth twitched into a fleeting smile, the frail smile of a vulnerable woman who knew not which way to turn should her husband never be seen in this world again.

Bolstered by her faint encouragement—the encouragement testified by her non-remonstrance—the pastor decided to venture further onto a terrain he had often visited in his dreams, ever since Jeanne Delpech first sat down at his table, like it was her rightful place, in his deceased wife's chair by the tiled stove.

'Jeanne, please do not think me too forward or inappropriate. But if for any reason your husband became . . . lost . . . then I want you to know that I would be honoured if you would become my wife. No, wait, please.' He held out his hands gently as if to ward off any reproach. Now that he was in train, he had to go all the way. 'I do say it with honourable intentions, Madame. It would simply mean that you and your dear boy would have a home here in Geneva. It would mean that one day, you might be able to welcome your other children here. And it would mean that I would have a ready-made family to cherish, that my dear late wife was unable to give me.'

'Thank you. Thank you for your thoughtfulness, Pastor Duveau,' said Jeanne, breaking eye contact. An awkward silence followed, neither of them quite knowing how to conclude. Then, seconds later, they were rescued by Paul clomping up the stairs with a pouch full of water. She rose to her feet.

The pastor had put forward his point, and the lady had not shown outrage or disgust, only slight embarrassment now that her son was on his way up. He knew enough about human nature to see she was reassured. Now he could leave her in the peace of her thoughts, and in the secret hope that—should Monsieur Jacob Delpech de Castanet not live through his terrible ordeal—he would stand every chance of taking care of the merchant's widow and children, whom he would cherish as his own.

That afternoon, Jeanne sat at her loom, weaving yarn recovered from used clothes. The act of weaving carried her away from her deepest fears for her husband, and threaded them into the fabric of a new pattern of thoughts. The new, albeit sad, notion that at least she would be saved from becoming a homeless wretch softened the pain of her sister's news.

NINE

GIVEN PROFESSOR BOURGET'S grand age and gout, Jacob took it upon himself to make evening calls at the slave shack over the ensuing weeks. He also accompanied the doctor in his general practice so that he might learn some of the professor's techniques and remedies. In this way Delpech was able to assist with burns, fractures, dislocations, and other wounds.

He brought down the child's fever by giving her barley water and oil of vitriol, as described in his medical book and confirmed by the professor. When she was up and laughing again, he made a point of dropping by no more than a few minutes at a time.

Elias Verbizier let him do as he pleased. After all, the Huguenot was doing him a favour by saving the girl. If all went well, in nine or ten years' time, she would be breeding home-grown slaves. A new generation of workforce that would not cost a sou, and would not have memories of Africa to distract them into lassitude and suicide. Moreover, soon the planter would stop importing worthless indentured male whites who had a limited term. Instead, to respect the race quota imposed by Paris, he would buy up white females only and get them to breed with the blacks. If only his old mother back in La Rochelle could see him now, he often thought; she always said he had a head for business. In the space of a generation, he would have a massive plantation and his own workforce of mulattos.

Jacob busied himself more and more with overseeing the slave workers. He could intervene when the slave drivers—some of whom were black Africans themselves, though of a different tribe—lashed out unnecessarily. And Verbizier again, at first, let him have his way.

However, after some discussion with Father Jeremy, it became apparent to the planter that this form of soft resistance was healthy neither for the plantation nor for the settlement. He sensed a wind of rebellion could well create havoc among his labour force, for even the indentured workers were beginning to talk back to their overseers.

So, after numerous warnings and efforts from both planter and clergy, it was decided that Jacob Delpech was beyond redemption. And now that the new mill and the wells were practically finished, he would have to be disposed of.

But that was easier said than done. Were he a rebellious, run-of-the-mill black slave or an indentured white labourer, it would have been as easy as putting a mad dog out of its misery. Article 38 of the Code Noir clearly endorsed it. *Fugitive slaves absent for a month should have their ears cut off and be branded. For another month their hamstring would be cut and they would be branded again. A third time they would be executed.* But Jacob Delpech was a Huguenot, and a gentleman.

Even Monsieur Dumas, the governor's lieutenant, was at ends with what to do with the shit-stirrer. The man was making everyone uptight.

'I know what to do, Sir,' said Captain Renfort as he and Father Jeremy deliberated over the matter with the lieutenant governor in his office.

'What is that, Captain?' said Dumas.

'Execution, Sir. Spaniards do it all the time. Takes away the rotten apple and decontaminates the rest by example.'

'We could have him on a charge of heresy if that's any help,' said Father Jeremy, eager to find a solution, it being nearly time for lunch. 'He has been blatantly divining in full sight of everyone.'

'He was searching for water, Father?' said Monsieur Dumas.

'Indeed, Sir, but it is still considered as witchery.'

'But you yourself have used one, Father,' said Captain Renfort.

Father Jeremy stared indignantly at the blockhead who was not getting the hint, and said, 'I am only trying to help, Captain!'

'I was thinking we could have him up for unlawfully assembling with that niece of his,' said Captain Renfort. 'I have a full report of their heretic movements and actions.'

'Yes,' said the lieutenant governor, pushing himself back in his mahogany chair, 'but that would mean burning him at the stake, as well as all those involved. It would stir up feelings.'

'I agree,' said Father Jeremy, raising an eyebrow slyly at the lieutenant governor, 'that's the last thing we want. There are far too many former Protestants here in the Antilles.'

Removing his hand from his chin, Monsieur Dumas said, 'I have an idea. Leave it with me.'

TEN

JEANNE SAT AT the sturdy kitchen table, cut out of a single piece of trunk. It stood solidly on trestles, and its edges were bevelled, the corners rounded. It perfectly illustrated the Fleuret family's abode and their nature, robust and effective, thought Jeanne.

She was half-turned towards Ginette, who was preparing flageolets in a copper pan at the sink, which was a hollowed-out stone slab with an outlet that channelled water through the stone wall. The fire smouldered and cracked in the deep hearth, and both women were rosy-cheeked, in the little cottage near the sawmill down by the river.

'You'll be eating with us, Madame Jeanne?' said Ginette.

'I wouldn't hear of it, what with all your preparations.'

'Preparations? Far as I can see, you're the one double-threading the buttons!'

'Well, it's no time to be giving you two extra mouths to feed.'

'Get away with yers. You ought to know by now no one escapes Ginette's kitchen without breaking bread and a warm bowl of stew inside of 'em! Besides, it's as much work for five as it is for seven!'

'All right then,' said Jeanne with a laugh, secretly glad to be with the Fleurets on their last day in Geneva. She had grown fond of going there to spin or to sew while Paul helped at the mill with Pierre. Ginette then changed the subject, as she often did to give vent to her thoughts.

'Do you really think Madame Rouget was a lady's maid?' she said, with large eyes.

'If she says so. Why?'

'Well, I think she was more a washerwoman. A lady's maid is chosen for her finesse, and Madame Rouget's got forearms like skittles. Haven't you noticed?'

Jeanne could only laugh. She would certainly miss their sessions and Ginette's exuberant talk about the church ladies.

'And what about the pauper?' said Ginette, pouring the washed flageolets onto a linen cloth.

'The who?' said Jeanne, already with a smile parting her lips.

'Monsieur Crespin. I call him the pauper 'cause he's got that scrounger's look about him.'

'Ginette! You are being unfair. He helps a lot, and he always takes the cloth from me so I don't have to carry it.'

'Yeah, does the same with my Jeannot, turns up to help just before lunchtime. That's what they do, you know, paupers, tramps, and profiteers. They make themselves useful just at the right time; then they get a free meal.'

'You are being harsh, Ginette. He used to be a woodworker, a cooper, I believe.'

'Jeannot says he's plenty resourceful and even useful, but a carpenter he's not.'

'Neither am I a proper weaver, and you might also say I've just turned up for a meal.'

101

'Get away with you!'

'Anyway, I'm just sorry it might well be our last together,' said Jeanne. 'There.' She placed the coat on a chair with a pile of other over-garments whose buttons she had reinforced. The humble abode with its functional furniture, and its bed alcoves in a bit of a shambles, might not be how Jeanne would have organised it, but it had Ginette's homeliness and her take-me-as-you-find-me feel about it. Jeanne then took up her own green coat and turned it inside out.

'And you and your boy, Madame Jeanne,' said Ginette, 'what are you going to do?'

Jeanne did not know what she was going to do. Her means to create revenue had been removed when the authorities had told her to sell her loom or risk having it seized. 'I am all at sea to be honest,' she said, scrutinising the stitching of the lining of her coat. 'Wait and hope. That is what I shall do.'

'That green coat of yours, I don't know how many times I've seen you darning it.'

'Strengthening it, Ginette.'

'Whatever. I will never forget the first time I saw it, like a song of hope, and I knew we would be all right. And I am not the only one. So, my dear Madame Delpech, if it don't bring you hope when it's been a ray of goodness for so many of us, then I say t'ain't fair!'

'I shall miss you too!' said Jeanne, pausing her needlework to look up with a smile.

'I s'pose it isn't bad at all at the vicar's, but if you choose otherwise, there's still time to come along with us.'

Ginette's empathetic nature lent itself to confidences,

and Jeanne had confided in her about the pastor's proposition, which he had reiterated. Now that she had lost her loom, he insisted that she take up residence at the vicarage until news came of her husband, especially as she now only had the revenue from spinning. Jeanne knew the pastor's offer to be honourable and sincere; however, she had so far refused. Otherwise, it would be like giving up on her husband, and by the same token, on her children.

She said, 'As much as I would like to, I cannot leave yet.'

'You know,' said Ginette, 'you have to let go, my dear lady, let go of your departed child. She is with God now, is she not?'

Ginette had hit the nail on the head, as she so often did. It was true; Jeanne felt that going a step further than Geneva would be physically removing herself further from her living children left in Montauban, and her dear Louise's and Anne's graves.

Pouring the flageolets into the cauldron of ragout hooked over the fire, Ginette continued, 'Your children will be with you in spirit and in your heart, whether you are in Geneva or Siberia.'

'God forbid,' said Jeanne, trying to hide her emotion under a jest, but Ginette was not duped.

After replacing the lid on the fat pot, she turned around to face Jeanne and said, 'Distance won't keep them from your mind. That is how I was able to leave Aigues-Mortes. My dearly departed children are all alive. They are with God, they live in my memories, and they are also here,' she said, patting the top side of her left bosom.

'Thank you, Ginette,' said Jeanne, 'but you have your husband to urge you on. I do not.'

'But I still often feel insecure, and afraid. We know not where we are setting our feet. But whenever the dark thoughts come on, especially at night, I try to force them to one side, because fear is a gnawing demon. It will suck all the puff out of your sails if you let it, till you lose all will to move forward. So, I decided I wouldn't let it. I decided I'll always travel with hope in my heart and God as my guide. My dear Jeanne, do we have any other choice?' she said, suddenly overcome with emotion.

Jeanne put down her coat to one side, got to her feet, and took her friend in her arms. 'Are you saying I am weak, Ginette Fleuret?' said Jeanne with false comedy, to show she was not offended.

'Oh no,' said Ginette drying her eyes with her pinafore. 'You are the strongest woman I've ever met. You can make a golden cloak out of a cast-off robe, you can make order where there's chaos, and you are as brave as they come. No, my dear, but allow me to say that you are only human, and you may have felt weak at some stage. But you must keep striving forward in hope. I say only this: live in hapless hope and fall into despair, or help yourself and God will help you.'

'I admit it is not always so easy. At the moment, I know not if my husband is dead or alive.'

'He's alive and kickin' in your heart, is he not?'

Before Jeanne could answer, the door burst open and in walked Pierre and Paul, followed by the pauper carrying a basket of wood cuttings and cones.

'When you talk of the wolf, eh . . .' said Ginette in a low voice, while Jeanne cast her a look of reproach.

'Good day, Mesdames,' said the pauper cheerfully and smiled at Jeanne, standing with her green coat still over her arm. 'Monsieur Fleuret told me to bring these down to the house,' he continued. He then proceeded to pour his load into the basket at the hearth so that it would not be empty in case they were delayed. 'Have you heard? There's news of a ship lost off the shores of Martinique, all but a few lost to the sea, they do say.'

*

It was ridiculous, and totally out of character, but Pastor Duveau had to know. The track lined with tender-leaved trees meandered round, and at last he could see the house near the mill, half-screened by a weeping willow. Paul playing in the distance with Pierre and his sisters, Rose and Aurore, confirmed what the baker's wife had told him, that she was helping the Fleurets down by the river. As he approached in his black soutane, he suddenly felt conspicuous and foolish, even though the children had not noticed him yet. He checked his step as if he had forgotten something.

'Turn back, you fool,' he said to himself.

But if he had been seen en route, how would he explain it if asked at church what he had been doing there? It wasn't as if he could present himself at another house either; they were few and far between on that side of the river. And the letter he had come to deliver to its addressee had travelled far. There was no reason that the news it carried could not wait another few hours. It now seemed obvious to him that the very act of bringing it so far out of his way made him look desperate. Yet he had to know.

He had thought up a story, to save face. He was on a visit to the Fleurets to thank them for their support; he had received the letter and thought he would take it along. That was the pretext that had driven his stride this far. But these people were not stupid. Where had he put his common sense? He now admitted freely to himself that he had left it in his heart, for he was in love. And love was now so near. 'Stupid, stupid, silly old fool!' he told himself as he realised he could not take another step forward. He was about to turn back when there came a voice from behind.

'Ah, Pastor. What brings you so far this side of the river?' It was Jeannot Fleuret. He was carrying a pair of snared rabbits slung over his shoulder.

'Monsieur Fleuret, ah, you quite made me jump.'

'Going down to the house, are ye, Pastor? Madame Delpech is there.'

'No. Yes. As a matter of fact, I thought I would call in on yourself and your good wife, to thank you for all your efforts. I rarely get enough time at church what with so much toing and froing, you know.'

'I see, Pastor. Well, that's jolly nice of you.'

They began to amble down to the house.

'When are you leaving, Monsieur Fleuret?'

'Tomorrow, weather permitting. And that's if we can get on the boat.'

'Yes, I am afraid they do get packed. I have asked the syndic to lay on more.'

'Oh, they have, Sir. It's just what with the mild weather, everyone's got the same idea, haven't they? It was bad enough in April. But now, the days are longer and the nights not so cold . . . And everyone wants to get to Brandenburg before the grand elector pops his clogs.'

'Actually, I believe he has.'

'Oh?' said Fleuret. 'Are you the bringer of bad news, Pastor?'

'Oh no, I wouldn't let it worry you. His son is as vehemently against your king as was his father before him.'

'Ah,' said Jeannot, reassured.

A few minutes later, they were met by the children outside the door. Jeannot opened it and offered the pastor to enter in front of him.

'Oh, Gigi, look who's come to visit.'

The two ladies inside had turned the moment the door was pushed open.

'Pastor Duveau, what a surprise to see you here,' said Ginette. 'I expect you've come to check on Madame Delpech,' she continued. She did not keep her tongue in her pocket at all.

'As I was telling your husband, I was on my way here anyway to bid you farewell. Though it is true, the baker's wife did mention Madame Delpech might be here, I thought . . .' He paused as it suddenly dawned on him that this was neither the time nor the place.

Locking her eyes on him, Jeanne said, 'Pastor, is there something the matter?'

'Goodness gracious, no, not as such. You have received a letter, Madame, that is all.'

'Do you have it?'

'As a matter of fact, I do,' he said, bringing out the letter from his pouch. 'Thoughtless of me. I should have thought you might like to read it alone, in your own time.'

Jeanne had been waiting for this moment, had been praying for it. 'You can hand it to me here. We are with friends,' she said. She knew she might have to face up to a catastrophe. But if catastrophe there was, she would rather know sooner than later—and she would rather be surrounded by friends.

She took the letter. On focussing her eyes, she instantly saw it was not the hand of her husband. Her heart sank; neither was it the hand of her sister. A stranger's hand had written this. Was it to notify her of a tragedy? She closed her eyes, then slipped the knife Ginette handed her beneath the Dutch seal.

Inside the letter, she found another one which made her take her seat on the chair in front of the table. Again she slipped the knife under the seal. It was the seal of Jacob, the one he carried in his writing case. With her hand to her mouth to avoid the show of emotion, she scanned the first words—*Cadix*, *La Marie*, *Islands*, *London*, *when I escape* . . . These were the words her eyes stumbled over.

'Seigneur!' she said, 'Oh, Lord. It is Jacob. He writes from Saint-Domingue! He is alive!'

'Dear God, hope. There's hope for you, my dear,' said Ginette.

The pastor stood holding his hat, a forlorn smile of defeat on his face. 'That is good, Madame, but pray,' he said with feeling, 'what is the date on the letter?'

'It matters not. All I care is that it is his hand that ran across it. For all I know, he is already on his way to London,' she said, and took her son in her arms. 'That is where we must go!'

'But, dear Madame,' said the pastor gently, 'look at the date.'

'The twenty-seventh day of February.'

'Is it wise to travel now? I mean, without confirmation.'

'It is neither wise nor reasonable. But my dear, kind Pastor Duveau, this is stronger than reason, it is hope! And to do nothing is to waste it, is it not?'

ELEVEN

THE LIEUTENANT GOVERNOR of Leogane had spent a restless night being jabbed by mosquitoes, followed by a whole morning deliberating how to dispose of the Huguenot without rousing suspicions. In his agitation, he had scratched the bites on his inner thigh, making them worse. He was in no mood for compromise when he summoned Delpech and his niece that afternoon to his office.

'Sir, I have no explanation to give you.'

'But—'

'You are condemned to leave, or face a more serious charge!' said the lieutenant governor to the Huguenot, who was standing on the other side of his desk.

Did the man not realise he was doing him a favour? In fact, he was saving his bloody life, and that of his 'niece' to boot. He had enough on them to have them both roasted for heresy. However, Lieutenant Dumas prided himself on being a gentleman of honour, loathe to have more killings under his jurisdiction than was strictly necessary.

To the left of Delpech stood Marianne Duvivier. Behind them stood two soldiers waiting to escort the prisoners out.

Dumas opened the drawer in front of him and took out three folded, wax-sealed letters, which he laid out one by one on his desk. Pointing successively to the handwritten documents, he said, 'These are your orders. One for the boat that leaves this night for Petit Goave. This, for passage aboard *La Charmante,* which will take you to Cow Island. As soon as you make landfall, hand this one to the commander of the island, Major de Graaf. He will arrange accommodation for you.' Dumas got to his feet. 'Take them. I wish you fair winds.' He nodded to his men to escort the Huguenots out.

'May the Lord be your guide, Sir,' said Jacob, picking up the orders and turning to Marianne, who was standing beside him. But she stood firm.

She said, 'Sir, have you news of my grandmother?'

Dumas looked levelly at the young lady who stood unflinchingly before him. She was clever, her clear voice was a model of articulate wisdom, and he was not insensitive to her becoming appearance. In truth, he was sorry to see her go. But Dumas was also a pragmatic man, and go she must, for she would never marry a Catholic, and so never bring forth new blood to the colony.

'Mademoiselle,' he said sternly, to stress his ascendance over youth and the fairer sex, 'you would do well to learn to speak when spoken to.' He knew it was the wrong thing to say the instant it slipped out.

'If I did, Sir, then I would never know what has become of my only family,' she said, indomitable as ever. 'Surely you can tell me if *La Concorde* made landfall or not. My grandmother is Madame de Fontenay of—'

'I know her name,' said the lieutenant governor, raising

a hand to stop her discourse. It was typical of the young woman. Would she never let up? 'I have already told you, I will send news to you in due course. My word is as good as my bond. Now, good day to you, Mademoiselle, Monsieur.' With a lordly flick of the hand, he signalled again to his men to accompany the prisoners out.

*

An hour later, Jacob was standing in the study of the planter's residence. It was past five o'clock. The afternoon heat had abated. Monsieur Verbizier was holding, of all things, a *toise,* which was a measuring stick of the length of one toise, or six French feet. He was showing Delpech another one of his tricks which, he was proud to say, adroitly summed up his philosophy on life. He was determined to give the gentleman another demonstration of his superior reasoning and perhaps leave him wondering how the son of a rope maker had made a success in Paradise, and how Jacob, the son of a physician, now lived in poverty.

The long wooden stick was graduated with notches representing inches, of which there were seventy-two, there being twelve inches to a French foot.

'So, Delpech, if this toise represents a man's life and each inch a year, this is where you are in your life right now. Provided, of course, you live to seventy-two.' Verbizier planted a thick digit on a notch which corresponded to the forty-second inch. 'So, this part represents what life there is remaining to you,' he said, indicating the space on the rod above the forty-second inch.

'Fascinating,' said Jacob. 'It certainly puts it into perspective. Thank you for showing me, Monsieur Verbizier.'

'Not a great deal, you will agree. So you may as well make it fruitful, my good fellow. I hope you shall seriously think the matter over. It might help you see reason yet.'

'I shall, Sir, I shall. And I should hope you do too.'

'Do what, Sir?'

'Seriously think the matter over. Because if I understand rightly, this is where you are on the toise of life, provided you live to seventy-two, of course. For you could die of a seizure tomorrow; God only knows.'

Delpech placed an index finger six inches above where Verbizier had put his. Indicating the space to the end of the rod, he said, 'And this is how much time you have left to save your soul, my good fellow! Good luck, Monsieur Verbizier.'

A few minutes later, Jacob was setting off down the track towards the township for the last time, with his escort in tow.

*

As he marched ahead of his escort between the neatly laboured fields, flanked by luxuriant jungle vegetation, Jacob admired the dazzling view. Set against the westering sun and the beautiful teal-blue sea, it could well have been a tableau of Paradise.

However, on one side, there were rows of men hacking down cane stalks and stripping them of their leaves; women piling them onto carts; carts being hauled away by oxen. As Jacob passed, some slaves dared to cast their eyes his way. The white water diviner had been good to them. Jacob gave a half nod, but then a barrage of insults, like a bark of triumph, heralded the crack of the whip. Jacob halted, turned, and protested to the black slave driver, but through pure insolence, the man cracked his whip again as the armed escort pushed Jacob onward.

On the other side of the plantation, he saw women clearing away new land, building retaining walls and planting poles. Verbizier had told Jacob the plantation was set to double its workforce in just two years. But how? If, God forbid, everyone in the French colony had the same obsession with sugar, it would take the population of an entire country to harvest the crop and work the mills.

He passed the mill, where unspeaking workers were feeding the diabolical crushing machine with cane. What did they think of? Home, most likely. And like Jacob, they yearned for their freedom, to put meat in the pot for their families, to dance on fete days, to hear women sing and their elders tell tales of old. The liberty to recall their past lives— among buffalos, tigers, and giraffes in ancestral forests, vast plains and great watering holes—was the only sanctuary left to them. Their minds were their only escape now, Jacob realised, but for how long? In a generation, even these memories would be gone.

Verbizier's banning chatter and song while feeding the machine had not helped the workers focus their minds on their labour at all. More lives had already been lost. Was it any wonder that these men were accident prone? But were they? A downcast moment in the day, the slip of a hand, and their torment was over. How horrible. At least, on Jacob's advice, now the cane feeders were allowed to alternate with the ox driver to get them out of the seat of temptation. No, this was not Paradise.

A pretty domestic slave girl strolled wearily by him on

her way up to the big house. She was carrying two dead hens in a basket. Though she must have been no more than thirteen, Jacob noticed her belly had grown considerably since he first came to the plantation. She used to be a favourite of Verbizier, full of smiles and bubbling with life. She glanced at Jacob for a fleeting moment, then at the soldier behind him, before casting her eyes downward and walking on.

He would miss the child. She had given him a cause in this godforsaken place. She was walking again; she was brave. How long would she live before her smile was stolen from her too? Had his time here counted for anything at all? A few lashings averted, perhaps, but that was already in the past. Would these black men and women remember that a white man had not accepted their condition of servitude? Or would their bitterness and hatred for all white men grow in their hearts and in those of their children?

He wished he could say goodbye to the child, at least to leave a seed in her memory, in her heart. But his escort had strict orders. The Huguenot was to retrieve his effects and go directly to the port. He was to see no one.

But then he saw the child's mother. Monifa was working in the indigo field. As he passed her by, she raised her head, then placed her free hand over her mouth. She was twenty yards away from him. They locked eyes for a brief, telling moment. Then he looked straight ahead again. He did not want her to feel the tongue of the whip.

He passed parallel to the last well, which was protected by a circular wall, as they all were now. He had deliberately placed this one as close as possible to the slave quarters so that the women and children would not have to carry the

115

water so far. But he knew their shacks could be shifted at any time as needs befit the expansion of the plantation.

He prayed inwardly that these people would find God's peace one day. Otherwise, what justice would there be in the world?

*

Two hours later, Jacob gave his first order to the skipper of the small cargo boat.

Huguenots were not allowed to congregate. But Madame Grosjean and Professor Bourget had braved the restriction to wave Delpech and Duvivier off. Marianne bade a tearful farewell. Jacob was about to offer the address of his house on the Quercy plain, all those leagues away. But then he remembered he no longer had an address to give.

'May God be with you, my friend,' said Professor Bourget. 'I shall watch over Madame Grosjean with Madame Colier,' he said to Marianne.

'And I shall watch over the doctor,' said Madame Grosjean, leaning on her cane.

Something in the surgeon's expression told Jacob he had resigned himself to his fate, that he would die here on the coast of Saint-Domingue, thousands of leagues from his homeland, like so many others. However, the esteemed professor seemed content with the consolation of the simple but jovial company of the old lady.

They embarked and cast off, waving as they left the township walls behind them, and sailed into the encroaching night.

The little vessel, rigged with a single sail, advanced slowly at first along the channel that led into the roadstead. Jacob scanned the shore to his left. Then he saw her. Lulu in her mother's arms, and Bono was there too, all waving.

Heavy-hearted but relieved to see them, he waved back. 'God be with you, my friends,' he called out. 'May God give you strength, Monifa, Bono, Lulu,' he shouted, waving harder. 'Goodbye. Goodbye, my friends . . . Goodbye, Lulu! Goodbye, Lulu!' They soon became a huddled shadow and were engulfed by the darkness.

This could well have been Paradise. But it was not.

TWELVE

WERE HE A Catholic, Pastor Duveau would have made the sign of the cross three times over.

But he was not, so he closed his eyes and prayed to God to give the boat safe passage. At least they would not be going out in the middle; they would be hugging the coast, he thought to himself. He had been helping Jeannot and Cephas lug the baggage aboard.

The boat to Lausanne via Morge was packed mostly with French refugees and their spartan baggage and knapsacks. Below deck was already packed solid. Above deck, families were staking their claim to every flat sheltered surface while trying to take refuge from the infuriating gusts of wind that made the gentlemen hold on to their hats and pulled wisps of hair from under ladies' bonnets. Some of the travellers had already begun breaking their bread and slicing dried sausage, for it was already past midday. The departure had been delayed because of a dispute.

Those at the end of the queue had been told they would have to wait for the next boat. For a good number of them, that meant having to wait another three days. So, having no place to stay, they remonstrated and pleaded.

'All right, I can take a dozen more,' the captain had said, in spite of protests from regular passengers from Morge. 'Long as you don't complain about seating arrangements, cause there ain't none!' The captain had given a loud roar into the wind that rivalled the cries of gulls and gestured to his men to let the remaining passengers board.

'Why does she always have to carry so much?' grumbled Jeannot, lugging another bagful of provisions.

'For the children, who do you think!' Ginette called back.

The pastor opened his eyes. Amid the assortment of people in their diversified garb, he saw the distinct green coat of Jeanne Delpech again. She was approaching after arranging a corner for her things on the lee side. Her smile was intelligent, sublime, and resolute, he thought.

'You should be in Morge in about three days if this wind keeps up,' he said, picking up the thread of their conversation.

'I shall miss Geneva, and my little rooms,' said Jeanne, with a smile. 'And I shall miss our outings.'

The pastor simply bowed his head in acquiescence.

Jeanne continued, 'But now you must start your life anew, Pastor.' He gave a smile. He was glad she said it. She was implying that she knew that his feelings for her had brought to the surface emotions that his wife's death had nullified. It was like a benediction to live again.

'I have much to do, as you well know, Madame Delpech. Summer is soon upon us. And frankly, I won't know which way to turn now that I have no one to lean on.'

'There will be another to take up the flame, I am sure.'

'Not like you, though. But you are right to move on, my dear Madame Delpech.'

'Thank you, and may the Lord bring you happiness.'

He mirrored her smile and took her hand with thanks. The Fleurets and Paul joined her in their farewells.

'My goodness, I nearly forgot!' he said, reaching inside his cape. 'Here. You must take these; you will need them on your travels.' He had made out an attestation for each family, and one even for Crespin, to enable them to travel on without hindrance.

He disembarked, and waved and nodded to other passengers who had known him through the church. It was a lone man, however, who stood on the lake wharf, but a man with perhaps a new lease of life. An odd thought occurred to him standing there: he could never have become a Catholic priest.

The main sail flapped in the wind, the lake surface was full of watery humps, but the captain, to the general relief, ordered the moorings to be detached.

'I do wish this wind would ease up, though,' said Ginette, glancing dubiously at the sky while tucking wisps of hair beneath Rose's bonnet.

'I am sure everything will be fine, with God's grace,' said Jeanne, doing likewise to Ginette's other daughter, Aurore, while Pierrot and Paul stood leaning over the side, waving.

'Oh aye, I'm sure you're right, because I'm not particularly in any hurry to meet Him just yet, are you?' said Ginette with a little chuckle.

The dockers, with burly, weather-browned forearms, released the lines, and the flat-bottomed vessel carrying forty-three passengers was soon setting sail north-eastward.

*

Goodness knows what it must be like on the open sea, thought Jeanne, remembering how Jacob was loathe to travel over water, as she covered her son with a blanket. The Fleurets were huddled next to them, the youngest children sleeping upon sacking placed on the decking. A number of passengers had already felt the effects of the Joran that swept off the slopes of the Jura, and which bunched up the waves that made the boat roll.

They passed Versoix, which was French territory; then they sailed on to the waters of Coppet, where they anchored as evening encroached. The lamps were turned on above and below deck, and despite the constant pitch, folk lay down their heads to sleep. The wind, however, fell off completely after dark, and the whiplashes against the mast became nothing more than a rattling in the rigging amid the ghostly sounds of cracking timbers.

Clouds scurrying by in the grey light of morning, and the faraway sight of vineyards on slopes, were what met the voyagers as they rubbed sleep from their eyes.

'That be French territory, just over that ridge,' said one man, a merchant from Morge, nodding and yawning towards the distant hills.

'Too close for comfort, I say,' said Jeannot Fleuret, chewing on his pipe while sitting on the port-side steps.

The wind that obeyed neither man nor beast picked up, despite the merchant's promise that the Joran wouldn't blow till evening.

'Whoa, steady as she goes!' he cried out as the ship seemed to dip into a deep trough and rise up again unexpectedly. Over the ensuing half hour, the dreaded Joran did pick up dramatically and now sent powerful gusts bowling into the square sail of the vessel.

Jeannot and the merchant were still sitting on the port-side steps when all of a sudden, a gush of cold lake water sprayed over the rim of the boat. Jeanne, Ginette, and the children, who were huddled together still half in slumber, let out screams of alarm. Some of the passengers shot up onto their feet. But the mountain wind that skimmed across the deck in quick successive gusts knocked some of them off balance, causing them to slip over, which brought an explosion of nervous laughter from some of the onlookers. However, any mirth was immediately dampened as another wave bowled over the side of the boat, then another.

Very quickly the lower deck was ankle deep in water. From the sombre hatch, the sound of frightened people replaced that of grunts and groans. Jeanne moved back from the dripping rim and held on tightly to her son; Ginette followed suit and pulled her clutch together around her. Jeannot, who had pocketed his pipe and risen to his feet, looked around from the steps to catch the captain's eye.

'She's too heavy, man,' he hollered. 'She's too low in the water. Let loose some cargo!'

'Nobody move, and she'll hold,' bayed the captain at the bar.

But the impetuous merchant at Jeannot's side was quick to pull out a knife. The next minute, he was cutting into the tethers of a batch of barrels.

'No, stop him!' yelled the captain. Jeannot understood the immediate danger. It was the wrong side to lighten the load, but it was already too late. With the next dip into the trough of a wave, four barrels went rolling overboard, causing the boat to suddenly bank to starboard.

Jeannot staggered over to port side with the intention to

lighten the load there to counterbalance the merchant's error. But the slippery deck, the tilt of the boat, and the gusts of wind sent him bowling against the side of the vessel, along with the merchant and several other passengers. Then the boat was lifted by a rising mound of water. Those on port side slid to starboard, and with the further shift in weight, the unthinkable became imminent.

Jeanne, who had managed to lodge herself with Ginette and the children under the port-side steps, shrieked out: 'If we go over, hold on to something that floats, children, and don't let go!'

No sooner said than the mountain wind slipped under the flat-bottomed hull and seemed to catch hold. It began heaving the boat over, sending merchandise, passengers, and crew overboard into the cold, cold water. Screams of women and terrified cries of children echoed from the hatch leading to the lower deck.

In those desperate seconds, Jeanne could not decide if they should hold on and hope the boat would become right again, or let themselves slide to the side that was taking in water and attempt to grab hold of a cask. Then she saw the dinghy being released and Cephas Crespin leaping into it. But as the glimmer of hope presented itself, to her horror she lost hold of her son, who went sliding inexorably towards the starboard now under water. Barrels and parcels rolled and tumbled freely, some clobbering people, making them fall unconscious into the lake that was whipped into a frenzy by the erratic wind sweeping down from the Jura. Young Pierrot, seeing his friend go, purposely let himself slide across the deck in his pursuit.

Jeanne would have jumped after him too, but she knew

Pierre, like his sisters, was used to jumping off the jetty in Aigues-Mortes and knew how to swim. Pierrot managed to grab Paul by the scruff of the neck after they hit the water. A cask landed beside them, as under the force of the wind and the waves, the boat continued to capsize. The girls and the ladies went sliding to their fate amid screams of terror as people hauled themselves out of the hatch turned into a death-trap.

Jeanne could not swim. But as she instinctively reached for the water's surface, her hand caught a floating punt used to push the barque away from the quay. It barely allowed her to float, but it sufficed to let her break the water's surface.

'Paul! Paul! Paul!' she screamed out, as the ghastly sight of lifeless bodies bobbed amid the tumultuous waves around her. She could not die now, after all she had been through; did it all mean nothing? Her strength was failing her, and she began thinking that if her son had drowned, it would be easier to let herself go too rather than endure the agony of his loss. At least she would be with him. But how? How would she find him in heaven? In her confusion and fear, she cried out: 'God help me, please!'

Rising up with another great wave, she quickly scanned her watery surroundings again, and this time caught a glimpse, she was sure, of her son holding onto a cask.

She was about to call out despite the penetrating cold that froze her jaw muscles, but her throat suddenly tightened. She began to choke from an invisible force, until it pulled her out of the water and she saw the edge of a rowboat. She realised she was being yanked out, and like a drowning cat, she scratched for a hold on the boat until, with an unceremonious tug at her bottom, she was hoisted aboard. Moments later, looking up, it was the pauper she saw, who was now letting the sopping body of an inert woman slip back into the lake. Inside the boat, she saw a pile of coins and rings.

She pretended not to take in the scene and, catching her breath as another cold cloak of water splashed over her back, she cried, 'Over there, please, my son.' Cephas Crespin held her gaze a moment. 'Please!' she beseeched. Then he put his back into the oars, while Jeanne focussed her remaining force on shouting to her son to keep holding on.

Paul was holding Pierre with his arm under his friend's chin, while desperately clasping the cask with his other arm.

'Pierrot . . . got hit . . . help!' he cried out, desperately trying to keep his friend's head above the water.

The pauper approached, pulled Pierre, inert, half into the boat, and felt in his pockets. Jeanne anticipated what he was about to do.

'My God, don't you dare!' she growled.

'He's dead. No point.'

'You don't know that. Get him aboard! Get them both, I tell you!' said Jeanne, who quickly slipped off her ring.

'Take it!'

'I'll take 'em both if you give me your coat and everything inside it,' bawled the pauper above the din. Was it Providence that put it into his hands now? He just had to take it with all its weighted lining.

'Get them in first!' said Jeanne, with fire in her eyes.

The pauper hauled in Pierre, then reached for Paul who, the moment he hit the bottom of the boat, was out cold.

Amid the turmoil, Jeanne placed the lads front down on the bench in an effort to bring them round.

By this time, help was arriving in the shape of rowboats manned by villagers. They were fast approaching the capsized vessel. The pauper, without looking for more survivors, put his back into the oars under cover of the grey light of morning, and within fifteen minutes they were within wading distance to the stony shore.

'Now give it to me!' said Cephas.

Distraught at the boys, who would not respond to her frantic attempts to bring them round, Jeanne reached in her pocket and brought out a handful of coins. 'I have nothing more,' she said. 'Now help me get them to shore!'

'I don't mean your bloody silver, woman!' he said. 'Give me yer coat!'

'I have nothing more in it!'

'You ain't foolin' me, you toff!' The man then lunged for her. Screaming, she kicked and fought back, clawed at his face with what strength was left to her. His mutilated thumbs prevented him from getting a firm grip on her throat, so he thumped her hard. She fell back into the bottom of the boat.

'Get away from me!' she growled between gritted teeth.

There was only one thing to do to shut her up. He snatched up an oar, then clobbered her across the face with it, and again until she fell unconscious on top of her son and Pierre, her face covered in blood.

At last, he wrenched off her coat, scavenged around for his little pile of booty, then waded speedily to shore.

THIRTEEN

AS THE SUN shone over the lake, having cleared the distant mountaintops, the pauper stopped in a pool of light.

He had climbed the wooded hill in order to cross the range westward, the shortest route into France. He had made good ground, and now he was rewarded by being able to settle in the first light of the sun, whereas the valley and port below were still in the dimness of a paling morning. It was a fitting start to the new day, a new life, bathed in golden sunlight. He brought out his knife. Might be better off keeping them sewn into the coat, he thought to himself, feeling the stones through the lining.

During the climb he had envisaged diamonds, sapphires, rubies, and emeralds. He took a deep breath of fresh morning air. Standing with Switzerland on one side with the lake below lit up like liquid gold, and France on the other side where the foothills rose into the Jura, he could already see himself mounting a magnificent steed. But first he would get himself a nice place to live. No, no, first, he would buy some fine clothes; he would dress as an alderman, he would need to look the part. Next he would go wenching with the finest. Then he would choose a place to live and get a wife, or perhaps the wife first, then the house, then the sprogs. That was the substance of his dream which had occupied his thoughts as he had climbed, for two hours solid, where neither horse nor cart could venture. There again, he would certainly need more coin than the measly amount he had collected, and how would he exchange the jewels without rousing suspicions? He put the thought to the back of his mind; it was but a minor obstacle. Was he not a resourceful man? Had he not obtained an attestation of good character from the stupid pastor?

He sat a while longer in the knowledge that he was untraceable, savouring the very moment that marked his change of fortune, from rags to riches. The jacket was of fine fabric, a little worn but still worth a fair price in itself, and cutting the silk lining was like throwing away good coin. So he started unpicking the thread at the seam, the very thread he had seen the Huguenot lady strengthen at the Fleurets' cottage down by the river. But then, with an irresistible urge to hold his fortune in his palms, he dug his knife into the lining and slit it carefully across the hem. His eyes widened as the stones tumbled to the ground. But they widened not in glee, they widened in shock and horror, and then narrowed in wrath. He let out a mighty roar from his tightened gut. 'Why? God! Is there no justice for a pauper? Jesus Christ!'

The stones his knife had let loose were just that, dull, lacklustre stones, devoid of any value.

*

Two days later, the death bells tolled over the little port of Nion. Thirty-eight people had perished; extra coffins had to be brought in from nearby towns in haste. The whole village had walked behind the coffins to the Protestant graveyard, where the deceased were laid to rest. It was a simple burial, in accordance with Protestant beliefs that they could not intercede on behalf of the dead for their entry into eternal life. No mass, no prayers, no superstitious ritual. They simply remembered.

'Your mother is in good hands,' said Jeannot to the boy after the funeral service. 'She will recover, but she must rest here. Tell her I have had to take our Ginette away from this place before the grief overtakes her, before I lose her too. You understand, my boy?'

'Yes, Sir,' said Paul, his face clouding over with sorrow. 'But I don't understand why Pierrot had to die and not me.'

The man and the boy were standing outside the tall house where Jeanne was bedridden. But for the rustling of birds in the trees and the trickle of a nearby fountain, all was calm—a calmness only broken from time to time by the distant snorts of horses in front of their carriages, on the adjoining road at the bottom of the lane. They were waiting to carry the surviving passengers on to Morge, the port town where the boat had scheduled to dock, and whence the refugees would take up their route northward.

'I know, Paul. I know,' said Jeannot, tears running into the cracks around his eyes. 'Now you listen here, my lad. Pierrot loved you like a brother, you know that.'

'And I loved him like my brother, Sir.'

'Well said, my boy. Remember, if you are the one who survived, it must be for a reason.'

'He will always be with me. Always, Sir,' said Paul, whose voice broke into a sob. Jeannot lifted the boy off his feet, and placed the lad's head on his powerful shoulder.

'Listen, my boy. You survived. Now you owe it to Pierrot to become a righteous man. Never forget to do him proud. You hear me?'

'I promise,' said the boy, controlling his sobs.

Jeannot put the boy back down but remained crouched at his level. 'Be brave, my little man. Look after your mother till I get back.'

'I will, Sir.'

'The doctor says she is over the worst. When she comes round, tell her we have gone to Schaffhausen. Tell her I will be back to collect you both when she is better.'

Getting up, Jeannot laid a gentle hand on the boy's mop of hair. Then he walked briskly to the waiting cart at the main lake road.

The boy wanted to see Ginette and Pierrot's sisters, but something prevented him from approaching the end of the narrow street: shyness, modesty, guilt perhaps. So he remained where he was, and watched the carriages from a distance roll away along the coast till they were screened by houses. He felt an urge to run down to the track as a horrible feeling of loneliness swept through him. But he did not want to be left alone in the road near the church where his best friend in the world lay six feet under. So he stayed in front of the house where his mother lay in convalescence, recovering from injuries that were caused, it was assumed, by a falling object. Though how she had managed to board the boat was very much a mystery.

*

On the wooded hill above the church, Cephas Crespin had a better view of the carriages. He watched the cortège rumble along the coast road, and saw the boy enter the house where his mother must be making a recovery.

Cephas was cold, hungry, and seething with ire. Enough niceties now, he thought to himself. He had come to claim his rightful reward, and it was all he could do to prevent himself from running down to the house and taking what was rightfully his, for saving the life of the bourgeois boy.

FOURTEEN

THE LITTLE BOAT arrived at Petit Goave the following day in the blue-grey light of morning.

'Would you like me to wait here with our effects while you find out about our passage?' said Marianne once they were standing on the landing stage. It was a pleasant place to be with the gentle sun on their backs, a clear view across the calm bay on one side, and the laboured fields and luxuriant island-scape on the other.

'Would certainly make sense,' said Jacob, looking about him further up the jetty which met with stone fortifications. 'But if looks are anything to go by, I think you had better stay close by me.'

He was referring to the little groups of matelots here and there who were already dozing, sitting, talking, smoking, and playing games of chance in the open air. These men, Jacob was to learn, were buccaneers recently in from a campaign.

However, it was not the robbery of their effects that concerned Jacob most, but that of Marianne's virtue. So they took up their things, which consisted of a canvas sack each and a small chest that Monsieur Bourget had given Jacob during his stay at Leogane. Inside it were instruments of surgery and vials of medicine that Bourget had in double.

They reported to the commander of the settlement, a certain Captain Capieu, who pointed out *La Charmante*, a small two-masted brigantine, which was sitting at the anchorage among other cargo ships, some being loaded, others offloaded. 'She's a shallow-draft vessel,' said Capieu, 'ideal for hugging the coast out of the reach of Spanish frigates.'

They found the captain of the brigantine, a certain Francis Poirier. He was overseeing a couple of crew members loading barrels into a dinghy for transit to the ship. The captain, an affable, burly man in middle age, wiped his hands on his baggy slops, then he read their order for their passage to Cow Island.

'We'll not be leaving for a day or two, M'sieur,' he said. 'Still waiting for provisions from Le Cap, see. But there's nothing keeping you and your niece from making yourself comfortable on board if that be your pleasure.'

The longer Jacob could remain on firm ground, the better. So he gave thanks to the skipper and told him that Captain Capieu had already mentioned board and a place to sleep. As prisoners of the king, they were, after all, under his jurisdiction.

The following day, Jacob and Marianne walked by the fort that looked over the bay. The mist had cleared, and the view was picturesque and peaceful. With nothing better to do, they soon found themselves in conversation with three of the buccaneers they had seen on arrival.

It so happened they too were expecting provisions from Le Cap. Neither Marianne nor Jacob had ever met a buccaneer before, and as a matter of fact, these turned out to be most civil and affable.

They explained they had got good pay from a recent expedition, so good, in fact, that they were deliberating whether to go on privateering, or to follow the governor's petition for them to withdraw from service and set themselves up in a more tranquil occupation.

'You being a man of culture, Monsieur Delpech, what would you do with the loot?' said the man who had introduced himself as Thomas Leberger.

It seemed quite abstract to be here in this idyllic scenery, tranquilly being asked advice by men who were mercenaries and killers, although you would not necessarily think it to hear them speak as they did in earnest. Even so, Marianne thought that a tactful tone would be the best to adopt, but Jacob, faithful to himself, said, 'Well, I should put down my sword, take a wife, and follow a more Christian way of life, and repent for the sins I have committed.'

After a brief, uncomfortable silence which made Marianne's pulse throb, the man glanced at her, looked levelly at Jacob, and said, 'I'm a religious man meself. We always pray before battle, don't we, lads?'

'Yeah, and after our last victory,' said the man to his right, 'Raveneau got us singing out a Te Deum, didn't he?'

'Aye,' said the man to his left. 'Best look after your soul. You can kill a man, but you can't take his soul, can ya?'

'No, you cannot take a man's soul,' said Jacob, 'because it is your soul that determines whether you go to heaven or hell.'

'I can see you've got a smart head on you, Monsieur,' said Leberger. 'And that be exactly what I was thinking 'n' all. Just needed to hear it out loud, like.'

The buccaneer reached into a pouch inside his jacket and

said, 'Here, take this as a token of my gratitude, Sir.' He ostentatiously handed Jacob a Spanish gold escudo, though what the man stalked in the tail of his eye was the niece's reaction.

Jacob was about to protest when Mademoiselle Duvivier, who had turned her head and was glancing into the bay, said, 'Is that the ship?'

Monsieur Leberger took a step towards her, so close that she could feel the heat of his suntanned body, and capped his eyes with a hand to reduce the glare from the sea. 'By the thunder of Neptune, I believe it is!' he said. Then, after a clap on the back from his mates, he cordially bid farewell, leaving Jacob one gold coin the richer, and Marianne all aquiver.

She seemed to stare out at the roadstead, still capping her brow with a hand, though the sun was behind her. But secretly, she was straining her eyes to watch the matelots as they hurried back along the quayside towards the township, to alert their other mates. Their smell, that of strong men, lingered with her a moment, as did their litheness. But then she shut them from her mind and followed Jacob's gaze over the roadstead where the cargo ship was dropping anchor.

They stood watching a good while as the crew offloaded the delivery of people and goods. The longboat was soon advancing at a good pace through the calm, dazzling water, carrying a small number of passengers, no doubt returning planters having bought provisions in Le Cap Français—or so thought Marianne and Jacob.

Delpech gave Mademoiselle Duvivier a gentle nudge as the longboat came closer. 'Marianne!' called a familiar voice, and the next instant, the young woman had shed her womanhood and, caught between tears and laughter, began running like a child to the wharf-side. The old lady, sitting beside a woman in her forties, was her grandmother.

A short while later, the girl wiped her eyes as she embraced her only relative, the witness of her identity, and her only link to her ancestry. She became filled with the irreplaceable love of generations, as her grandmother held her head to her bosom.

Was it an incredible coincidence? Or was it a noble act of kindness that brought them together again? Jacob suspected the latter, and he was now beginning to understand why, of all places, Lieutenant Dumas had sent them to Cow Island, the place where everyone knew ships stopped to water before continuing their voyage to Jamaica. Was it not to give them a chance to abscond?

By late afternoon, the brigantine was loaded, and the captain chose to sail out with the land breeze along the coast.

The evening below deck was spent in conversation, with the two parties sharing their stories under lamplight. Madame de Fontenay and her friend, whose name was Madame Charlotte Odet, were unaware of the shipwreck which many aboard *La Marie* had mistaken for *La Concorde*. However, Madame Odet recounted how the ship that brought her from France, *L'Espérance*, was indeed shipwrecked off Martinique. There were only forty survivors who were taken to CapFrançais, where not long after, *La Concorde* came to moor and delivered her load of Huguenots. The two ladies joined forces and formed a religious resistance. They urged everyone to refuse to join the Catholic Church and encouraged recently converted colonists to convert back.

'We supposed they could not put up with us any longer,'

said Madame de Fontenay. 'And I knew you were further down the coast and hoped that was where we were headed. And here we are!'

It became apparent to the young woman now that her continual remonstrance had not fallen upon deaf ears after all.

'But why did the lieutenant governor not tell you about your grandmother?' said Madame Odet.

'I do not know,' said Marianne.

'I can only surmise,' said Jacob, 'that it is the policy of the government to separate families in an attempt to break their will. And in the case of Monsieur Dumas, being formerly of Protestant stock himself, he did not want to risk looking as if he would favour a Calvinist. I suspect he knew he would be doubly watched by the clergy.'

'Anyway, I am pleased to see my granddaughter looking so well,' said Madame de Fontenay, smiling at Monsieur Delpech and Marianne sitting opposite her. She sensed they had become close and was not surprised to hear of their uncle-and-niece act.

'Jolly good for you,' she said. 'I knew I could count on you, Sir, the moment I set eyes on you!'

It was a joyful reunion, only darkened by the horrible stories of brutality and bondage, and the fact they were still prisoners themselves. Jacob asked Madame de Fontenay what her intentions were now.

She said, 'I have decided not to think of tomorrow. Not to regret the past. Just to live life in the present, in the company of my dear granddaughter until I see her wed.'

'Grandmother!' said Mademoiselle Duvivier.

'You are nearly eighteen, my dear. It is that time in a woman's life.'

The old lady was certainly an inspiration, thought Jacob. She managed to battle on despite her age, having lost her family, home, and heritage. But his own situation was not that of Madame de Fontenay, and he could not share her outlook. As they tucked in for the night trip, he could think of nothing but a future day when he would be reunited with Jeanne and his children. He was as eager as ever to make his escape.

*

A few days later, they dropped anchor in front of Grand-Anse, a small village without defences that had been constantly harassed and plundered by the Spanish. Perhaps they did it, thought Jacob, in retaliation of French buccaneers such as Monsieur Leberger, who plundered and sacked Spanish townships on the great island of Cuba. Did these filibusters realise that while they were filling their coffers with stolen riches, the civilian population was losing their livelihood through no aggression of their own? But would they care? Probably not. It was becoming more and more apparent to Jacob that the New World was in fact a self-destructive society, centred on individual wealth and success. A world where barbarians could become masters.

A good number of these villagers mounted aboard *La Charmante*, in the hope they would be better protected on the fortified Cow Island.

There followed a hullabaloo of hoisting, packing, and securing what possessions they had before the brigantine was ready to take to the sea again.

'I bet you weren't expecting us lot,' said a man in banter from the group of colonists that settled near the Huguenots. They sat, squatted, or lay down as best they could among the ropes and barrels, baskets and chests, pieces of furniture, chickens and goats. 'I bet you ain't never been packed so close,' he said, which Jacob understood as being a reference to their normal respective stations in life. Or was he fishing to see if they were Huguenots?

'Oh, I find it rather cosy,' said Madame de Fontenay. 'One can even kick out one's limbs to their full extent!'

The man laughed out loud at what he took as fair banter from the old lady. Then he said, 'You might not see it the same way come this time next week, though, Ma'am.'

The Huguenots gave a polite and merry utterance, but said nothing of their five-month voyage packed like cattle. It was nonetheless a quiet victory to be treated as ordinary passengers.

It was clear by their conversation and the way they spoke that these folk must have been indentured workers, now freed of their bondage, looking to establish a new life for themselves. Now that the bridge had been established between the classes, conversation turned to planting and crop cultivation, and Jacob was glad to impart some of his knowledge to the man who had first addressed them. He was a smallholder whose name was Jacques Rouchon, thirty-seven years old and originally from Nantes. He said he might even cross over to Jamaica from Cow Island, which gave Jacob further reason to believe his deliverance was nigh.

It was the tenth of June, and they set sail on a fair wind along the coast around the southwest leg of Hispaniola. They arrived at their destination eight days later as a new dawn was breaking.

Upon landfall, as instructed, Jacob handed his third order to the commander of the isle, Major Laurent de Graaf, the notorious buccaneer.

FIFTEEN

A SUMMER HAZE filled the air with scent, and the pleasing buzz of a bee collecting nectar accompanied the visions of Jeanne.

She saw her daughters and Paul playing in a meadow knee-deep in grass and wild flowers, then the girls in their summer dresses, opening a stable door where Paul was making a hay camp with Pierrot. But the sky suddenly darkened. Then there was rain, torrential rain, a river, and a soldier with a stern stance. Fear stabbed her heart as the eyes turned to murderous rage, and she saw the pauper raising a cudgel above her as she placed herself in front of her son in the bottom of a boat.

'No, no!' she called out, and immediately a new light, soft and dazzling, came over her as beads of perspiration shimmered upon her brow. She opened her eyes, dazzled by colours, and she found herself in a snug wooden bed, in a room with flowers on the balconette. A large-boned woman was attaching a shutter so that it would not slam shut, and bees were dancing in the geraniums.

'Mother.'

Jeanne tried to open wide her eyes, which made her wince, and cupping the side of her swollen face, she turned her head to see her son. He had leapt out of a chair and approached her. Under his smile, she saw a trauma, and she knew, even before tears welled in the boy's eyes, the tragedy of Pierre.

'You are to stay as long as it takes to mend your head, Madame Delpech. I have been given instructions.' It was the large lady who spoke the words in her slow Swiss accent, thickened by guttural intonations. She was evidently from the northern parts and introduced herself as the housekeeper.

For the next few days, the nightmares and the dizziness kept Jeanne mostly to her bed. It was not until she was able to dress and go down for dinner that she met her host.

As Paul led his mother from her room, she discovered a spacious house of solid build, timber-framed and clad in stone. The wooden staircase creaked as they descended. At its foot stood a tall, finely carved case clock that counted time peacefully. It sounded its pleasant chime as Jeanne and Paul entered the solidly furnished dining room, where a white-haired gentleman stood up and smiled on their arrival.

'Madame, you were brought here and now you are under my protection,' he said, after the pleasantries of introduction. 'And I might add, I am a good friend of Pastor Duveau, who sends his kind regards but has had to remain in Geneva to carry out his duties. You are welcome to stay as long as you wish in my household, Madame.'

'You are most kind, Sir. I will repay you for your hospitality . . . and for these clothes,' said Jeanne. The housemaid had laid them out for her and explained that they had belonged to the gentleman's daughter, who had moved

141

to another town with her new husband. He wanted her to have them.

'Shan't hear of it. I am but an old man, and I crave company. It is I who thank you, Madame Delpech. And your son is charming. We have been entertaining ourselves during your convalescence by playing chess. I might add, he has talent!'

Monsieur Gaugin was a jovial gentleman, an alderman with a scholar's stoop. At table over leek soup, he said, 'I am myself of French heritage; my father came here when he was still a child. So, my dear Madame, my forbears were in the same situation as you find yourself today. And I consider it a duty and a pleasure to welcome you here where my grandfather was welcomed, by none other than his future father-in-law!'

'You are most generous, Sir. However, I really must make my way north. First to Schaffhausen,' said Jeanne, taking care not to show the side of her face that was black and blue.

'My dear lady, are you sure you are fit to travel?'

'My wounds will heal. Those of my friend's are much deeper. She lost her son.'

'Yes, I know, a terrible tragedy for many. Well, the difficulty will reside in finding transport, it being the busy season in the fields, you know. Moreover, did Monsieur Fleuret not say he would be back for you?'

'I am not so sure he would leave his wife and children alone now. And I would not expect him to. We shall go on foot.'

'All the way to Schaffhausen?'

'Yes,' said Jeanne, touching Paul's head. 'Then on to London, if that is what it will take to recover my children with my husband.'

'In that case, I will advise you which route to take to Schaffhausen. For it would be unwise to walk for long stretches after the fall and the knock to your head. We all wondered how you got it. Were you hit by a barrel?'

Jeanne realised that no one was any the wiser as to the pauper's appalling behaviour; her son had not then revealed anything, but had he seen? Not wanting to delay further, she decided to keep it to herself. What concerned her more was reaching Ginette. She could well imagine her pain at losing her only son.

The following day, Monsieur Gaugin brought good news. There would be a charabanc to Morge, from where he knew daily journeys were made northward. It would not be difficult to reach Yverdon. From there she should take the boat across the lake to Neuchatel.

*

Holding Paul firmly by the hand, Jeanne paced through the milling crowd at the lakeside port of Yverdon, to find out about the passage to the other side. Her eye was suddenly caught by a flash of green. She stopped to focus her gaze on a small group of ladies by the wharf chattering, their young children playing at their skirts. A shudder of horror seized her, and she grasped Paul more firmly by the hand.

'What is it, Mother?'

'Nothing. It is nothing.'

But Paul had followed her gaze to the clutch of chatting ladies and saw the reason for his mother's sudden anguish. One of the women was wearing her green coat. It had been cleaned and was adorned with a brooch, but it could not possibly be anything other than the one she had cherished.

It was evident from the lady's hat and shoes that the coat did not suit her budget. She must have bought it at an old-clothes stand or from a stranger.

'I see,' said Paul, as his mother turned and instinctively glanced around her, as if searching for an invisible menace.

But the boy slipped his hand from her grasp and ran towards the lady. On approach, just six feet from where the brood of ladies was chatting, he deliberately tripped himself up—a trick he had learnt from Pierrot. As he went down, he let out a yelp.

'Ah, my knee! My knee!' he wailed out.

Seeing the lady she took as the boy's mother in simple but quality clothing, the ladies reacted to the child's cries, and one of them broke away to tend to the lad. It was the woman in green.

'You alright, my love?' she said while Jeanne was rushing over to him. 'He yours, Madame?'

'Yes, no, I'm his aunt. Always slipping away and finding trouble, he is,' said Jeanne, taking the boy by the arm to pull him onto his feet. But the boy still clutched his knee.

'Kids these days, eh? Well, he shan't be hopping away anymore today.'

'Come on, Jacob, now, please. I've told you before, stop running off. What will your mother say if I lose you?'

'Oh, mine's just as bad,' said the lady. Jeanne looked at the boy next to the woman, two inches shorter than Paul, who was standing beside her with a big-eyed grin and a naughty smile.

'Ouch, it hurts!'

'Serves you right, young man!' said the lady, siding with the boy's aunt. 'You ought to learn to do as your aunt says.'

'I'm taking him to see his grandparents. Travelling yourself?'

'Payerme. We are travelling to Payerme.'

'Well, Madame, I shan't keep you. Come along, Jacob, up you get. Thank you, Madame.'

'Ouch, stop pulling, my aunt,' said Paul, walking with a limp. 'It still hurts!'

'Oh, I am sorry,' said Jeanne, continuing in a low voice, 'I thought you were playacting.'

'That was the plan, but my knee landed on a cobblestone.'

'And to think I thought you were overdoing the acting!'

'So? Is it or isn't it?' said the boy.

Jeanne looked down at her son, and realised at that moment how very astute and adult he had grown. She realised she now had more than a son; she had a clever accomplice. In a low voice, walking as fast through the crowd as Paul's limp would allow, she said, 'It is. I recognised my threading where I patched it up under the arm.'

'Thought so.' Paul had justly sensed her anxiety. 'Was it stolen, then?'

At first Jeanne did not want to let him in on her secret. But given the turn of events, she led him away from the crowd to the side of the wharf, and told him briefly about the aggression that took place while he lay unconscious in the boat.

'I thought there was something awry. Monsieur Cephas was nowhere to be seen among the survivors. So you think he might be wanting to get what he thought he stole?'

'You can never be too prudent when it comes to individuals of that sort. And by the way, your name is Jacob from now on,' she said, keeping her voice down.

145

'Jacob and the coat of many colours!' said Paul, with a clever grin.

'Jacob Delgarde de Castanet,' said Jeanne a moment later, as she smudged and scraped the attestation—already subjected to soaking from the boat accident—on a stone mooring bollard.

*

The Swiss Confederacy had by this time become relatively organised. Not wanting people to linger too long, it had set up road and boat links which conveyed refugees onward in their trek north. In most places, the local inhabitants had become used to the continuous flow of travellers, and were in the main prepared to harbour passers-by for the night until transport was arranged.

A short while later, Jeanne and Paul stood in the queue for the boat from Yverdon to Neuchatel. Since the tragedy—especially as the captain had been publicly shamed and sent to prison—checks had become more rigorous and boarding more controlled, with priority given to Huguenot women, children, and old folk.

The agent studied Jeanne's attestation.

'It got soaked, Monsieur. I was on board the ship that capsized.'

'I am sorry, Madame, a tragedy from what have heard. I was just trying to decipher your name. I have been asked to look out for a lady and a boy, and you seem to fit the description.'

Jeanne gave her son's hand a light squeeze. 'I don't think so, Monsieur, what was the name?'

'Delpech.'

Jeanne tried to keep her face from revealing her shock as she said, 'Well, as you can see, I am Delgarde de Castanet.'

'Yes, that's what I was wondering. See, there's a water mark on Del—.'

'—garde, Delgarde.'

'Pity, would have saved you from travelling alone.'

How could the pauper have the audacity? thought Jeanne. But then again, he had fooled everyone once. There was no reason why such a conniving mind would not try to do so again.

'I assure you, it is Delgarde. Delgarde de Castanet.'

'Yes, I see, please take your place aboard, Madame. Next.'

SIXTEEN

SURROUNDED BY TREACHEROUS shoals and reefs, Cow Island was a perilous place for the unsuspecting captain, which, Jacob deduced, made it consequently more difficult to raid. However, for the knowing master and commander, it was a choice spot, a place to shelter and careen, which was doubly why Laurent de Graaf had made it his base, and all the more so now that his command of it had been officialised by the French governor of Saint-Domingue. It was for this reason that the group of freed indentured colonists had elected to establish themselves here.

The buccaneer, revered by the French and feared by the Spanish, did not look at all like the callous man Jacob had been expecting. He was very tall, blond, and with his goatee, there was something of the elegance of a musketeer about him. In fact, he was disarmingly charming and refused to let Jacob reside any place other than in his own house, which, he said, had enough room to accommodate the ladies, if they did not mind sharing.

'Well, Sir, I do not know what to say,' said Jacob as they approached the promontory where the house was perched.

It overlooked the northwest bay and the little natural harbour below. Madame Odet, Madame de Fontenay, and Mademoiselle Duvivier were walking along with them.

'Then say nothing, Monsieur Delpech,' said the newly appointed major, who motioned to the ladies to enter the modest abode before him. 'Ladies. I pray you enjoy your stay here at Cow Island.'

It was a modest house with a tin roof, and yet it was more convivial than the residence of Monsieur Verbizier.

The following morning, as the sun was rising, Jacob was woken by hollering sailors, banging and rolling noises, and all sorts of hubbub coming from down at the cove where de Graaf's great frigate was anchored. From his whitewashed window, Jacob could easily see the tall, energetic figure of the young major, directing operations.

An hour later, on striding up to the house in front of which Jacob was now standing, de Graaf said, 'Ah, Monsieur Delpech, you must excuse me, I have urgent business at my plantation in Petit Goave.'

Jacob had acquired a certain empathy for the man, knowing from their talk of the previous evening about how he himself had been a slave in the hands of the Spanish on the Canary Islands. He no doubt inspired the same feeling of kinship in his men which made him such a charismatic commander to fight for.

'I hope there is nothing awry, Monsieur de Graaf,' said Jacob, glancing across the harbour. It was a beautiful morning over the limpid aquamarine bay, rimmed with immaculate strips of sand where coconut trees grew. And there was not a ripple on the water.

'Just routine,' said the buccaneer, 'nothing I cannot handle.'

He did not halt but followed his stride into the study, where he retrieved some rolled charts. Then, on his way back through the hall, he said, 'During my absence, an English merchant ship will call by here. Do not be alarmed. The captain is a friend of mine. Daniel Darlington is his name. He will be arriving from Saint Thomas.'

'An Englishman?'

'I trust I can count on you to give him a warm welcome on my behalf?' said Laurent de Graaf, with an eloquent smile.

This was clearly a tacit invitation to leave the island, was it not?

'You may indeed, Sir,' said Jacob with discretion.

'Good man,' said de Graaf, tapping Jacob on the round of his shoulder. 'And I am certain you will find him receptive to your cause.'

'Understood, and I must thank you for your hospitality, Sir,' said Jacob.

'You are most welcome. And, please do not think me pert, but I hope to find my house empty when I return!' The tall Dutchman gave a short bow, then continued out through the door. 'My regards to the ladies!' he called back. 'Oh, and there are men I have left in charge here. They are here to guard against outside aggression, but they have orders to leave you in peace.'

*

Within the hour, the famous captain had departed as he had planned. And over the coming weeks, several times a day, Jacob looked through the brass spyglass he found in the salon, in the hope of spotting the silhouette of a ship on the eastern horizon.

During this time, he also explored the islet high and low, in its length and breadth. He made sketches, read up on medicinal plants, and, having found a musket in a cupboard, went hunting with Jacques Rouchon, the indentured worker he met on board *La Charmante* at Grand Anse. Rouchon was jovial company, rustic but practical-minded; he was also a crack shot and an excellent trapper. During their hunting jaunts, he recounted the exploits of de Graaf, how the colossus had defended the coast of Saint-Domingue against the Spaniards from Cuba, and how he had made a fortune plundering their treasure fleet and settlements.

'Very clever man, de Graaf. Can speak to his men in four different languages, you know,' said Rouchon one day as they were resting on the hilltop. It offered an impressive view over the lush mangrove forest on one side, and the harbour inlet fringed with golden beach on the other. 'And shrewd with it,' he continued. 'Do you know why else he's so attached to this here island?'

'I should think because it is easy to defend, for one,' said Delpech, scanning the eastern horizon through his spyglass.

'And because of the sunken treasure!'

'Treasure?'

'Aye, down there somewhere be the treasure of Captain Morgan of Jamaica,' said Rouchon, motioning towards the inlet, which prompted Jacob to swing round with the spyglass. Rouchon then recounted the story of how the islet used to be one of Morgan's assembly points, where pirates from all around the Caribbean would come together and join forces before heading out on a campaign against the Spaniards.

'Then one day, while they were making merry and letting

off muskets and guns and what have you, a spark flew into the gunpowder room and blew up Morgan's ship! That weren't all. She took down with her the two captured French ships laden with treasure! Just think, it could be at the bottom of that there inlet.'

'Then why does nobody fetch it up?'

'It be cursed; not even Morgan can touch it. He came back for it only to wreck another ship!'

'But why would it be cursed?' said Jacob, who was less interested in Morgan's treasure than the moral of the tale.

'Because the explosion took with it three hundred men, most of 'em so sozzled out of their brains, they couldn't swim even if they knew how! Three hundred souls haunt that very cove. Makes yer shiver, dunnit.'

On another occasion, Rouchon admitted he had come to the island with the other colonists, just to see with his own eyes where the treasure might lie. But given the curse, and now that he had been and seen, he was finding the mosquito-infested islet too small. He was wondering if he should try his hand on a larger island, one far from Santo Domingo and the Spanish raiders of Cuba. And one place that sprang to mind was again the one he briefly evoked on the brigantine. It was Jamaica.

With a free reign on the islet and with want of what to do, both Rouchon and Delpech also lent a hand to the other colonists. They had settled on the southwest slopes on the other side of the freshwater pond, though still only a short distance from the northwest harbour.

The eastern part was mostly avoided. Being low-lying, it was full of unhealthy swampland infested with mosquitoes, the island's biggest blight. Since their arrival, the new settlers had, despite the stifling heat and the incommodious insects blown by the breeze, already built rudimentary accommodation, churned and turned over the soil, planted crops, and located the best places to catch the massive manatee—a native delicacy—and the wild boar that roamed freely on the big island opposite.

To pass the time, Jacob had acquired an interest in sketching. He found the island offered incredible diversity for such a relatively small area. It seemed moreover to bring him closer to God; it gave him an even greater appreciation of His intricate creation. These were times he preferred to be alone. But of late, he had invited Mademoiselle Duvivier to join him.

One of the guards, a young man of some vigour, in the absence of normal social boundaries, had become helpful, then amiable, then forward. And he now was in danger of becoming blatantly disrespectful, taking it upon himself to call upon the ladies morning and afternoon under the pretext of proposing his aid for anything they desired. It was becoming awkward. Private Guillaume Girard was a simple commoner but a guard all the same, and they were theoretically his prisoners. What was more, he tended to pass by while Jacob was on one of his jaunts.

Marianne going out sketching with Jacob had curbed young Girard's ardour. At least, so it seemed.

Marianne enjoyed sketching out in the field as much as Jacob did. And when he attempted to explain to her the rudiments of art, it turned out that she had a far greater talent for it than he had. At times she wished she could be in a place where she could enjoy the same rights as men, so that she could learn to become a proper artist.

It was while they were out sketching the mangrove forest one morning that Jacob at last spotted the English merchant ship. They collected their apparatus, borrowed from the house—a spoil from a Spanish settlement—and together they hurried back to break the news to the ladies.

*

That was almost a week ago. Delpech had hoped he would be on his way to London by now. He was gazing out across the cove where the merchant ship lay on its flank like a beached whale in the shallow water. He had heard vaguely about careening. Now he was seeing it with his own eyes.

The ship was lashed down by ropes that were tied to the masts at one end and wrapped around palm trees at the other. The sun had been up only an hour, and already shipmates were working alongside her in a row—a few standing in the longboat, others on wooden platforms— chipping away the barnacles and scraping off the seagrass and seaweed on the exposed surface of the hull.

Captain Daniel Darlington, a well-spoken gentleman, not yet thirty, had explained to Jacob that if they did not careen and repair the ship, they would be at a serious disadvantage if they came across a Spanish patrol or vulgar freebooters. As it was, his ship *La Belle* had only just escaped pursuit coming round Puerto Rico. The embedded weed and molluscs had restricted manoeuvrability and created drag that had considerably slowed her down. She had received damage at mid-port just above the waterline, before she could get away with all the sail she could make.

So it was time to fix her up and give her a smooth hull. They would have to replace any splintered or worm-eaten timbers, and caulk and shellac gaps between planks, before applying a coat of amber-coloured tar to the whole for optimum protection.

Once repaired, the vessel would have to be hauled out and floated, then ballasted, balanced, and loaded with all the cargo, tackle, water, and supplies that had been removed to make her lighter for hauling. The whole job would probably take a couple of weeks, the crew being no more than a handful of seafarers.

Jacob had waited three years to be set free. He would gladly wait a few weeks more rather than risk foundering at sea.

Moreover, Darlington was not heading for London as Jacob had hoped, but up along the east coast of North America, to the province where he was born of a Dutch mother and an English pastor. Mr Darlington had nonetheless assured Monsieur Delpech that it was easy to get a passage back to Europe from New York.

Daniel Darlington spoke some French and lent a sympathetic ear when his replacement hosts recounted their odyssey, especially—and this did not escape Jacob's attention—when Marianne spoke. During the first dinner at the house given in his honour, Marianne seemed to glow with inner contentment which made her even more poised, fresh, and beautiful. It was the glow of youth, of youth eager to shine, of youth in search of a soul-mate. The young captain was captivated by her metropolitan manners. She was as refined as porcelain, which made him feel at moments coarser than he really was.

He was nonetheless a wealthy man, and showed the spirit of nonconformist nonchalance common to men of means.

He was of the first generation of the English fledgling township of New York. And he was proud of it, although he would certainly not swear allegiance to the English crown, or to any other crown for that matter.

Upon that first dinner—Darlington would dine at the house every evening thereon—Jacob saw clearly that a mutual empathy had been borne between the young people. An empathy which neither he nor Madame de Fontenay cared to discourage.

After the arrival of *La Belle* in the natural harbour, instead of accompanying Jacob, Marianne took to sketching the ship being hauled and secured for careening, and the operations thereafter, Darlington ever at hand to explain each operation to her. Her grandmother was never far away, chatting with Madame Odet and darning or embroidering new coifs, while secretly reporting to each other any signs of first love.

So Delpech suspected why the previous evening, Mr Darlington had insisted that the two of them spend the morning hunting together. He now turned to face the young man as he strode up to the house from the harbour, kitted out with his fusil over his shoulder.

Daniel Darlington said, 'Please forgive me if I am a little late, Monsieur Delpech. I was just going over the hull with my carpenter. It seems there is more damage than we initially anticipated. Several more planks need replacing.'

'That is unfortunate,' said Jacob, standing with his leather pouch strapped over his shoulder and his flintlock musket at his side.

'Thankfully, however, our absent host is as far-sighted as he is courageous; he always has seasoned lumber lying around in the storehouse for such cases.'

'Good, it would not do to take in water,' said Jacob with a congenial smile, despite the extra setback. 'But come, let us be off, before the sun gets too high.'

The two men stepped off at a brisk pace in the freshness of the beautiful morning.

'Would you believe, I always water here on the way from Saint Thomas, and yet I have never ventured further inland than the port beach?'

'Then be prepared to see some delights of God's nature, Mr Darlington!'

They took a forest trail past swamps. And as they climbed the hillock to dominate the scenery, they spoke again about the news from England, fresh from Darlington's contacts in Saint Thomas. It was not what Jacob had hoped. James II was still trying to establish Catholicism. There was even talk of the Protestant clergy inviting the Dutch king to take his place. This could mean yet another civil war in England. Jacob might have to set his sights on Amsterdam instead.

*

'That is where you will find turtles and manatees,' said Jacob, pointing to the expanse of seagrass and remarking that it grew as lush as the meadows of Holland.

'My friend, de Graaf, must feel quite at home then,' said Daniel Darlington.

'Except that in Holland, there are no slaves, sugar cane, or buccaneers!' said Jacob.

'I have been to England and Amsterdam. I realise that it is a very different world from here,' said the young captain, showing he would not shy from a challenge. 'But here, it is a world where only the fittest can survive. It is a land of opportunity; almost any man can live out his dream . . .'

'Or nightmare,' said Jacob. 'Do you know how many human lives your cargo of sugar has probably cost?'

'No, Sir, but I suspect there is injustice in all man's endeavours, and that most people turn a blind eye.'

'So you agree with slavery?'

'I do not, Sir. I am wholly against it. And I might add that I intend to stop this commerce and settle down. For the past five years, I have been going to and from these mosquito-infested lands. I have been shot at and chased, seen my ship pillaged and three times almost shipwrecked, and I can count myself lucky, compared to many of my past acquaintances who are no longer of this world.'

Jacob was about to make a sardonic remark as to the wealth Darlington had acquired, albeit indirectly, on the backs of slaves. But this time, he held his tongue, for he suspected the young man was ready to disclose the real reason for their jaunt around the island. Besides, he was right about how easily people turned a blind eye to recurrent atrocities. Did Jacob himself not turn a blind eye to galley slaves when he was a bourgeois in France not so long ago? Had he not financed an unspecified cargo lost at sea with his legal colleagues when in Montauban?

In a less controversial tone, Jacob said, 'And what might you do, Sir?'

'I plan to invest in my hometown and build a family before this life gets the better of me too.'

'I was given to believe you were unattached,' said Jacob, who had decided to make it easy for him.

'Yes, Sir, that is so, but the time has come for me to take a wife.'

'Indeed.'

'Yes, Monsieur Delpech, which brings me round to why I have asked you to walk with me this morning. I would like to speak about your niece.'

During their evening meals, Marianne had continued to address Jacob as her uncle—she had become so used to doing it in Leogane that it had become an automatism, and it still brought her reassurance while upholding the boundaries of their relationship, for Jacob Delpech still cut an attractive figure.

So Jacob thought he had better set the young captain right. Casting his gaze away from the expanse of seagrass, he turned to Darlington and said, 'Well, wait a moment. I must put you straight about one thing—'

'With all due respect, Sir, please hear me out,' said Darlington, afraid that Jacob was about to nip his prepared rhetoric in the bud, and his affections with it. 'I know you intend to return to Europe. However, I have struck up a rare fondness for Miss Duvivier, and I believe it is, or at least I hope, it is reciprocated.'

'What does she say?'

'She has no plans for the future, which is why I would like to ask your consent to ask for her hand.'

'Are you not precipitating things somewhat, Sir?'

'If I wait, she may get used to the idea of going back to Europe.'

'Have you spoken to her about your feelings?'

'I wanted to ask her uncle his consent first, so that what I will offer her will be free of obstacle. I mean, not that I mean you would be an obstacle, Sir . . .'

'Indeed, I shall not,' said Jacob. There was really no point beating about the bush, and the truth was, Jacob and Madame de Fontenay had already spoken about the eventuality. It would be a godsend.

'But, Sir, I beg you,' said the young man, his face flushed with a sense of injustice, 'please hear me out before making a rash decision. I realise that you wish to rebuild your heritage in Europe, but . . . I love her . . .'

'I am afraid you have misunderstood, Mr Darlington. I said I shall not. I shall not constitute a hindrance,' said Jacob. A visible wave of joy spread over the young man's face. Jacob continued, 'If you both desire to create a life together, then you must. As long as she finds the comfort she deserves, and her grandmother is well looked after in her advancing years.'

'Oh, she will, Sir,' said the young man eagerly.

'Good. And by the way, I was going to say I am not actually her uncle. At least, not by blood, although I have looked over her as if she were my own daughter.'

It could not have turned out better, and Jacob was delighted for the girl and relieved to have the responsibility removed. The young man was strong, his father was a pastor, he had resources—the cargo alone would make him a rich man—and to be frank, her breeding would certainly refine any coarseness Darlington had acquired owing to his birth and New World way of life. And with her strength of character, he trusted that she would make Darlington see the senseless savagery of slavery. Yes, it could not have turned out better. And now he would be able to concentrate on getting back to his own family.

The sun was near its highest point, and the heat was already stifling, so they decided to turn back westward towards the natural harbour. As he turned, Jacob caught sight of a distant ship. On seeing it too, Darlington was seized by a sense of urgency, and in a falsely calm voice, he said, 'If she consents, I dearly hope you will give her away.'

'Before you speak of marriage, should you not get to know each other better first?'

'Of course, of course, I am jumping the gun. She must know where I live, meet my family. No doubt I have seen too many of my friends die too young. Life is not like in Europe, as you well know. Here you have to seize the opportunity before it passes you by.'

But fate would have it otherwise. Delpech would not give her away to Mr Darlington after all.

*

Earlier that morning, a little after eight o'clock, Marianne Duvivier emerged from the house, fuming.

She had hardly slept a wink all night, what with the heat and the mosquitoes buzzing around her ears, and then with silly, rambling thoughts of Mr Darlington. How dare he laugh at her efforts to speak English during dinner! His French was hardly the epitome of eloquence either. Although it did occur to her that she had a tendency to correct his grammar, often. But then why did he insist that his ship was feminine when the proper language dictated it to be *le* and not *la navire*? And yet he would not have it any other way.

And how dare Monsieur Delpech accept to take him on a jaunt without her, as if it were too dangerous. After all she had been through, honestly, she had faced more terrors than many a trooper! Did they really take her for a silly young girl? And Monsieur Delpech, of all people; she thought he at least was on her side. She might have all the inconveniences of her sex—her periodical discharge, the cumbersome layers of clothing that made a woman of quality ostensibly decent—but that did not make her inept. And to top it all, now squalls of wind kept upsetting her hair.

But she would not be compounded just because there was no man about. Besides, the days had become far too warm and sticky to stay indoors, even behind closed shutters. So after her coffee, she took up her sketching equipment and the little folding stool which Jacob had fitted with straps. And despite her grandmother's remonstrance—none too insistent, as the old lady had not slept either—she headed off past the swamp area to the hillock on the south side of the little island.

Three quarters of an hour later, she was setting up on the clifftop to finish her sketch of the farmstead huts which spread along the low ground in the distance. She unfolded her stool close to the ledge, where the sea breeze kept the mosquitoes at bay, and sat with her knees supporting her drawing.

By the time she had finished her landscape piece, the big golden sun was blazing high in the sky. It was sweltering. She stood up, capped her eyes with her right hand, and looked eastward. There was still no sign of the amblers, not that she was expecting them, of course, but in the distance, she could see the outline of an approaching ship.

Then she moved her gear back forty yards to the shade of the trees on the edge of the wood.

*

Private Guillaume Girard was twenty-three. Until a few days ago, he had high hopes of declaring his flame—a flame that still raged inside despite the arrival of the Englishman. In fact, now it raged even more fiercely, for it was also fuelled by the feeling of injustice and the power of jealousy.

Girard knew he was better-looking than the merchant captain, and more practical too, and yet the Englishman walked in with a hull full of sugar, and she practically fell at his feet. Girard saw her turn on her charm like a soft glow in a warm night, as she had done with him: a smile that any man would die for, and the way she let her hand lightly touch his arm so he just melted into submission.

For five weeks, he had been shadowing her. Normal enough; he had been given the job of keeping an eye on the Huguenots. The old captain of the garrison—which consisted of just a handful of men—knew too well you had to keep reports up to date no matter what your commander said, because commanders could come and go as quickly as the turn of the tide. And that meant keeping your eye out in case questions were asked.

What the old captain did not foresee, though, was that Girard would get a twinkle in the eye for Miss Huguenot.

The soldier now often thought back at how he had cherished every one of her smiles at the beginning of their "relationship". How she had encouraged their nascent camaraderie, asking him a multitude of favours, and each time he obliged unfailingly. Would you bring us some fresh water, Monsieur Girard? Could you fetch some wood for the stove, Monsieur Girard? Do you think you could possibly retrieve that coconut up there, Guillaume? What a bloody baboon he had been! What a lackey! And yet he had felt a real complicity grow between them. That is, until the old crow poked her beak in.

Nevertheless, he still had been able to observe her from the woods, from behind the rocks, and at night from the top of the slope that overlooked her room. He had learnt her every move. He had even seen her piss twice. Once in her room, and another time out in the field during a sketching session. It had taken all his willpower to keep himself from appearing in front of her. A whore once told him that women have an extra sense that tells them when a man is watching. And that they watched men even more than men watched them. It was obvious, of course, but it was nice to hear it confirmed by an expert on human nature.

Yes, Mademoiselle Duvivier knew what she was doing all along. Of course she was leading him on. It was time to see how far she would go now that he had her alone at last.

*

Girard had been crouching in the cover of the woods, doing his job, spying on her. He was now leaning behind a group of trees, and stood there in hiding, liberated and eroticised as she approached.

Two minutes later, she was unfolding her stool; then she sat back to take in the view of the sea and the faraway ship. She was in a lethargic, dreamy mood, and was roasting hot. She proceeded to untie her corset from the front, and then slipped her hand inside to open and close her blouse in order to let out hot puffs of air.

She let her thoughts run wild, as she often did at this time of day. Of course she was still a virgin. But she knew about lovemaking; she had seen a horse mount a nag when she was eleven. The image often played on her mind, and when she saw a man, she sometimes found herself wondering what he was like. Despite her prayers, this longing would never go away completely, so she had learnt to live with it, and let herself flirt with the idea in the privacy of her mind.

She now pictured the handsome Captain Darlington, his lips, his regular teeth, and his large hands. She felt like a woman in his eyes; he had known her no other way. Would he or wouldn't he? she wondered. Then she imagined him nude and her head level with his chest, her hands exploring his body.

She tugged at the lace of her corset to loosen it further. Sitting astride the stool with her back arched, she softly squeezed her plump breast through the fabric of her blouse. She then looked left and right, and brought out both her breasts, one after the other, and felt the air on her intimate skin like a liberation.

He had seen her do this before. This time, he was closer than he had ever been; barely half a dozen yards separated them. But she had her back to him, and he could not feast his eyes on her breasts, which he knew were as plump as pigeons. He had to move a step closer.

A noise in the trees, a bird perhaps, made her start. She swiftly tucked her breasts back into her corset, then spun round to face the woods.

Behind the screen of vegetation, he held his breath.

'Who's there?' she said in a steady voice, for the sake of her own conscience. But then she really did sense someone was spying on her. She had experienced the sensation before.

'Who's there?' she repeated with her hand on her collarbone, her blouse still undone.

'You know who's here, Miss Marianne,' said a man's voice. The girl gasped. Private Girard continued, 'We're drawn together, you and me. And you need me as much as I need you.'

He knew when a girl was ripe to shed her virginity, and he stepped slowly forward till he appeared just a few yards in front of her.

'Stand back, Guillaume!' she ordered, fighting off panic.

With confidence and feeling, he said, 'We just need to hold each other.' He took another step forward and held out his hand. 'Just once.'

'Get back or I shall scream!' she said, pushing back the stool, and she began to draw back slowly.

'No one will know of our little rendezvous.'

'You are drunk, Guillaume! I shall report you to your commander.'

'And I'll tell everyone what you get up to when you're on your own. Admit it, Marianne, you need it the same as I do.'

'Get away from me!' she said, scowling at him defiantly. He lunged for her. She turned to run. But in her panic, she tripped over the stool.

He was soon on top of her, smothering her in the smell of male sweat and rum, holding her in his arms despite her battling to get free.

He flipped her over, sat astride her, and slapped her full on the side of the face to calm her down. It shocked her, numbed her for a moment.

Then she felt his hands fall on her breasts, bunch them up, and squeeze them till they hurt.

'Get off!' she shrieked desperately, struggling to break free.

Having given full vent to her voice, she screamed out again, and again. 'Help! Help! Someone! Jacob! Help!'

But Girard was determined now. Even if it meant throwing her off the cliff once he was done with her. The rocks would break her bones, and the sea would carry her body away. It would be an accident. He would arrange her equipment near the clifftop. The squalls could be strong and treacherous on that south-facing ledge.

She continued to battle and scream, so this time, he punched her hard. He clamped her neck with one hand as a warning. Then he pinned down her shoulders.

She lay still, her head seething. She did not want to be hit again. Neither did she want to pass out.

He then removed his right hand from her left shoulder to feel for the top of his breeches, and to lift up her dress. Clamping her down with his left forearm, with his right hand he cupped her crotch, in the firm belief that she was bound to succumb in the end, just like the other virgins that had gone before her.

Her fingers reached out and touched a hard, cold object the size of a fist. She took it in her hand, but hesitated.

If she hit him, he would be sure to throttle her. He was capable of it. His hands were immeasurably strong. But then she remembered the promise she had made to herself and to Jacob on board the ship from France. She had promised never to succumb to the sovereign force of the male predator. So she clenched the rock tightly and struck Girard's ear as hard as she could.

The blow knocked him off her. She shot up and bolted, screaming for help, up a natural embankment so she might be seen. Despite his bloody ear, he was up after her, as swift as a falcon, and pounced on her shoulders with all his weight.

In the commotion of the ensuing struggle, there came a

loud shot. It made both victim and predator freeze for an instant. Private Girard then instinctively wrapped his arms around his prey, rolling her over.

'Move and I kill you,' shouted the voice of Daniel Darlington, from a distance of twenty-five yards. Girard got to his feet, lifting her with him so that she formed a human shield.

'She's a witch, Sir,' he shouted to Darlington. 'She has bewitched me like she has bewitched you!'

He whipped out his knife from its sheath.

'Do you know what she does when she's alone?'

Marianne felt his powerful forearm on her neck, so tight that it blocked her windpipe. But suddenly the pressure was released, and she sank to her knees, gasping for air. She hung her head while recovering her breath as Darlington ran up to her. The side of her face was heavily bruised, but she told him she was all right. She motioned for him to help Jacob, who was at present wrestling with the soldier twenty years his junior.

Delpech and Darlington had split up as they had come to the opposite side of the wood. They had taken different routes to increase the chances of one of them arriving in time to prevent whatever danger it was that had caused Marianne to scream. Darlington had come round the west flank first; then Jacob had appeared behind Girard, moments after the gunshot.

Girard and Delpech were now locked in a fierce embrace. Jacob had latched onto the soldier's arm to stave off the knife from Marianne's throat. Before Darlington could intervene, they both tripped on a rock that jutted through the turf, and they fell where the ground stepped down just a few feet.

Delpech rolled swiftly away from the soldier so that Darlington could pin the man down with his musket. But there was no need.

Private Girard got to his feet, holding his belly, his face suddenly sobered. He looked down at his hand which he had pulled away. It was covered in blood.

'My God,' said Jacob.

The soldier staggered a few steps before sinking to his knees.

'I loved her,' he said. Then he collapsed completely, face down on the patchy grass.

Jacob was quickly upon the young man, turned him over, felt his pulse. 'My God, he's dead,' he said in horror.

Darlington picked up the bloody knife, glistening on the grass where it fell. He wiped the blade on Girard's shirt and replaced it in the soldier's sheath.

'We must throw him over. He will be taken by the current,' he said, latching onto the body by the ankles.

'My God, man, you cannot . . .'

'His captain will want to know who killed him.'

'But he fell on his own blade, Sir. You bore witness.'

'Doesn't matter,' said Darlington, dragging the body towards the ledge of the cliff. 'I am an English American. You are a Huguenot. You will be placed under arrest, and sent to Leogane to face trial. What chance do you think you will have?'

'He is right, Jacob,' said Marianne, visibly holding back her emotion. 'I hate to say it, but he is right.' She was still in shock, but was herself surprised to find her thoughts lucid and practical. 'His death will condemn you. We cannot let that happen.'

'The man had been drinking. His disappearance will be put down to a tragic accident,' said Darlington, brandishing the soldier's rum flask. 'We will leave this on the edge. We have no choice, Monsieur Delpech. He is dead, and thanks be to God, you and Mademoiselle Duvivier are alive!'

The man's soul had left him, and it was true nothing would be gained by taking the body back; there was no family to mourn him here on the island. It would most likely be buried at sea anyway. So at length, after a short prayer, Jacob agreed to the Englishman's course of action.

The two men solemnly took the body by its wrists and ankles, carried it the rest of the way to the cliff ledge, then swung it twice and let go.

All three of them looked over the edge to see that Girard's body had landed in the shallows. However, instead of being swept out to sea, it soon became apparent that it was being washed to shore.

SEVENTEEN

IT WAS AN hour past noon when the *Sally-Ann* put into the natural harbour to refill with water, venison, and a barrel of fruit.

The two-masted sloop, armed with six guns, was on her way to Jamaica. She displaced 120 tons, was manned by fourteen crew members—composed of a mixed bag of nationalities, led by a French captain—and was carrying a delivery of French wine and fineries procured from merchants in Martinique. Jacob could do worse than to pay for his passage aboard.

Darlington's ship would be flopped on its side for weeks to come, and Girard's body, beached on the south shore, could be discovered at any moment. Once the soldier was reported missing, the garrison commander would put together a search party. So, Jacob concluded, it would be foolish not to take the providential ride to freedom.

He would not be entirely alone. Jacques Rouchon, who knew his way around a ship and could tie knots, had paid his passage by joining the crew. Delpech had told him he lacked the patience to wait another few weeks for Mr

Darlington's ship, laid up as it was, and that he must find a passage to Europe to reunite with his family.

Rouchon had put Jacob's edginess down to the imminent departure when he said: 'Aye, Monsieur Delpech, sure as day follows night, yer bound to find a passage across the Atlantic from Port Royal.'

By early evening, the sloop was ready to slip out with the land wind. Thankfully, Girard's absence had still gone unnoticed. Jacob reckoned his mates were covering for him, thinking he must be sleeping off a drunken stupor somewhere under a tree.

It was a good easterly that blew, and the fat, gleaming sun still had an hour to go before it turned orange and sank into the horizon. Moreover, there was nought on Cow Island that could temp the crew to pass the night there. Truth was, nothing could compare with Port Royal, and they were all eager as hell to get there.

Jacob, aided by Darlington, placed his effects with his medical chest into the longboat. Jacques Rouchon was there with another sailor, loading the last runlets of rum. Marianne, Madame de Fontenay, and Madame Odet were standing thirty yards up from the foreshore to see Jacob off.

A few hours earlier, Madame de Fontenay, informed of the accident, had said to Jacob, 'I encourage you to run with the wind and never stop till you reach your goal, Mr Delpech. We do not want to see you fall short now!' But the thought now entered his mind that it might be premature to abandon them all to the care of Mr Darlington, whom, after all, he hardly knew.

However, the young Englishman must have read his thoughts. Striding back with him towards the waiting women, in a confidential tone of voice, he said, 'Fear not for the ladies, Monsieur Delpech, nor for Mademoiselle Duvivier. I shall take good care of them. You have my word, Sir.'

'It heartens me to hear you say so. Thank you, Mr Darlington.'

'It is I who am indebted to you, Sir, for looking after my future wife!'

Jacob could not resist a friendly chuckle and said, 'I am glad you have found more than what you had bargained for on this voyage.'

Darlington said, 'By God's grace, I have found what I have been seeking for many a year! I have found my true love!' As they came within hearing distance of the ladies, he handed Delpech a card. 'Please, take this,' he said. 'It is my address, should one day you find yourself in New York. You never know.'

Jacob was satisfied, his mind put at ease. He was learning to let go of his country gentleman's reserve, and realising that here more than anywhere, it was important to quickly get the sway of a man. For in this world of pioneers, people continually resettled from place to place by trial and error, and came and went with the winds of conflict and changing frontiers.

It was not without a pinch of sadness that Jacob bade farewell to the ladies, especially his "niece". She had thrown a shawl over her head, to protect from the gusts of wind, but also to cover her swollen cheek.

Teary-eyed, she thanked him for his unrelenting attentiveness and said, 'Please do not worry on our account, nor on anyone else's. You must concentrate your efforts on finding your family now, my dear uncle Jacob.'

She was right; there was no time for guilt. Like her, he should put the whole tragic accident behind him. He must focus on his next goal: his return to Europe.

Marianne was standing beside Darlington now. Jacob noted with satisfaction that they already looked like a young couple. And there was a new and profound complicity between them. They shared a terrible secret.

EIGHTEEN

THE CROSSING TO Jamaica usually took three days. Jacob took enough provisions for four, in case the wind fell off. Jacques Rouchon was mostly kept busy with the crew, which suited Delpech well, as he could traverse his moments of melancholy and seasickness in relative solitude.

For the first two days, they made excellent headway under a steady easterly. But as the third night fell, the wind became more erratic, and the swell began to grow. Despite his rising nausea, Jacob had at last managed to drift off to much-needed sleep.

His dreams weaved in and out of recent traumatic events, and he saw Private Girard's face as the man rolled over him, driven by a desire to kill. A horrid swirl in the gut and a loud cry suddenly brought him smartly out of his fearful slumber, and into the living nightmare occurring about him.

'Get the sails off her, mates!' he heard the captain roar, as his eyes were met with a flash of lightning that lit up the sky through the hatch above. Almost instantly, it was followed by a sickening volley of thunder.

Hand over mouth, Jacob staggered to his feet and made

a dash towards the gun port. But the chaotic pitch and roll of the ship sent him tumbling backward, and he was sick over the deck. A heavy gush of cold water then burst through the hatch and washed the planks clean, leaving Jacob drenched.

'Mister Rouchon, check the hold!' he heard the captain yell out, before another wave came crashing down on the upper deck.

Jacob was clutching the capstan as Jacques Rouchon, soaked to the skin, came sliding down the steps on his way to the cargo space below.

'What can I do?' shouted Delpech, now rid of the nauseating ball in his gut. Amid the din of booming waves, Rouchon motioned to follow him below into the hold. Already it was two foot deep in sludge and water.

'Can yer man the pump?' he shouted.

Jacob read his lips in the dim light of a lantern and made a sign that he could if shown how. Rouchon gave a quick demonstration before letting Jacob take over the task. It stunk to high heaven of bilge, but he kept to his station and pumped unrelentingly through the darkness. It allowed more qualified hands to perform on deck, reef the mainsail, and point into the wind.

The swell raged with fury the night through; it was worse than anything Jacob had ever experienced. Then, with the dull light of morning that began to seep through the hatch, the storm began to abate. The inpouring of sea gradually ceased. However, after such a battering, the timbers now presented a multitude of small leaks. And there was worse to come.

*

The storm had petered away as quickly as it had risen up, and barely left in its wake a sigh to power the sails. What was more, with a closed ceiling of dense grey cloud, it was impossible to pinpoint the sun. They were temporarily lost. Lost, with hardly enough provisions to last another day, save for the fruit in a barrel standing on deck, now full of seawater.

By the fifth day, Jacob's own victuals had run out. The water was rationed to just a cupful doused with a dram of rum, every three hours. 'Barely enough to wipe the salt from your lips!' groused Rouchon.

On the sixth day, the biscuit ran out, and there was no more cassava bread either, most of it having been spoiled in the storm. The captain allowed a cask to be tapped to lengthen the water. So the diet was watered-down French wine, and tobacco which was chewed or smoked to deceive hunger and prevent exhaustion.

There is nothing worse for a matelot than a stagnant sea. The crew were soon on edge. The captain had to keep the most volatile of them from each other's throats by sending them on duties at opposite ends of the ship. One of these mates was called Harry, an English rigger with a scar from his left ear to his nose. He was short, lithe, and as nimble on the top spar as he was deft with a blade. The other was a big Dutchman by the name of Piet, who could throttle a man with just one hand.

Jacob realised that it would not take much provocation for these men to kill, and he was all the more glad for the company of Jacques Rouchon. The tension was palpable as the two newcomers to the ship sat on the gun deck, each on a cask, smoking their clay pipes. In a low, gravelly voice, Rouchon explained a seafaring custom. 'I think you should know, Monsieur Delpech, that in the extreme case of starvation, one man's life can be sacrificed to save many others. Straws are drawn and the loser killed, bled like a sow, and eaten.'

'My God, that is inhumane, Sir, it is criminal!' said Jacob in an equally low voice, to quell his surprise.

'It is the custom of the sea,' said Rouchon. 'And if it comes to it, Monsieur Delpech, be sure to keep a close watch on the straw-holder's eyes.'

'Why the eyes?' said Jacob, who took another sip from his ration of drink.

'Because this crew be thick as thieves despite appearances. They'll not think twice about singling out the newcomer by the simple bat of an eyelid.'

'What do you mean?'

Jacques Rouchon blew another hoop of smoke from his pipe and said, 'For example, three blinks from the holder could mean the third straw is the one not to take, get it? You gotta keep an eye out, Monsieur Delpech, if you don't wanna end up their next meal!'

'Unless you are the first to take the pick, which would mean better odds.'

'If you say so, Sir, if you say so. Though I'd rather watch for the count. Anything else might be tempting the devil.'

'Or putting your faith in God!'

However, two hours later, the wind picked up. The stagnant cloud began to break up, revealing rags of blue sky here and there. The captain was at last able to locate their position. They had slipped off the shipping lane completely. He estimated it was another two days to the Jamaican port, God willing.

*

On the morning of the nineteenth of August, seven days out of Cow Island, the *Sally-Ann*'s sails began to lose their tautness and to flap. By three in the afternoon, the wind had volt-faced. The sky in the west began to bulge and toss and to turn an angry purple. The captain knew—they all knew— that what they saw rapidly advancing towards them was the most devastating phenomenon known to the Caribbean. The Caribs saw it as a manifestation of Maboya, the evil spirit. And they called it *hurricane*.

Despite their thirst, hunger and fatigue, all hands aboard swiftly set to work preparing the sloop for the battle ahead. They fastened down gun port flaps, secured cannons, strapped down any loose gear, and prepared the longboat for quick and easy release in case an emergency launch should be required.

Their only chance was to abandon course, again reef the mainsail, and steer as close to the eye of the wind as possible. By the time the crew had finished striking the sails, the prow had become awash with huge waves crashing down on it. The sea, cold and frothing, had begun its demoniac dance with the wind howling like hell's hounds all around them. Then the captain gave the ultimate command to strike the reefed mainsail, and let the ship run with the wind and steer by the whipstaff. There was nothing more for most of the mariners to do than to take refuge below deck.

Jacob read fear in their eyes, something he had not seen

on the previous occasion. Some prayed in earnest, others remained silent, but all sat with the mark of dread etched into their stern expressions. One mate next to him mumbled incantations.

'Course I believe in God, course, I do, course I believe in God,' he garbled over and over again in French, so panicked he had not the presence of mind to think of anything else.

It came to Jacob how the apostles had feared the storm on the Sea of Galilee because they too doubted their faith in Jesus. Delpech took it upon himself to help the terrified matelot by reciting the Lord's Prayer at the top of his voice, so that anyone in any language could join in.

The timbers now screamed with every battering as if the ship would break in half, and men were soon rolling about like skittles. Piet, the Dutchman, fell and cracked his head on the cascabel of a cannon, but there was nothing anyone could do for the big man, out cold as he was on the planks. 'He'll not fall any further,' growled one mate.

Another gigantic wall of water slammed over the ship from port side, and another smashed into the hull. And through the howling boom came the appalling sound of splitting timber.

'She's breaking up!' shouted Rouchon from the hatch of the hold, before another great screeching of timber resounded throughout the whole ship. Every man fit to stand scrambled above deck, where the captain ordered them to the longboat on the starboard side.

At the same time, a gigantic roller reared up and snatched three mates near the retaining cordage. Another wave wrenched away the longboat, and Jacob saw it go scudding away into the great folds of the sea.

'The gig, lads, prepare the gig!' cried the captain.

Despite the terrible conditions, the small boat was positioned in minutes. In the short time it took to carry out the operation, the sea had ripped away plants, expanding the opening in the ship's hull, and she was beginning to list. Great rollers now beat over the sloop from every side, like glutinous fingers trying to pull her down, trying to prevent the men from escaping.

Another three men were swept away in one go as they were about to lower themselves into the gig. One of them was Jacques Rouchon.

But through the roaring elements, Jacob could hear cries for help. The planter had managed to latch onto a trailing line and was hanging on for dear life over the side of the ship. Delpech pulled and heaved the rope till Rouchon was hauled back on deck.

The timbers let out another appalling screech. Not a second was there to lose. The bosun and two other men were already aboard the gig when it came to Jacob's turn to climb down the cordage. He hardly had the force to stand, let alone grasp the rigging, but in a last push of strength, he clambered over the side.

'Hurry, man!' shouted Rouchon behind him. But Jacob had given all he had, and he lost his grip. He slid down the side of the hull. However, by good fortune, the small boat was heaved by the swell, and Jacob was able to use the hull to throw himself aboard, narrowly missing Harry the rigger.

The next moment, a huge mass of water clobbered the ship on her windward side and weighted her down further. There came another appalling crack—it must have been the keel. Rouchon jumped aboard the gig behind Jacob. The ship began to turn up her long bowsprit as her stern began to go under.

'Cut her away, man!'

'Wait!' shouted Jacob. 'There's still men aboard!'

But the flash of a knife appeared before Jacob's eyes. It belonged to Harry, the lithe Englishman, who proceeded to cut the ropes that attached the gig to the ship.

The little craft was instantly whisked away over the waves as the 120 tonner turned up her nose, then slid downward like a giant sea monster.

*

Of the sixteen men who set out from Cow Island, only five had made it into the gig: the bosun, Jacob Delpech, Jacques Rouchon, Harry the rigger, and the tiller mate. Every slide into the deep trough of a wave seemed like it would be their last, and time after time, each man committed his soul to God. And indeed, had they embarked on the heavier longboat, they would certainly have gone under by now. But the gig just kept bobbing up and over the waves as good as a cork.

By first light, the steep watery hills began to roll out into smooth undulations, and the sea became navigable once more. The five men in the boat were already half-starved; they had no rations, and just enough water to last the day at a push. But they were still alive.

Jacob promised God that he would fight tooth and claw to survive his terrible ordeal, and live thereafter as living proof of God's grace. But all was not written, and as Jacob well knew, mortal danger lay ahead.

They put up the mast and opened the sail to steer the

craft west by southwest, according to the reckoning of the bosun. They then sat or lay for the better part of the day, recovering from their sleepless night of bailing out the little boat.

Come sundown, they used the sail to collect rain water that fell in light showers during the night. But it was a dismal collection, especially compared to the sea miles they had sacrificed.

The following morning, with not a cud of tobacco left to chew on and hardly a drop left in their flasks, the question Jacob most dreaded was put forward.

'Custom of the sea?' said Harry, who then laid the only musket down on the bench beside him. His eyes blazed with the fire of desperation. 'There's one shot,' he said. 'Otherwise there's the blade.' He flashed his knife in the garish sunlight.

The men looked solemnly at one another. Only Jacob was truly horrified, as much at the prospect of being slaughtered as at the thought of seeing man eat man.

'No, wait,' he said. He then pleaded on the grounds that, according to the rule, all present must give their consent, and concluded, 'It is unchristian. It is sinful. I say we first pray to God for deliverance.'

'All right, go on then,' said Harry in all simplicity. 'Then we get to it. Right?'

Jacob reached for his hessian sack, still strapped over his shoulder. It contained two precious items, his medical book and his Bible. The latter he took out, opened the damp pages, and read in French from the Gospel of Mathew that spoke of the storm. Each word grazed his parched throat, but he persisted, translating the words as best he could into English. 'And his disciples came to him and awoke him,

183

saying, Lord, save us, we perish. And he said to them, why fear you, you of little faith?'

During the prayer spoken in English, Harry cut off a piece of rope and untwisted the twines, which he sliced up into different lengths. He then looked up with a sigh of impatience bordering on fury as Delpech at last concluded, 'Dear Lord, we ask for forgiveness for our mortal sins, and we ask for forgiveness if we have lacked faith. We pray, oh Lord, for the safety of our loved ones far across the ocean sea. And for our lost brethren, so they may rest in heavenly peace. And, dear Jesus, we pray for Your grace so that we may be saved from the mortal sin of murder. Amen.'

'Amen,' said Harry, businesslike. He glared around intensely at each one of the group. 'Now we draw straws. Right?' he said. 'Right?'

The mates replied with a solemn *aye*, even Jacques Rouchon. While all eyes were on Jacob, the planter from Nantes discreetly motioned to Delpech with his two fingers to watch Harry's eyes. Jacob gave a short nod.

But Delpech did not take heed of Rouchon's suggestion. Instead, he quickly put out his hand to take first pick. At least this way, there was no chance of being cheated.

Jacob did not choose the shortest straw. It was poor Rouchon who, only recently freed from his indenture, was about to be bled like a sow. The thought was unbearable, but this was the custom which he had accepted.

Jacob nevertheless tried to make a plea for Christianity, but there was nothing doing. Even the bosun, who was normally a charitable man, had the look of someone possessed by an insatiable urge, like that of Private Girard just before he fell on his own weapon. It was the look of a bloodthirsty killer.

184

Jacques Rouchon, seeing his fate was sealed, burst into a parched but brazen chuckle. 'Come on, Harry,' he said, 'make it quick, and drink to my soul!'

He laid down his head on the gunwale, keeping his eyes wide open. Harry hungrily placed the musket near the planter's temple and waited an instant to get the timing right between the bobs of the boat.

'Wait!' shouted Jacob, quite agitated, which made the gig bob out of time. He was now pointing to the sky where a squawking gull came nearer. Fuelled by the sudden adrenaline, he got unsteadily to his feet and looked straight ahead. 'By God, it is land!' he declared. 'Land ahoy, I say. Land ahoy!'

'Sit yerself down, man!' said Harry. ''Tis the trick of the sea!'

The bosun held up a hand to pause Rouchon's execution while the tiller mate seized the barrel of the musket. Careful not to disturb the balance of the boat, the bosun also rose to his feet.

'That be bloody land all right, lads!' he croaked, 'or I'll eat my own boot leather!'

A feeling of fraternity instantly supplanted the feral instinct of survival, and the men now wept dry tears of joy and clasped each other heartily. Only Harry, who would have eaten his own mother, wore the sneer of disgust on his face.

Whether it was a miracle or due to the bosun's navigational skills, before long, not only could they see land, but the distant masts of tall ships that told them they had reached the port of Jamaica. They had made it to Port Royal! Commonly known as the wickedest town on earth . . .

NINETEEN

THE TEAL-COLOURED waterways and the breathtaking views through the Swiss valley—with the lush plateau to her right and the foothills of the Jura to her left—brought Jeanne a measure of tranquillity.

Monsieur Gaugin's mention of her head injury on her travel document had allowed her to travel with Paul by lake, canal, and river, from Yverdon across Lake Neuchatel, over Lake Bienne, and then all the way up the river Aar to the pretty village of Brugg. They arrived late in the day. A gathering of villagers headed by the mayor, a benevolent man, greeted them as they disembarked.

'You are welcome to stay in our homes, brethren,' he said. 'You will find food and a bed for the night.' He gestured to the good people standing behind him, who offered bows and nods and utterances of welcome. Jeanne was feeling faint after the long journey, which surely could not explain what she saw next.

It was a face in the crowd that stared back at her. It was the face of the pauper. She wanted to shout out, but first instinctively turned to her son and clasped his hand. When she looked again, the man was gone, and it was a different face that looked inquisitively back at her. The next moment, faces were spinning around her, and Paul was kneeling by her side.

'Fetch some water,' said one lady, who had been travelling with her since Yverdon. 'You fainted, Madame,' she said. Had Jeanne seen the man who was responsible for the mark on her face and the bump on her head? Or was it the bump that was responsible for her vision of that man? Jeanne no longer knew what to think as she was helped to a bench.

'Now,' said the mayor, clearing his throat, 'I have a message for a certain Madame Delpech if she is among you.'

Fortunately Jeanne, seated by now, this time retained an outer composure as he asked again. 'Madame Delpech. Do we have a Madame Delpech among us?' said the mayor, sweeping his gaze around the group at the quayside. His eyes seemed to linger over Jeanne and her boy. Jeanne also looked around as if she were searching for this Madame Delpech to step forward.

'Oh well, if anyone comes across her, I would be most obliged if you would ask her to see me. I have been given a message for her to remain here in Brugg.'

The audacity of the wretch made her want to step forward and shout out her story: How the man she had just seen had clubbed her and left her for dead for the sake of her jacket, believing it contained gemstones. How he had gone through the pockets of the drowned people, and then thrown their bodies back into the water without knowing if they had expelled their last breath or not. But what proof did she have to lock someone away, even if they did find him?

So she bit her tongue and kept the peace. It was written on her paper that she had received a head injury; they could well retain her. Then what would become of Paul? Moreover, the aldermen of the village certainly had far more to worry about herding refugees northward than the imaginings of a French bourgeoise. No, she had kept it under her hat till now. She had already made her mind up that the less anyone knew of her story, the fewer chances she had of being tracked down.

Jeanne joined the small group of people queuing to be led to the tavern; most of them would have felt out of place in a bourgeois home. On their way to the tavern, they passed a wondrous clock above the city gate that captured the admiration of all. Set in a recess above it, the painted figure of a Swiss countryman brought much-needed merriment to the group as it came out and counted the hours on its right hand, like a living person. But as Jeanne turned her head again, a sickness in her heart replaced the fleeting gaiety as she thought she saw the pauper skulking away. Could it truly be that her mind was playing tricks on her?

*

Early next morning, she waited in the fog, wrapped in her summer shawl with the other refugees who had been conducted to the wharf. Four flat-bottomed riverboats, attached two by two, were waiting for them to board. The leading boats that would carry the majority of the passengers were headed for Basle by way of the Rhine; from there, the passengers would head north. The second two boats were scheduled to let their load of twenty or thirty passengers disembark at a landing stage a league's distance from Zurzach.

'Paul, come and say goodbye,' said Jeanne to her son, who was throwing sticks into the current just a couple of yards behind her. She smiled back at the lady with whom she had exchanged a few pleasantries during the previous day's journey, and who had come to her aid when she had swooned. The lady and her adolescent daughter were waiting to board one of the first two boats headed for Basle, from where they intended to travel to Brandenburg.

'It's the best season for travelling north, if that is where you're headed, Madame,' she said.

'Thank you,' said Jeanne, 'but really, I have to see a friend at Schaffhausen.' Jeanne regretted the slip as soon as it was out and instinctively turned to see if anyone was listening. There was no one; most of the crowd were advancing towards the boats. With a half-smile, Jeanne continued, 'I pray you find your sons and your husband.'

'Oh, I am sure they are in Brandenburg. I must admit, though, I am not going to enjoy the river ride, specially not this one, from what I've heard. I'd much rather travel by cart, and I'd gladly put up with all the bone-shaking as long as I had the firm ground beneath me, for I am like a brick to water, Madame.' So was Jeanne, but she did not say so.

'I am sure everything will be fine, Madame. With God's grace, you will get over it.' Again Jeanne regretted her slip of the tongue. Had she not said the same to Ginette before leaving Geneva? 'I bid you farewell,' she said, as the lady followed the movement of the crowd into the first two embarkations.

'Bon voyage to Schaff . . . Schaff . . . whatever you call it,' called the lady. Jeanne did not try to correct her. Instead, she waved back, then set about gathering her effects to board one of the other boats.

No more than twenty yards from the quayside, the leading pair of flat-bottomed boats vanished, engulfed as they were in the thick, morning fog. The clock eerily tolled six dampened chimes as the second pair of boats were pushed away from the wharf and floated into the swift current of the river Aar.

For two hours solid, the mist rolled closely along the water's surface. It was impossible to make out the opposite bank most of the time, let alone the boats ahead. And certain narrow passages gave cause for hearts to pound quicker and women to yelp as they clutched their broods. But the captain bore a reassuring appearance: his impressive moustache was as impeccably trimmed as the garb of his profession. He was mindful to forewarn in a tenor voice of any bumpy rides ahead, and soon, most aboard became inured to the rapidly flowing waters. However, a small incident came about that for Jeanne would have dramatic consequences.

By mid-morning, the mist had lifted, and the sun was warming rigid muscles. Paul, at the prow, was the first to sight the two vessels travelling just one hundred yards ahead. He yelled out none too soon, because shortly after the sighting, the leading craft slowed.

'What be the matter?' called out the captain in German across the water, as the trailing boats managed to overtake the leading craft at a wide part of the river.

The answer was barked back in the same language, and judging from the hand-talk, it became clear to the French speakers that the two leading vessels had become untethered. In fact, they had become entangled in floating branches and other matter. The captain of both leading vessels preferred to pull over at the nearest quayside to re-tether properly.

The overtaking boats slipped through the widening waterway without further hindrance and continued through the epic Swiss riverscape.

'Steady as she goes!' the captain called out, and German accents all around seemed to fall upon Jeanne's ear, now that they were moving deeper into German-speaking territory.

There was no call to be miserable in such a beautiful environment. But though she sat bathed in sunlight, from time to time, her face clouded over as her thoughts spiralled back to the recent tragedy. What she would say to Ginette she knew not, so she did her best to empty her mind, to just let the gentle heat of the sun soak into her tumefied face.

By high noon, they arrived at a landing stage, where they took their lunch of bread, cheese, pâté, and beer that had been packed for them by their generous hosts in Brugg. Led by guides paid by the confederacy, the group of refugees then trekked at an easy pace to the small town of Zurzach, which they reached by late afternoon. From Zurzach, Jeanne and Paul climbed on a charabanc that took them and a handful of other travellers to the village of Neunkirch. Here, they dined on broth and were given a place to sleep.

'How far is it to Schaffhausen, Madame?' said Jeanne to the good lady who was ladling the soup, and who spoke some French.

'T'ain't far, Ma'am,' she said, 'not more than a two-hour walk across the plain, but they've arranged a cart for you. Not tomorrow, of course, but the day after the Lord's Day.'

*

Doubt filled Jeanne's thoughts as she lay holding her son, in the large room where other travellers snored in their sleep.

Should she have travelled north with the vast majority of Huguenots? At least they spoke her language, whereas the Germanic utterances she overheard now made her nervous. These people seemed good and kind, but when she overheard them laugh out loud that evening, it had almost seemed as if the jokes were on her. But she could not bear the thought of leaving the Fleurets with no manifestation of love, sorrow, loss, and condolence. If she had headed north, she would never have seen them again. She would forever regret not having reached out to them in their grief. But what if they were no longer in Schaffhausen? And why had they decided to stop there anyway, when everyone else was headed for Brandenburg, where the grand elector's successor had extended his welcome to Huguenots to settle in his province? Could it be that Jeannot Fleuret had found work there? Just a few hours separated her from the township, and from knowing.

'Why can't we wait for the cart?' whispered Paul an hour later as Jeanne, having found a quill, scribbled a thank-you note on the kitchen table.

'Because it would mean waiting another day,' she said, keeping her voice down. 'That's if we're lucky, what with the season. And what if the cart is delayed?'

She silently led the way out into the freshness of the breaking morning and strode onto the stony track, as though she had decided to embrace her fate. Paul knew there was no debate to be had when his mother got the bit between her teeth, so he trotted along beside her with his load on his back and a long stick that had served him well the day before, on the path to Zurzach.

'I hope they won't think us ungrateful, but we must press on.'

'I hope there are no bandits!' said Paul.

'Well,' said Jeanne, 'your father always much prefers to travel by early morning when the day is new and fresh . . .'

'And when the riffraff has not yet stirred,' continued the boy, quoting his father by heart. 'But what about Monsieur Cephas?'

Jeanne checked her step as she said: 'What about him?'

'I thought you . . .'

'Saw him? Seeing things, more like,' she said, resuming her resolute gait.

'Didn't you see him then, in the crowd? I thought that's why you fainted.'

'No, my mind playing tricks.'

'Then that would make two of us,' said the boy, looking up at his mother with the frank gaze of his father.

'Oh, I see,' said Jeanne.

She pulled her shawl over her shoulders, held her boy's hand tight, and, with her stick in her other hand, dug into the earthen track that took them towards the gold and blue light of the nascent day.

*

Sometimes, Jeanne thought, you have to live in the present, for the here and now. It enables you to put distance between life's tides; it saves you from getting muddled in future plans and from worries that have not yet even emerged. So, for the time being, she let past and future fall into oblivion as she walked hand in hand with her son, along the path that narrowed from the open plain into thick woodland. She felt young again, like she did in her country home when she used to run through the long grass with her other children, back in the days when the world seemed so simple, when men had not given up their sense of Christian virtue for the malice of a king.

Paul, sensing the bounce in her step soften, tugged her hand, and they ran together as if they were siblings. For a fleeting instant, the boy saw his mother as a little girl, and that the little girl needed protection and love like every child.

A cart coming towards them on a bend in the narrow road made them resume a more orderly gait. It turned out to be a couple with their three children. Early birds, no doubt, on their way to church. It reassured her to know that other like-minded folk would soon be following in their tracks. Hats were doffed, smiles exchanged, and as soon as they were alone again on the forest thoroughfare, Paul resumed his playful pranks, running into the dense wood and leaping out at her.

'Paul, stop it now,' she said, but the lack of conviction in her voice only encouraged the boy. He played stalk the deer, running from tree to tree, trying to get as close as he could to startle her again. The boy needed this time for play, she sensed. After all, despite the young man already budding inside, he was still only a boy of ten. So she let him have his free rein and continued along the narrow path at a good pace, pretending not to see him.

Walking on her own, her thoughts meandered back to her deceased children. Ginette was right; Louise and Anne would travel with her always, because she carried them in her heart. It was liberating to know she could travel the world, and they would still be with her. Just because they had been called to God did not mean she was not their mother. She still had five beautiful children.

But first she must get to Schaffhausen to give her support to the Fleurets. Then she would head up the Rhine and travel across country to Amsterdam. From the Dutch port, she would cross over to London, where she hoped to reunite with her husband. Together they would somehow recover their children who remained in Montauban: Elisabeth, who must be a young lady by now, and sweet Isabelle, who was no longer a baby. That was what she must do now.

But what if Jacob had not made it to London yet? What if the Fleurets had left Schaffhausen? Had her innate optimism got the better of her judgement again? A movement in the trees made her look left, to the edge of the forest.

'Paul. Paul,' she said, striding into the vegetation that skirted the wood. 'Paul, come out now.'

There was a muffled call and a loud rustle, like that of a heavy animal.

'Paul, don't be silly. Come out now, please!' she said in the uncompromising voice of a worried mother. But it was a large form that emerged from the dark undergrowth which quickened her pulse. And it was accompanied by a coarse voice.

'You want the boy?' said the pauper, stepping forward. 'I want the stones, the precious ones this time!'

Jeanne, rooted to the spot, for a long second just stared at the sight of the man, standing on the edge of the forest with one hand over her son's mouth and a hunting knife gleaming against his soft, white throat.

'Cephas Crespin, don't you dare!' growled Jeanne in the voice of a mother ready to die to defend her child. At the same time, she flashed her gaze at her son and read determination in his eyes. She knew that he had no sense of the danger he was in. 'Paul, don't move!'

Too late. The boy sank his teeth into his captor's hand.

'Ouch! You little tyke!' yelped the pauper. Then he grabbed the boy by the hair, lifted him onto his toes, and pressed the blade against his skin. 'Give me the stones, or I'll slit his throat now!'

'All right,' said Jeanne, holding out her hands, as much for the pauper not to draw his blade across as to prevent her son from trying to break free. 'Paul, don't move, please, for me, darling,' she pleaded. She knew that it would take just a quick lateral slice, and her son would be dead.

'The bloody jewels, woman!' bellowed Cephas Crespin while the lad struggled and kicked.

'All right, all right,' she said, hand on her shoulder strap to remove her sack. 'Paul! Please, keep still.' But as the man tried to tighten his grip and slowly pressed the blade into the boy's throat, Paul jerked back his head, and stamped and kicked for all his life. 'NO!' screamed Jeanne. Wasting not a second, and remembering the man's maimed thumbs that prevented him from clasping tightly, she took up her stick and in one movement brought it down with all her strength onto his hand, knocking the knife to the ground. The pauper tossed the boy to one side. Jeanne stood holding her stick, ready for another swing.

'No you don't, Cephas Crespin, or I promise I'll . . .'

She swung back her stick, but he was inside her reach too quickly and grabbed her by the throat, making her drop it. He snarled: 'Or you'll what?'

Her only answer was to gouge at his ill-shaven face like a wildcat. He punched her to the ground, then dived on top of her. He thumped her in the gut, slammed back her head, and flipped her over so she lay on her belly. Sitting on her posterior, he wrenched her sack from her shoulders, almost pulling her arms out of her sockets. She screamed with frustration at being clamped down. She cared not for the sack but kept up her struggle to give Paul time to get back to the thoroughfare, where he might find help from people on their way to church.

Pinning her torso down with his knees, the pauper plunged a hand into the sack to make sure the stones were there. But a dull, heavy blow sent him sideways.

On the relief of the pressure on her nape, she looked round to see Paul standing there, holding her stick. Then the boy swiped away her bag from the pauper, who was cupping his right ear.

'Leave it, Paul!' she cried out before the man, still on his knees, lunged for it like a rabid beast.

Still in a daze from the blows, she scrambled onto her hands and knees and threw herself between the pauper and her son. She was not going to lose another child while there was still life in her. The pauper staggered to his feet and booted the boy, who fell to the ground winded, and then stamped his booted foot down on Jeanne's shoulder.

Amid the leaves and insects of the woodland litter, she saw her son lying on the ground where the pauper's knife had fallen. With a feral scream, she crawled desperately to reach him. Two powerful blasts of a gun were the last things she heard before closing her eyes.

*

Jeanne saw herself standing, pregnant, holding her two-year-old daughter in her arms, with Paul and his elder sister, watching the cows being led into Mon Plaisir meadow, which lay between the house and old Renac's farm. The meadow had been given over to pasture that year. The gentle warmth of the sun made her face tingle as everything became a blur. Then her gaze met the soft yellow canvas of a moving cart, illuminated by the sun shining on the other side. Realising she was no longer in a dream, she turned her stiff neck. 'Paul,' she said. The boy was looking out into the moving landscape, where a river ran parallel to the track behind them. He turned towards her. In a calmed voice, she continued, 'Paul, my boy.'

'You are safe now, Mama,' he said as she gestured for him to move closer. She felt the twinge of her swollen skin when she brought his face to hers. But it did not matter. She just needed to feel the cheek of her child on her bare skin.

The cart slowed. Before Paul could give any explanation, Jeanne heard a familiar voice.

'We found her. On the road from Neunkirch.' She recognised the voice of Etienne Lambrois.

'And not a moment too soon neither, by God,' said the voice of Jeannot Fleuret.

'She's in a poor state,' said Lambrois as the carriage came to a halt. The flap was pulled to one side.

'My God, my poor woman,' said Claire. Slowly, Jeanne removed herself from the cart. She embraced Claire—Claire with her large bump. Then she was met by Ginette. The two women fell into each other's arms.

'My God, look at you. I shouldn't have left you,' said Ginette, tears in her eyes, 'but I couldn't stay . . . I lost my boy.'

'I know, Ginette, I know,' said Jeanne gently. 'That's why I came as soon as I found out.'

'But he's still here, isn't he?' said Ginette, touching her large bosom. 'Where I keep my other darling butterflies.'

'Yes, my Ginette,' said Jeanne, with her hand on her own heart, 'and he is here too.'

TWENTY

ON THE AFTERNOON of August 24, five haggard and thirst-bitten castaways staggered from their gig onto the boardwalk at North Dock.

The port town was only just rousing from its siesta as they paused outside Customs House. It was closed. So they proceeded opposite onto Lime Street, where a tavern or three showed signs of life. On the veranda of the first establishment, a group of pretty painted ladies were sitting on stools or leaning on posts. They were smoking, chatting, or just drowsily watching the world and his mistress go by.

'Hey, prince!' called one of the temptresses in accented English, but the five men did not even turn their heads. Instead they dived into the cool tavern opposite, where the sawdust was freshly laid, and they ordered beer, broth, bread, and a pipe of wine to begin with. Two hours later, only Jacques Rouchon, Jacob Delpech, and the bosun—whose name was Benjamin Fry—re-emerged to report the shipwreck.

It was past six o'clock. The street was alive now with walkers, lookers and drinkers, and labourers rolling barrels towards the dock. The colourful painted ladies of the bawdy house across the street were down to three and busy in banter with a disparate bunch of matelots, five or six in number. They must have come from aboard the tall ship newly moored in the bay, thought Jacob as he and his mates made their way back towards Customs House.

'Up there's the Exchange,' said Benjamin Fry, who nodded to a building up the street on the right where groups of merchants were in discussion. 'And further up's the governor's place.'

They were crossing Queen Street, which was lined with rum shops and half-timbered houses. It led to the lieutenant governor's stone-built mansion. Soldiers in red coats, darkies carrying baskets, and a whole array of ladies and gentlemen in fashionable attire created the colourful street scene. It did not seem so wicked a place as all that, thought Jacob.

'I wager that's where a buccaneer will fetch his letters,' said Rouchon, turning to Delpech with a cheeky grin. Jacob knew he was referring to letters of mark, which gave privateers a legal right to attack Spanish ships and settlements. They had spoken about them in the tavern where Fry and Harry had given a brief rundown.

But Jacob was no longer listening. In fact, he suddenly found himself struggling to even put one foot in front of the other. Must be the heat or perhaps the fatigue, he thought to himself as he wiped his brow.

They continued across the east-west road, bathed in sunlight, and strolled to the door of Customs House to report the shipwreck. Rouchon turned to say something to Jacob, but then checked himself and said: 'You all right, Monsieur Delpech? You look a bit green around the gills, I must say.'

'Ye—yes, thank you. Must be the effects of the . . . the . . .'

'Of the what?' said Rouchon.

But Jacob was unable to think: his mind was swimming; the words to describe his meal eluded him. He bent over and touched his knees to catch his breath, and he felt like he was standing aboard the *Sally-Ann* again. As he looked up, his eyes were met by a whirling landscape of sky, sun, and buildings. Then his legs collapsed beneath him.

Face up, the next thing he saw was a succession of talking faces. They belonged to Rouchon, the bosun, a soldier in scarlet uniform, and a big-bosomed lady in a flamboyant feathered hat.

'He's got the fever,' she said.

Jacob closed his eyes, and for a second, he saw his wife and his children playing in their country home in France.

'Just shows, doctors are as vulnerable as the next man,' said the bosun.

Benjamin Fry thought Jacob's medical chest—now at the bottom of the Caribbean Sea—had carried the tools of his profession, in the same way a tradesman carries the tools of his trade. Jacques Rouchon did not attempt a foray into English to rectify what he knew to be a misinterpretation, so the error stood. Indeed, it was even upheld by the medical literature found in Jacob's sack.

'It's a chance I've a spare room, vacated only this morning,' said the large and exuberant lady. 'If he has coin, you can bring him round.'

In Port Royal, reputedly the richest town in the English Indies, not only was every service the object of payment, but people expected to be paid in ready cash.

During Rouchon's numerous jaunts with Jacob on Cow Island, he had spied the bulge of Jacob's *bourse* under his shirt. So he was able to reassure the lady of Jacob's solvency whether he lived or died. His level of English, however, only allowed him to make three-word sentences that reflected his bodily needs, such as *we go eat, give me wine, you me go*, and so on. So the planter's gesturing was just as eloquent as his words when he said, 'Oh, coin he has, Madame!'

Mrs Angela Evens was a Welsh-born matron and the respected widow of a tavern keeper. With the sale of her husband's assets, she was able to purchase a relatively peaceful lodging house, just a stone's throw away from the graveyard.

Rouchon, with his forthright air, was convincing enough for Mrs Evens to hail down a man with a cart who had been delivering barrels of beer. She ordered the man, whose name was Isaac, to deliver the sick "doctor" to her lodgings. The bosun continued into Customs House to report the loss of the *Sally-Ann* and most of the mates aboard, while Rouchon followed Jacob, slumped in the handcart, to his new lodgings.

*

At the height of his delirium, Delpech dreamt a Catholic mob was coming to lynch him. But the hundreds of people streaming by outside his second-floor window were in fact returning from the funeral of Port Royal's most illustrious privateer, Captain Henry Morgan. The former governor of Jamaica had passed away on his plantation the day after Jacob collapsed. The clamour of revellers drinking and singing was enough to rouse the dead, and Delpech wondered at one point during the commotion for what reason he was lying in hell. He was not, of course, although the captain's after-funeral celebrations would later indirectly bring Jacob grief of a distinctly mortal nature.

Jacques Rouchon visited the stone-built, three-storey lodging house every day around noon, for the first fortnight of Jacob's distemper. During the first moments of lucidity, Delpech mustered all his strength to give the planter money to buy laudanum, to dull the pain in his belly and help him sleep. He had read that more than anything, a sick body needed rest to be able to resist the ailment and be cured.

He also handed Rouchon a list of ingredients with which to make a draught for the calenture. This consisted— according to *The Surgeon's Mate*—of barley, two gallons of freshwater, liquorice juice, cloves, oil of vitriol spirit for his ailing head, and a spoonful of rose wine to take away the bitterness. Along with the doses of laudanum, the resulting decoction was about all Jacob could take down during the initial stages of his illness.

At the same time, other elements were combining that would pin Jacob down far longer than his present calenture and dysentery. These elements included Jacob's taking laudanum, Jacques's meeting up with Harry, and Morgan's funeral that acted as a catalyst for vice in the shape of dice.

*

One Tuesday, a little over two weeks after he had collapsed in front of Customs House, Jacob at last was able to sit up and spoon down the chicken broth Mrs Evens had concocted specially for him. He felt alert now that he had not taken any laudanum since Sunday, having heard how easily it could take root in the seat of a man's desire.

He was looking forward to seeing Rouchon, who usually showed up around noon. But noon came and went, as did the night, and the next day, without a sign of the planter. By the following Wednesday, Jacob prayed nothing untoward had befallen his friend, and he got to mulling over their last conversation together.

'You have been most generous,' Jacob had said. 'You may well have saved my life.'

'As you have saved mine, I might say,' Rouchon had returned.

At the time, it had struck Jacob, albeit fleetingly, that Rouchon had not used the preterit, as one would on relating a past event such as the one on the *Sally-Ann*, when Jacob hauled the planter from the side of the hull. He had used the present perfect tense as if the event had just happened and was ongoing.

'Although I don't deserve it,' he had continued, ''cause I have dabbled in the vice of dice, Monsieur Delpech. And the worst of it is that I won at first! Now I wish I'd lost.'

He had then related how, on the night of Captain Morgan's funeral, he had run into Harry, who had taken him to a dicing house.

'But I swear to God, it is not a place for a poor planter, and I fear I must soon leave, Monsieur Delpech, before it is the ruin of me.' But Jacob had not realised how soon.

There was a knock at the door. Instead of Jacques Rouchon, in walked Mrs Evens with his broth, which was as good a consolation as any, now that he was recovering his appetite.

'There you are, Doctor,' she said, sliding the tray over his lap once he had managed to prop himself up against his pillows.

'Thank you, Mrs Evens. You are so kind.'

The French doctor was a charming man, and she was not indifferent to his soft baritone voice and accent. But there were nevertheless practical matters to be addressed.

She picked up his bedpan, matron-like, and proceeded past a little round table dressed with flowers, to the window.

'It is a fine day, Doctor,' she said. Leaning her generous bust out of the window, she threw out the contents of the pan into the street below. Turning back into the room, with a smile she said, 'Now that you are back among the living, Doctor, do you think you can pay me?'

'Pay you?' For a second, Jacob was taken aback, fearing the lady had misread his intentions.

'For bed and board, Doctor,' she said affably. 'I can only go on feeding you if I have food in the larder, and for that, I'm going to need some rent.'

'Oh, yes, of course, Mrs Evens, forgive me. I err have still a light head.'

How naïve he had been to imagine she had taken him in out of the goodness of her heart. He asked her what he owed her.

'It's seven shillings a week for the room, and three shillings for board, and a further shilling for care, which amounts to four crown and two shillings for the two weeks past, or four pieces of eight if you prefer.'

It was a hefty price to pay, he thought, considering that an indentured servant cost twenty pieces of eight, and that was for a three-year term. Yet it was a small price to pay for still being alive, although had he known the cost sooner, no matter how weak he was, he would certainly have chosen to stay in a more "godly" establishment. For the opposite wall often let through the intimate sighs and the most eccentric squeals of ladies and gentlemen in the clutches of their primal passions. He told Mrs Evens he would have some coin ready for her when she came back for the bowl. She exited the room with one eyebrow raised and her nostrils flared.

Once Jacob had finished his broth, he took the key hanging from his neck and reached across to the locked drawer where he kept his valuables. He pulled out the drawer and grabbed his plump little *bourse*. But the instant he did so, he knew something did not tally. His heart sank as he tipped up the sack. His eyes widened in shock, then horror, as one by one, instead of twenty-eight gold louis, an assortment of farthings and pennies fell into his hand. His hopes of boarding a ship to Europe were dashed. Not only that, he now found himself in debt.

Ten minutes later, there was a knock at the door. Mrs Evens's large figure filled the doorway. She stepped into the room and looked down at the drawer still open, then at Jacob, whose gaunt face was an open book.

'I knew it. He's taken your coin, hasn't he, Doctor?'

Jacob gave a nod. 'I must see the governor,' he said with incredulity.

'With all due respect, you are in no state to go anywhere. And besides, your friend is gone.'

'Gone? Why did you not tell me?'

'Only just found out myself. My maid says she saw him hopping onto a ship to Lord knows where. He was with a man with a scar across his face.'

'Harry,' murmured Delpech, recalling how the English rigger had once nearly skinned the planter for his flesh, and then had introduced him to dice for the planter to be fleeced.

'I did hear he was dicing, and losing. It's commonplace round here, you know. They live it up and goad each other on till there's nothing left, and they're back in debt and having to put out to sea again.'

'So, as I am his creditor, I am also the loser.'

'The only one who really wins is the tavern keeper. That's why there are so many of them. You're still going to have to cough up, though, Doctor, if you'll pardon the expression.'

'Madame, I have no other means,' said Jacob, taking in the immediate implications of the theft.

'You might try looking in your jacket, and if that's not enough, you'll have to write me out an IOU, Doctor. I do believe you to be a gentleman true to his word,' she said, with one hand on her hip, the other hand pointing to his jacket on a hook behind the door.

'Yes,' said Jacob, remembering the gold escudo he had been given at Petit Goave. But it was only worth sixteen reals, or two pieces of eight. So he was obliged to make out an IOU.

*

By the end of September, Jacob had put some flesh back on his bones, and was strong enough to go for strolls around the town and its port. Being in Mrs Evens's debt had obliged him to remain in her lodging house. He had, however, moved to a smaller room on the third floor which consisted of four bare walls with a single bed and a chest of drawers. She treated him kindly and agreed to continue to give him board and lodging in exchange for IOUs, which, by the time he was able to stand and walk about, amounted to five pieces of eight. And that did not include her deceased husband's clothes that she insisted he wear, for she would not have a gentleman walk about town in tatters.

*

Thursday, 30 September, was no different than the previous days, except that, instead of wondering how he could pay his passage on board a ship to Europe, he found himself pondering over Mrs Evens's proposition.

She had offered to let him stay on at her house. She would forget his debt and even pay for his medical instruments so that he could practice from home. In short, she was offering him freedom from debt in exchange for marriage.

Despite it being a very fair deal, he knew in advance what conclusion he would arrive at. The tricky part was how to let her down gently. After all, she was his creditor and had his IOUs, which she could well sell to the highest bidder.

From the quayside near Fort James, where gulls were pecking into a pile of fish guts, he had a good view of the dockers unloading barrels from a ship. He might not have the means to work as a merchant, he once thought, but loading and unloading merchandise was something he could do. However, he had dropped the idea as soon as he found out that any menial work would barely bring him enough to live on, which meant it would take many years to pay back his debt. She really did have him over a barrel, did Mrs Evens.

As he unravelled the whole farce in his mind, it was becoming more and more absurd. She would not even believe he was not really a doctor, so set was she on her ideal. He now realised why she had not kicked him out when she saw he was penniless. She had seen him as a good client from the start. Then she saw the theft of his money as an opportunity to move up from being a Welsh tavern keeper's widow to a respectable French doctor's wife. And having once taken root in her mind, the notion had grown till this morning, when she popped the question.

'I want you first to think it over before giving me your answer,' she had said.

Not wanting to provoke her immediate disappointment and have her flying into a direction she might later regret, he had promised he would.

As he ambled down Lime Street among the fashionable gentlemen and stylish ladies, he realised that in this town, where fortunes were made and thrown away on the roll of a dice, anything could go. And he could be anyone. He could call himself a doctor and no one would object, because everyone here was also trying to be someone else. Even Mrs Evens, whom he suspected of once being an indentured servant, then a lady of lesser morals before becoming a tavern keeper's wife, could aspire to become a doctor's wife.

The whole town, with its assortment of pretty brick buildings, its shop fronts, taverns, and cobblestones, was in fact a sham of a civilised settlement. And its morals were no less shallow than its foundations, built as they were on a spit of sand. Its pretty façades hid the lies and vice and sin at its heart, which entertained wicked men like Harry and corrupted good men like Rouchon, the planter, who, having once felt the lure of easy money, might well die without planting a seed as a free man.

He continued up the cobbled lane, passed the fish market, and turned into York Street, which led to the church and was lined with fine houses. He stopped at a large dwelling as per his habit and knocked. It was the maid who appeared at the door. She told him that Mrs Evens would like the pleasure of his company for a cordial before he went up to his room.

*

'I have a surprise for you,' said Mrs Evens excitedly, after the initial exchange of pleasantries.

They were sitting in the lavishly furnished parlour, where the patterned wallpaper and gaudy window hangings were in the image of its exuberant owner. She was sitting on her two-seater sofa covered in red brocade, which catered amply for her skirts. He was seated on the edge of the French wing chair opposite her. A low marble-topped table formed a respectable barrier between them. Upon it stood a carafe of lemon drink, two glasses three-quarters full, and a tray of sweetmeats leftover from the great rejoicings of the birth of the new Prince of Wales, celebrations which had been postponed to September because of the burial of Captain Morgan in August.

From the side of the settee, she brought out a large leather bag. She said, 'Your new tools of your trade, Doctor.'

Decidedly, she had resolved to make it as difficult as she could for him to refuse her offer.

'Dear Mrs Evens,' he began, 'you have been my . . . my guardian angel, and I deserve not your continued err kindness. I have thought over your err fine proposition, however.' Her nostrils widened and her brow pleated with concern, which almost caused Jacob to lose his thread. He continued. 'However, I am sure you will not err be able to live with a man who betrays his own wife and children, would you?'

'For you, Monsieur Delpech, I would bear up,' she said bravely, and with fervour.

It was no good. He would just have to hammer it home harder to make her see clearly.

'But really, I must return to Europe, Mrs Evens . . .'

'Monsieur Delpech, you cannot. You cannot refuse me after all I have done. I have nursed you back to life. Fed you when you were delirious . . .'

'And I am, and err will be forever, in your debt,' he said, which he regretted the moment it was out.

'You are indeed, Monsieur Delpech. And here, there are laws. It is bondage for a man who cannot pay. You are aware of that?'

'I cannot lie to you. Neither can I betray my family, Mrs Evens. I do, however, sincerely hope we can be good friends.'

Friends. It was the word she dreaded most. She did not want a good friend. She wanted a husband, but not any drunken riff-raff that came ten to a penny in these parts. She wanted a man of culture who would accompany her in the increasingly refined circles of the town whose gentrification was well in train. Especially since the new governor, the second Duke of Albemarle no less, had brought his entire entourage from England. No longer did the swelling bourgeoisie want to put up with uncouth sailors and coarse pirates. And Mrs Evens had the means to enter the bourgeoning society; she just needed a gentleman for a husband.

Jacob's refusal was all the harder to swallow in that she had not even contemplated it. Moreover, she had opened up her heart, for she really did have feelings for this man whose voice and imperfect English made her heart tremble like she never thought it would again.

In her disappointment, she turned sour. Coldly and haughtily, she said, 'Then I have no alternative but to take the matter of your debt to Chief Justice Ellerson.'

*

Later in the afternoon, two royal guards came knocking at Jacob's door. He put his meagre possessions into his hessian sack and was marched, not to the courtroom, but to the deputy governor's sumptuous house. Delpech thought this odd, as he knew the house was being rented at present by the new lieutenant governor, none other than Sir Christopher Monck, His Grace the second Duke of Albemarle. Why would he be taken to see the chief official?

'I asked you here for two reasons,' said Sir Christopher. 'One, to allow you to pay off your debt in the quickest fashion possible so that you may regain your liberty. And two, for you to tell me your cure against the fever.'

Of late, the Duke had been suffering from a tropical illness that his wife and entourage feared would carry him to an early grave. He was only thirty-four. However, yesterday his temperature had dropped, and this morning he was in fine spirits and well enough to get up and dress. And there was nothing the Duke liked more than to dress—apart perhaps from good company and Madeira wine—which gave some cause for distress as one could not pile on layers of clothing in Jamaica as one did in England.

Nevertheless, standing with one hand on the diamond-studded knob of his beautifully gilded walking stick, the duke was still a feast for the eyes. Indeed, Jacob at present was filled with awe at the dazzling array of blue satin and gold tassels that seemed to outshine everything and everyone in the opulently furnished room. Lord Monck was certainly larger than life, taller too. The piled hair of his enormous wig and his high-heeled shoes with jewelled buckles meant that he towered over the Frenchman standing humbly before him.

It took a minute or two for Jacob to realise that a man was standing on either side of Albemarle. To the duke's right stood Mr Ellerson, the chief justice, and to his left a young man twenty years Jacob's junior, with a serious demeanour and an intellectual brow. This was Doctor Sloane, the Duke's travelling physician.

Albemarle gave a brief glance to his right. Then, turning back to Jacob, he said, 'The chief justice tells me you cured yourself of the tropical illness.'

Jacob answered in the affirmative and gave a brief account of his concoction and how much laudanum he had taken.

'The body needs to be err unfatigued in order to be able to combat the illness with the tincture,' he said in a precise and pondered manner, so that his strong French accent would not hinder the comprehension.

'I agree, Doctor,' said Sloane with indifference, 'although that is nothing we do not already know.'

Though ruthlessly down-to-earth, Sloane's answer nevertheless gave Jacob instant relief. It meant he did not take Jacob for an impostor.

'If it is nothing we do not already know,' said Albemarle, 'then why have I not been advised to take some?'

'Because you have been advised to first refrain from entertaining, my Lord,' said Sloane uncompromisingly.

Turning back to Jacob with a grunt, the duke continued, 'And would you believe the local practitioner insists I take bird peppers in a poached egg, because, he says, parrots eat them when they are poorly? I ask you, do I look like a parrot?'

Jacob forced himself to say that he did not, despite the Duke's dazzling appearance.

'And what about my jaundice? It is of great discomfort to my wife. She tells me I have gone Chinaman yellow! And yet, Doctor Sloane here refuses to bleed me. What do you make of that, Doctor?'

'With all due respect, my Lord, I would not bleed you either,' said Jacob, who sensed it would be unwise to go against the advice of the trained practitioner.

Doctor Sloane removed his finger from where it pressed against his upper lip, and gave a short nod of approval.

'I would take rest,' continued Jacob. 'For the body must be invigorated physically to be able to fight the fever. And I would take a tincture as my principal source of nourishment. No wine.'

During Jacob's conversations with Mrs Evens, she had often spoken about the duke's reputation as a party head. A reputation that had been confirmed to her by one of the many servants the duke had brought with him in his yacht from England. And a reputation embraced by the rich, fun-loving Jamaican colonists.

'No wine?' said the duke grouchily. 'Would your tincture

help deafen my ears to these midges? I do not think so. Would it refresh my rasping gullet? Certainly not. I do declare that wine is the only beverage drinkable in this godforsaken place! However.' The duke turned to his doctor. 'We shall take you up on the laudanum.'

'You would also do well to take a Spanish hacienda rather than a brick-built palace, my Lord,' said Sloane. 'I am sure the French would never have built their governor's house in infernal red bricks in this climate.'

'Brick reminds me of home,' replied the duke. 'A white Spanish dwelling does not!'

Albemarle faltered an instant, then took three steps back and slumped into his strategically placed armchair. After a little fussing from the Lord Justice and Doctor Sloane, the duke called for his secretary to bring him his tincture of wine.

Once he had taken his restorative, the duke was able to recover his dignified posture with his hand on his walking stick, albeit now sitting down. He said, 'In order to avoid putting you under bond, I have purchased your debt.'

Jacob thanked him.

'I did consider keeping you with me. However, you are French. Furthermore, I happen to know a captain who requires a surgeon for his next voyage, so I have sold your debt to him. I believe it is for the best. There might be an element of danger, naturally—there always is aboard a ship. However, if the captain's campaign proves successful, you shall be able to pay for your liberty and have enough coin to set yourself up wherever you mean to go.'

Jacob was suspicious of the "element of danger". But when Albemarle asked him if he was satisfied with the arrangement, he said, 'If it is God's will, then it is also mine, my Lord.'

Delpech was nonetheless glad to be leaving the Jamaican port, steeped as it was in sin, vice, and disease.

The chief justice handed Doctor Delpech the leather medical bag that Mrs Evens must have cunningly sold with Jacob's debts. He then ordered the guards to accompany the freshly indentured surgeon-barber to the north dock for immediate embarkation on the *Joseph*, a seventy-ton sloop with eight guns and forty-six men under the command of Captain Brook.

As Jacob walked down High Street between his guards, he found himself thinking with horror that he had never cut off a lock of hair in his life.

The doctor was ferried to the ship along with a pirate, detained between two other soldiers, who introduced himself as Captain Cox.

'What's your name and station?' snarled the pirate.

'I am Jacob Delpech, Sir. I have been appointed as surgeon-barber.'

'That's all right then, but you'll not be needing shears on this ship. A good sharp knife and a solid saw might come in handy, though!'

The pirate chuckled to himself and said no more.

TWENTY-ONE

TEN MINUTES LATER, Jacob and Captain Cox were climbing aboard the *Joseph*.

Men were heaving lines, scuttling up and down the rigging, and getting ready to unfurl sails. From his vantage point on the quarterdeck, Captain Brook gave Cox a short nod of approval. The pirate was led below deck with his wrought iron chest, which was lugged behind him by two mates. Captain Brook then looped his gaze down at Delpech, who was holding his sack over a shoulder and his leather bag in his hand.

'So you be the French doctor,' boomed the captain, who had a permanent snarl that made him look disgruntled at everything he set his eyes on.

Looking up, Jacob noticed he was hideously ugly with a pockmarked face, was of average height with powerful shoulders, and was clad, not in English uniform, but in a frock coat that must have once belonged to a Spaniard.

Although it went against his moral grain, Jacob had no choice but to play out his fraud to the full. 'Yes, Sir. Doctor Jacob Delpech at your service,' he said. The captain waved him up to the navigation deck.

As Delpech went to climb the steps, a crewmate scurrying down the port side stopped in his tracks. He held Jacob's gaze for an instant. Jacob had the shock of his life at the sight of the man, who then hastened towards the capstan. Although he was bearded and his hair was tied back in the fashion of seafaring rovers, this man could be none other than Ducamp, the dragoon lieutenant who had ransacked his home three years earlier.

Jacob continued to the quarterdeck.

'Indentured to me, you are now,' said the captain in a gravelly voice. 'And so as you know, all aboard this ship is equal and shall be treated as such, till death do us part.'

'Of course, Sir,' said Jacob, whose mind was still half on the bearded mate.

'And we share the rewards of the catch.' The captain rubbed his greying goatee as if he were evaluating an estimable beast. Then he said, 'And two hundred pieces of eight will buy you back your liberty!'

This was Jacob's second shock, and he had barely been aboard five minutes.

'There must be a mistake, Sir,' he said, shaken with indignation. 'I owed not a tenth of that sum.'

With impulsive scorn and sudden fury, the captain bayed, 'Are yer saying a doctor is worth no more than a slave or a swabber?'

'No, Sir . . .' said Jacob, searching for his words.

But before he could get another one in, the captain—whose rage died down as quickly as it had flared up—said in his resonantly deep voice, 'As I said, Doctor, we share the rewards of our toil with all aboard. And there will be plenty of coin to be made where we are headed. As surgeon-barber on this here ship, you are entitled to one and a quarter shares of any spoils of war taken along the way. Fear not, Doctor, I'm not asking you to go on the account.'

What could the man possibly mean? Jacob wondered.

Captain Brook now clasped Delpech in a comradely manner on the shoulder, but his attempted smile and fixed gaze, which were perhaps supposed to express fellowship, did not reassure Jacob one bit.

'Show Doctor Delpech to his quarters,' said the captain to Jacob's escort. Brook then turned and gave a word to his quartermaster—a thickset, bald, and bearded man named Blunt—who in turn shouted the order to haul up the large anchor.

As Doctor Delpech continued towards his quarters, he heard the bosun, whom Jacob had known as Lieutenant Ducamp, call out in French for his mates to start winding the capstan.

Jacob continued to a space at the front of the ship down on the orlop deck, partitioned on one side by canvas drapes. The dimly lit enclosure, ten feet square, was furnished with cabinets and shelves containing the various gruesome implements of his profession. They included saws, knives, pliers, extractors, and lines of bottles and jars of ingredients, no doubt left by the previous surgeon-barber.

He opened his medical bag, which contained drawings that showed the various operative stages of amputation and other modi operandi. This unexpected wealth of know-how bolstered Jacob's morale and allowed his mind to put aside the bearded face of Ducamp for the time being. He plunged into the fascinating diagrams and instructions, neatly drawn and written in English.

As the *Joseph* slipped out of the port under light sail, Jacob gave a thought for Mrs Evens. She had cared for him, given him food and shelter in the hope of catching a suitable husband. Then she had set out to punish him for not succumbing to her attentions. But he felt no animosity towards her, for had she not ultimately set him on the road to freedom, to England? At least, that is what he wanted to believe.

*

An hour into the voyage and two hours before sundown, there were footsteps outside Jacob's quarters. In walked the bosun.

There was no one else on the orlop deck, but Ducamp closed the sheet behind him anyway. The two men stood eye to eye, both as fake personas, and aware of the power they potentially held over each other. Jacob was not a doctor. Ducamp was not a French Huguenot seeking asylum on an English merchantman.

'You have changed, but I knew who you were the moment I saw you, *Monsieur* Delpech.'

He glanced at the instruments that Jacob had laid out on the table before him for study. But Jacob had already instinctively grabbed a dismembering knife.

'You have equally changed since we last met, Lieutenant Ducamp. When you ransacked my house.'

Ducamp stood calm and still. He said, 'For sure, I am a changed man, ever since I left the king's service. On this ship, see, we respect every man's creed, colour, and class. And there is no majesty, no bourgeois, just good men, and a right salty bunch they are too. I have not come seeking an

221

argument, but to suggest that what happened in France, stays in France. So you can put down your knife before you cut someone.'

Jacob stared at the face that brought back memories of humiliation, of pain, and of his separation from his wife and children. And now it brought him news he had been dreading to hear, that he must be on a freebooting buccaneer ship.

'So, have we a deal, Doctor?' continued the bosun.

Jacob gave a reluctant nod, and said, 'I see now why the crew are not in uniform.'

'We're not pirates, if that's what you're thinking. We're on a commission to transport Captain Cox to the settlement of Virginia. From there, he'll take a frigate back to London with his spoils of war, so he can fulfil the contract of his amnesty. But we are not pirates.'

*

Delpech settled into his new role quickly and, to his surprise, without much queasiness. Apart from a splinter removal, a successful tooth extraction, and the treatment of a gunpowder burn, all of which earned him the respect of the crew, there was little to do during the first few days. He read extensively, prayed frequently, and prepared lotions to remove gunpowder from flesh and a decoction of wine vinegar to treat burns, should the need arise for them again.

Jacob was at first taken aback by the crew's apparent lack of unity in dress and naval rigour—they slept or lounged, some with legs interlaced, wherever they chose to lie on their mats or hitch up their hammocks. But he soon saw it did not seem to hinder the progress of the ship. And they did not drink excessively, nor was there any dicing for coin. These privateers, as they were known, seemed to Jacob's now more discerning eye competent enough in performing their tasks, which gave him some cause for reassurance.

The heat was bearable, food and drink were in plentiful supply, and the *Joseph* was making good headway. So far, the voyage was turning out to be, both in the figurative and the literal sense, one he could easily stomach.

He and the bosun managed to keep their distance from each other until the third day, when Jacob heard a sudden clamour above deck. It was mid-morning. He was reading in his cramped enclosure by lamplight.

He looked up from his book as someone scuttled down the steps from the deck above. A moment later, a young crewmate of slight build and with soft facial hair was standing in front of the canvas partition of the surgeon's quarters.

'Beg your pardon, Doctor, you are needed on deck,' said the young man, catching his breath.

'What is it, Steven?' said Jacob, putting his book to one side and getting up. He liked the lad, who was respectful, willing to help, and desirous to learn to read, which Jacob encouraged by setting him lessons in English.

'It's the bosun, Doctor,' said young Steven, accompanying Jacob towards the steps. 'I reckon he must have misjudged the distance sliding down the rigging. Don't think he's used to it. Rope burns yer palms, and when that happens, you come unstuck, and down you go.'

By the time Jacob arrived on the scene, Ducamp was regaining consciousness, though still lying where he had landed. He gave a loud cry as his arm collapsed beneath him, when he tried to push himself up off the deck.

'Broken collarbone,' said Blunt, the quartermaster.

'I don't think so,' said Jacob, inspecting the wound. 'Pray, help him to his feet, and bring him to my quarters. He will suffer less out of the sun.'

This was not entirely true, for already the surgeon's den was like a bakehouse. The truth was, Jacob strode back below deck not for the comfort of the patient, but to glance over his charts and literature on dislocation.

Ten minutes later, Ducamp was lying on a table in the privacy of the surgeon's quarters, where the injured limb was dowsed in camomile oil. Next, Jacob gave Ducamp a piece of cloth to put in his mouth, to keep him from biting off his tongue. Then he asked Steven and the accompanying mates to hold the patient down. Remaining aloof to the muffled grunts of agony, he pulled and worked the bone back into its joint until the bump of the bone had disappeared, and the patient was calmed.

Wiping his soaked brow, he turned to the men. 'Thank you, that will be all,' he said.

He proceeded to apply a cataplasm made of oatmeal to the bruised and tender shoulder. Next, he began binding it. Ducamp, relieved to feel his shoulder tightly bandaged, at last broke the silence.

'I thank you, Doctor,' he said.

'I am carrying out my duty, Monsieur Ducamp. That is all.'

'Look, you cannot blame me for the dragonnades. I was only carrying out orders, and frankly, it was one reason why I left.'

Jacob finished tying the knot. 'It is done,' he said. 'You are free to go.'

But Ducamp remained seated, and in a conciliatory tone of voice, he said, 'I kept your wife and your children from my men. I stayed awake to make sure they were not touched, Monsieur Delpech. See, my own lad would have been about your boy's age.'

Jacob took a cloth to wipe his hands, and in a voice of controlled patience, he said, 'My wife is now a refugee in a foreign country without resources, my children have been taken from her, and my young daughter is dead, Monsieur Ducamp.'

'I am sorry to hear that, truly, but I tried.'

Jacob did not answer.

Holding his arm, Ducamp got up from the table and crossed the floor to the canvas partition. As he opened the flap, he said, 'Listen. There's been a change of plan. And there may be fighting at some point along the way. If there is, stay close to me.'

The bosun exited the surgeon's den, leaving Jacob perplexed. His puzzlement was doubled that afternoon when, going by the poop deck, he overheard the pirate in a discussion with the captain over the destination of their voyage. Captain Brook wanted to head for the Gulf of Mexico; the pirate preferred the Bay of Honduras. Yet was this man not supposed to be on board as a detainee? It certainly did not appear so. Moreover, Jacob was not aware that the latter port of call was en route to Virginia.

*

On the fourth morning out of Port Royal, the lookout spotted land. Jacob was busy cleaning his instruments. Using his medical book, he was able to identify the many and varied gruesome tools of the trade for dismembering, cauterising, and bullet extraction. He climbed the deck steps to see for himself the distant island, dotted with palm trees. And with grim irony, he noticed crewmates here and there cleaning their instruments too, though theirs were made to maim and kill—cutlasses, axes, muskets, and pistols.

By the time the sun had shifted an hour past its zenith, they were putting into a commodious cove where another sloop was already anchored.

As the *Joseph* carefully ventured into the clear blue waters of the natural harbour, there came a gut-churning explosion that made Jacob wonder about the intentions of the moored vessel. But when Captain Cox, standing at the bow, removed his hat and swept it before him in a gesture of salutation, a great roaring cheer rose up from the other ship's deck.

Jacob's suspicions were confirmed. This whole commission was a farce planned in advance to free Captain Cox.

Ducamp's offer of protection now became clear, as did the captain's claim that Jacob would find means to pay off his indenture. They were about to go freebooting.

*

The following day, the crew emerged as fresh as bilge rats. If any Spanish *guardacostas* should come upon them now, Jacob knew they would be as good as pigs to the slaughter. He had remained on board, preferring his own company to revelling ashore with the mates of the *Fortuna*, who had recovered their captain. He also chose to turn a blind eye to their drunken antics along the beach with the fall of the evening.

What had he done to end up in this devil's lair? He could

not for the life of him fathom why it had pleased God to lead him to bear witness to the devil's machinations. All he could do was continue to breathe through it, upholding his faith until God showed him the way to freedom.

After a sluggish start, the *Joseph* and the *Fortuna* left the island that Jacob had found out to be Caiman Grande. They set sail westward towards the Yucatan Passage, which would take them through the Gulf of Mexico.

As they sailed on to the south side of Cuba, the lookout sighted the distant masts of a lone frigate. The captain was with Doctor Delpech, who was treating his syphilis.

'What she be flying?' he asked Quartermaster Blunt, waiting on the other side of the canvas sheet.

'French colours, Cap'ain, and she be a biggen.'

Jacob had finished applying the mercury ointment to the captain's skin. Brook grunted thanks to the doctor, then went swiftly to the quarterdeck to scrutinise the French vessel.

Jacob was left wondering if being captured by the French navy could be the answer to his prayers. Could it be the lesser of the two evils? But then, it suddenly did not seem so bad to be committing fraud as a privateer's doctor. At least, it was something he would rather do than find himself back in a French prison, where he might well face execution. And besides, was he not doing goodness among these outcasts that society had disowned?

Then he remembered the treaty signed by James II and Louis XIV while he was in his prison in France. It meant there was normally no cause for hostilities between the two nations. There again, affairs in Europe did not seem to be of great importance in everyday dealings in these faraway lands, which Jacob now realised were very much a law unto themselves.

But Captain Brook did not turn against the wind to escape the French warship. Instead, with the prevailing westerly full in her sails, the *Joseph* veered north by northwest, closely followed by the *Fortuna*, to give chase to the massive frigate.

Leading the way at a steady ten knots, the *Joseph* closed the gap within a matter of hours. By late afternoon, it became clear that the French ship was heading to Isla de los Pinos, the large island off the southwest coast of Cuba.

As the buccaneers approached under English colours, the French ship struck her main sails and sat waiting on the south side of the *isla*. She was colossal, twice the size of the English sloop. Yet Captain Brook continued his approach.

Jacob stood nervously near the main mast, inwardly praying for his wife and children, that they might find peace and safety from their tortures, should he perish this day. And he hoped to God he would stand courageous at his station, should a battle arise.

The *Joseph*, which had cut through the waves faster than the *Fortuna*, was within gunshot of the brigantine's prow. As the English sloop slipped closer through the lapping waters, Delpech could now perceive the tall stature of the French master, standing on the quarterdeck with his back to the westering sun. He could only make out the French captain's outline, but it was enough for him to recognise the man who had lent him his house on Cow Island.

The sloop, having shortened her sails, was now within shouting distance.

'What brings ol' Captain Brook a roving in these waters?'

called Captain Laurent de Graaf over the bulwark using a loud hailer. 'Hunting sharks, are we?'

'Aye,' barked back Brook, 'and it looks like we've found a ship full of 'em!'

De Graaf let out a loud laugh.

*

Within the hour, both sloops and the French frigate had weighed anchor at a musket shot from the south-facing shore of Pinos Island.

The Dutchman quit his ship with a mulatto and was soon climbing aboard the *Joseph*, where Captain Brook met him with a welcome. 'Young scamp still tempting the devil, is he?'

'Indeed,' said de Graaf, 'and it looks like I've found 'im!'

The two men clasped each other's shoulders affably.

As they strode to the captain's cabin, a familiar face caught the Dutchman's eye. De Graaf offered a civil nod of recognition to Jacob, then proceeded to the stern of the ship without a word. There, he lowered his head into the captain's cabin, where Captain Cox was already waiting. Crewmates crowded around the open door to listen in on the conversation. It was their democratic right.

*

Decidedly, nothing was made to be clear in this world where English privateers mingled with senior French officials. An hour later, feeling abandoned to his fate, Jacob looked up at the man who had just settled against the bulwark beside him. He said, 'It seems, Lieutenant, that you were right about the change of plan.'

'That's de Graaf,' said Ducamp.

'Yes, I have already made his acquaintance, in different circumstances.'

'I wager he wants us to join him on a foray on Cuba.'

'On land? But that would equate to piracy.'

'Not if he has a letter of marque for it. Cheer up, Monsieur Delpech, 'cause if he has, it means you can buy back your freedom sooner than you thought. Long as you don't get killed, that is.'

There was a movement of the crowd around the captain's cabin. Brook stepped out, followed by de Graaf, the mulatto, and Cox. The expectant crew gathered around them or climbed up the standing rigging. Jacob and Ducamp approached.

'I have here a letter of Marque and Reprisal,' said de Graaf, holding up a wax-stamped document, 'to punish our Spanish neighbours for their barbarism. And the more we are, the merrier!'

Captain Brook then roared out, 'Are we up to it, lads?' The whole ship rocked with a hearty cheer.

The Dutchman left behind his mulatto named Joe, captured on a previous coastal foray. Joe, a former Cuban slave, knew the coast waters well and would serve as guide, should the ships become separated. De Graaf then made his way along the deck, accompanied by Captains Brook and Cox. He stopped in front of Jacob, who was now standing by the main mast.

'Delpech?' he said.

'You know our doctor?' said Captain Brook.

'Indentured doctor,' corrected Jacob. He could only hope the Dutchman would not question his occupation.

'We met on Cow Island,' said de Graaf with a quizzical look. But without further comment, he walked on, climbed down to his boat, and joined his vessel.

The face-to-face with the Dutchman had been awkward. What more could Jacob have said in front of fifty pairs of eyes? He could hardly explain his circumstances, or complain about his lot. And would there have been any point, given that the man was part and parcel of this association of rovers?

TWENTY-TWO

THERE WAS SOMETHING bracing about being in the middle of a seafaring force, something that almost made Jacob forget the immorality of the imminent raid.

It was early October. The Caribbean winds had become more variable, and the flotilla was tacking back along the luxuriant south-facing shore of Cuba. With time on their hands, the crew prepped their weapons or practised their aim with pistols and muskets. Jacob admired how these well-seasoned hunters invariably hit their marks, despite the pitch of the ship.

One afternoon on the main deck, the bosun insisted Jacob learn something of swordplay for the sake of his welfare, and consequently for that of the entire crew. But Jacob was not keen.

'At least learn defence, man,' said Ducamp, holding out a sword to the doctor. ''Cause neither Jehovah nor Neptune will stop a steel blade from running through your spleen!'

Albeit reluctantly, Delpech took the sword, which won him a resounding cheer from the crew. Their cheers abated, however, when he declared he would not kill a man. He had made it his duty to save rather than destroy life.

On hearing the cheer, Captain Brook had ventured out from his cabin. 'You'll soon get a taste for it, Doctor,' he said, swaggering up to Delpech.

An intimacy had grown between them after Jacob treated his syphilis, which consisted of applying a mercury ointment to his facial and genital sores. And, with scientific gravitas, Delpech showed all those infected by the painful disease how to rub in the unction.

Cupping a large hand on the ball of Jacob's shoulder, Brook said, 'Then before you know it, the smell of black powder and blood on steel will be the perfume of your dreams!'

'I very much doubt that, Sir, with all due respect,' said Jacob, whose new-found importance among captain and crew allowed him a certain liberty of expression.

The captain let out gruff snarls, which was his form of laughter. 'Kill or be killed, Doctor!' he said.

He then turned to Ducamp with a look of exasperation which told the bosun to make the man see sense. The doctor was too precious to lose.

Brook went back to his cabin, where he continued to extract navigation information from Joe the mulatto in exchange for kindness, food, and coin. Joe was already planning ahead.

Meanwhile, Ducamp turned to Jacob and said in French, 'He's right, you know. It's kill or be killed. And you best make up your mind now, because when you've a cut-throat in your face, it will be too late!'

*

Bound by language and culture, the two men very often sat together, smoking tobacco on a chest or on steps. Jacob had long since adopted the pipe. Even when not lit, it was invariably planted in his beak nowadays. For if smoking on land kept mosquitoes from his ears, at sea it kept the foul bilge waters from infesting his nose.

On one occasion, Jacob let the bosun steer the conversation to something that was clearly on his mind. He had been beating about the bush, especially now that Jacob read the Bible aloud to any mates who would listen—and many of the men did, including Quartermaster Blunt. Jacob sensed Ducamp needed to get something off his chest.

'You say you obey God's will, but so do Catholics. How do you know God listens to you and not to them?'

'God listens to all who have faith.'

'You sure? I've seen many a religious man, good and bad, Catholic and Calvinist, pray for mercy and be cut down by the sword, no different from any imp or scoundrel. Then nothingness. No cries, no lights, no ghost, just the stillness of death. But you haven't seen it yet, have you?'

Jacob had stopped hating this man who had brought calamity upon his family. So he obliged with a question. He said, 'You are angry with God, are you not, Lieutenant Ducamp?'

'Angry? Not angry. How can a man be angry at nothing? Because if there were something, then why did he let my wife and son be killed while I was away defending his religion?'

Ducamp's eyes watered slightly, surely from pipe smoke. It could not be from emotion, could it? Again Jacob helped the bosun empty his bile of bitterness. He said, 'How did they die?'

'Swept away by disease. When I went home, the place was bare and lifeless. No older than your lad, my boy was. A bright lad, and now just gone. Nothing left to prove they even lived.'

'The rendezvous is in heaven, Monsieur Ducamp. It is the only hope.'

'Heaven? Even if there was a heaven, how would *I* get in? I have sinned. I have killed, and I prepare to do so again.'

'The choice is yours, but you must make it now. For when the musket shot flies to your head, it will be too late. Remember, if you repent, you may regain God's love through Jesus Christ, He is our Saviour.'

'And why not through Mohamed or Yahweh?' said Ducamp, who had lost some of the bitterness in his voice now that he had got his story off his chest—now that he had made it clear to Jacob that he too had suffered the grief of loss.

'I will pray for you,' said Jacob. By offering to pray for the man, Jacob realised he was forgiving him. And he felt relieved of his own ball of bitterness.

The bosun gazed through the gun port towards the approaching shore of Cuba. He considered for a moment that it was inhabited by people he was conditioned to kill.

After drawing on his pipe, he said, 'Don't make sense.' Then he climbed the sun-filled hatchway to prepare for manoeuvres.

*

Laurent de Graaf knew the southeast coast of Cuba well. The previous year, he had defeated Biscayan privateers off Jucaro who had been commissioned by the king of Spain to track

235

him down. But the coast was still frequently patrolled by the *guardacostas*. So under the Dutchman's lead, the three ships slipped into the cove of a cay located a few leagues from the mouth of the Cauto River.

The warm smell of the land, of trees and fresh flowers and vegetation, was once again in Jacob's nose as evening encroached. He had joined two hundred men or more ashore, sitting, squatting, or standing around a cluster of rocks where the three captains made their case.

De Graaf proposed to draw any patrolling Spanish ships away from the Cauto estuary so that the other parties could slip into the river mouth aboard longboats and canoes. From there, they could follow the river upstream toward the township of Bayamo, one of the richest commercial and agricultural settlements on Cuba.

Once de Graaf had dispatched any *guardacostas* ships, he would lead his forces along the Manzanillo land route, shorter and more direct than the winding river. The idea was to attack the township from both sides, north and south.

It would be a daring inland campaign for sure, one that had never been attempted, which was all the more reason to suspect the place would be full of complacent merchants and planters with coffers full to the brim. And according to Joe, the little mulatto, the township, having never been harassed, lay pretty much open to attack.

'I got a question,' boomed a great bull of a man who had got to his feet at the front. 'What if they get news in Santiago? You can bet your breaches a full fleet will come chasing quicker than you can say *rumbullion*!'

'Winds are against a ship reaching Santiago,' said de Graaf. 'It would take a week for a runner to get there by land.

Then a fleet would take three days at best to round the cape. That gives us ten days to take the town and carry the plunder back to the cays!'

Captain Brook stepped forward, and with his usual gruff charisma, he roared: 'What you say there, lads? Are we here for plunder?'

The little cove was filled with a resounding *aye* and a thunderous cheer that shook flocks of colourful birds from their perches.

The buccaneers immediately set about making ready all the boats at their disposal—including those from de Graaf's frigate—which would carry them to pots of gold, or to their death.

*

De Graaf boldly sailed his frigate away from the setting sun into Spanish waters. Captain Brook waited. The first stars appeared, and an hour after that, there still had been no shot fired, which could only indicate that de Graaf had not encountered any Spanish ships.

Brook's boat led the way over the starlit water of the placid coastal shoals. Thirty men had been left behind to defend and manoeuvre the ships if need be. Jacob at first assumed he would be among them, but Brook told him his services would be needed in the field. Barely an hour later, the eight-boat flotilla reached the mouth of the Cauto River.

The estuary, which once thrived with contraband activity, was still. The massive flood of 1616 had altered the river's course. It no longer offered an easy link to the embarcadero where, back in the day, merchandise to and from Bayamo used to be loaded and unloaded. These days, merchants preferred the route by land, which had the advantage of running straight to the township.

Brook, with the help of de Graaf's mulatto, led the way through the dark, winding waters of the Cauto River. Captain Cox, Quartermaster Blunt, and five other senior crewmates followed in silence, each commanding a boat containing up to twenty-five men who took turns to row against the gentle current. Jacob sat in the one Ducamp was given to command.

They paddled along in Indian file in the white light of the rising moon, which was three-quarters full. They kept to the middle of the river, well away from the banks where the odd splash announced the presence of crocodiles. On a few occasions, they had to carry their embarkations over the marshy ground to the next navigable portion, and took shortcuts across strips of land whenever the river snaked round on itself.

A new day was dawning by the time they reached the old embarcadero. Only twenty miles now separated them from the township of Bayamo.

The boats were swiftly and quietly lifted out of the water and placed upside down in the long grass along the riverbank. Standing on the embarcadero, Captain Brook surveyed the surrounding vegetation and the rough dirt track ahead with satisfaction. Then he swung his arm around the little mulatto's neck in a gesture of companionship.

'Well done, Joe!' he said with a paternalistic glow, and puckered a kiss on the mulatto's forehead.

Jacob could not help but notice the new twinkle in the captain's eyes that, since their first night out of Pinos Island, seemed to search for the mulatto whenever he was out of sight. It was the same look many a mate shared with his chosen partner. It might be difficult to admit, but Jacob knew it was the look of trust, and love. The mulatto looked up at his protector with gratitude.

But as they proceeded into the track surrounded by woodland, the captain soon recovered his sardonic snarl. After fifteen minutes of marching, he stopped.

'Hold it, lads!' he growled, holding up a hand to halt the movement of the group. Fifty yards ahead, the road was strewn with felled trees. Fresh sap still hung heavy in the early morning air. It was a barricade. Somehow the Spaniards had gotten wind of the buccaneers' approach.

Something moved in the tangle of logs and branches. A head, then a barrel of a musket became visible. The first shot went off, closely followed by a cracking volley. It was a warning shot. Brook, a cunning and quick-thinking fellow, wanting the Spaniards to think he and his men had taken heed, signalled to everyone to turn tail.

The Spaniards must have worked all night, thought Jacob, as he ran with the group back to the embarcadero.

'We can take 'em easy,' said Captain Cox, once Brook had assembled with the other chiefs on the bank of the river.

'Nah, man. They'll have set up ambushes all along the route,' said Brook. 'We'll be well knackered by the time we get through to the township.' He put a hand on the mulatto's shoulder. 'Joe'll show us the way through the woods, won't you, Joe?'

'Yes, Captain Brook, Sir, I show you what you want!'

'Good lad!'

Cox made no attempt to debate his case; he had seen Brook this way before.

Brook's plan was swiftly put to a vote, and then put into action. The advancing men took turns to beat through the vegetation so as not to dull their blades.

Their relentless march through woodland and thick undergrowth at last brought them to the edge of a thicket north of the township, which was not open, as was initially thought. It was protected by a stockade. Between the wall of timber posts and the thicket lay a field that had recently been laboured.

To Jacob's disappointment, all these unexpected barriers did nothing to deter the fervour of the buccaneers who, on the contrary, now made no secret of their presence. They beat the flat of their swords with relish and howled like baboons, sounds which would instil the fear of the devil into any man or beast.

*

The mayor of Bayamo was Guiseppi de la Firma, well born, and like all Spanish nobility, proud of his heritage. So proud, in fact, that he added five extra syllables to his already many-syllabled name, making it Senor Guiseppi Alonzo de la Firma del Barro Bravo. Guiseppi was also an important landowner whose fields of cocoa and tobacco stretched far and wide along the south-facing slopes of the township. Needless to say, being such a proud man, he was very clever too.

It was his idea to impede the onslaught of the assailants by setting up ambushes. A devout Catholic, Guiseppi also had the luck of the devil, and it so happened that a company of cavalry was at present stationed in his town. They had been patrolling across the hills from Santiago to Bayamo as an exercise to train up cadets.

Guiseppi now peered through the stockade at the disorderly rabble of rovers lined up on the edge of the thicket. Their slaughter would be his proudest achievement and might possibly earn him a place in Spanish history.

*

Jacob was standing with Ducamp. Captain Brook was just a few yards away.

'Most likely take 'em tomorrow,' said the captain, 'soon as de Graaf shows up.'

It had been agreed with the Dutchman that they should wait until he sent word of his arrival on the opposite side of the township. They probably wouldn't even have to raise their hangers, De Graaf had said in jest, thinking of the surprise on the faces of the townsfolk when they found themselves surrounded.

But the chief of the Catholics had other plans. At his disposal, he had a company of young, brave cavaliers, a captain ready to do battle, and he surmised that the insolent bucks in the near distance must have already suffered ambush after ambush till they had been pushed into the woods. Their attempt at intimidation, a ruse to hide their fatigue, did not fool him.

So, urged on by the company captain, who was impatient to put his training to good use, and despite no news from the barricades, the mayor ordered his surprise force of cavaliers to assemble in front of the stockade. And he sent word to the soldiers stationed at the ambush sites to cut the rovers down as they retreated. Not one of the rovers should get away; all must be stopped, dead or alive.

The buccaneers' cacophony was silenced as the horsemen took their positions for the two-hundred-yard charge across the laboured field. Captain Brook's eyes widened with surprise, then narrowed with a sort of glee.

'What have we here, lads?' he roared. 'Looks like playtime's come sooner than later!' The men hallooed and bat their swords, once again making a terrifying din.

The horsemen, three lines deep, began steering their steeds towards the horde. But the horde was already spreading out into a treacherous crescent.

'Make 'em count, lads!' hurled Brook as the buccaneers drew their muskets.

The rovers did not run to meet them on the battlefield; they were not prepared to meet swords travelling at forty miles an hour. Buccaneers did not fight fair like proper soldiers: they fought to win. So instead they took aim with their muskets, and they began picking off their prey with an almost nonchalant precision. By the time the cavalry had reached the middle of the field, a third of them had fallen, whereas not a buccaneer was wounded.

Jacob was at first mesmerized. From the edge of the wood, he contemplated the scene with a strange fascination as tens of determined young men were struck down on the squeeze of a trigger. He watched the buccaneer next to him take aim with one eye half-closed, and fire his musket. Jacob followed the trajectory of the shot, as if time were slowed down, and a few moments later saw it sink into the head of a young Spaniard who then tumbled backward off his mount.

The acrid smell of gun smoke and the rumble of fast-approaching hooves jolted his senses and made him remember his station. But precisely where was it that he was supposed to stand?

He scanned left to right, where scores of buccaneers were popping away with their guns. As the sun was becoming stronger, his reflex was to back into the wood, where he put down his leather bag at the foot of a tree.

The shooting suddenly ceased. The thunder of hooves and the snorting of beasts grew louder. Then Jacob heard the roar of Brook. 'Step back, lads! Back to cover!'

A cavalier barely twenty yards away blasted out in Spanish, 'Lascars! Stand and fight like men!' It was the Spanish captain. He must certainly have felt cheated, for the lascars were not playing by the rules at all. Instead they backed into the thicket while bringing out their cutlasses in order to parry the onslaught.

The caballeros nevertheless continued their course over the undergrowth and straight into the wood, swiping at everything that moved as they went. But the trees, though sparse in places, made their horses swerve and reduce their gait.

The rovers were not slow to seize their chance. They rushed the confused steeds as they turned, pulling down their riders to the ground where a heavy razor-sharp blade awaited them.

The battle quickly evolved into a mass melee. Jacob found himself standing alone amid the raging fracas and hellish commotion made by steel and the many contrasted roars of men killing each other. He stood by his bag like an uninvited guest at a ball. It seemed like everyone in the wood had gone into a frenzied dance, and he was the only sane soul among them. There were practically two rovers to every caballero, which meant that Jacob lacked a partner to dance with. Not for long, though.

A young cavalier on foot, tall, lanky, and smooth-skinned, appeared before him. This was the kill-or-be-killed moment Brook and Ducamp had spoken of.

Delpech drew his sword just in time to parry a blow. The muchacho was visibly inexperienced, clumsy, and probably terrified. Maybe this was his first melee outing. Maybe he lacked the killer instinct that came naturally to some folk. Maybe he had not made that kill-or-be-killed decision either. He struck with wild, sweeping blows, leaving himself open to a poke in the ribcage. But instead of a lunge forward, Jacob backed off, parrying again and again, until his back came up against a tree.

Unable to move backward as the caballero continued his attack, Jacob could only dodge and stick out his sword. Delpech felt his blade run through flesh and muscle till it butted against bone. The young man dropped his sword in mid-swing. 'Madre!' he cried in one short, horror-filled breath. He then deflated like a pig's bladder, and fell to the floor as blood leaked out profusely from the perforation in his side. Jacob looked down aghast at the fallen lad lying on the thicket bed. He felt sick. He let fall his dripping sword from his hand.

'Pick it up, man!' yelled a voice from a few yards away. It came from Ducamp, who was deflecting a blow from his adversary.

But Jacob could not.

A mounted Spaniard charged out of the sun into the

dusty thicket. He reared his horse and pointed his pistol at the bastard at the tree with the muchacho lying at his feet.

Delpech, paralysed, gritted his teeth in terror and shame. Then there came an almighty explosion from behind his left ear, and the next instant, the Spaniard's head jolted back with the force of a cluster of shot that peppered his face.

'Pull yourself together, man,' shouted Ducamp, now standing next to him with a smoking double-barrelled pistol, which he holstered.

Jacob suddenly drew his own pistol and without a thought fired. Ducamp turned round to see the Spaniard who would have lopped off the lieutenant's head, had Jacob not sent a shot into his chest first. Ducamp finished him off and continued the fight.

'Go with Joe!' commanded Captain Brook to Jacob, ten yards further along and visibly relishing every kill. Nothing seemed able to resist him as he wielded sword and pistols with equal delight and dexterity.

The mulatto who had appeared at Jacob's side led the doctor deeper into the woods, away from the killing zone, away from the chaos of bloodletting and the flashes of steel and powder.

The fight was short-lived, and in less than an hour, the Spanish, seeing their numbers drastically dwindle, retreated across the field running and limping, some bowed over on horseback. But the distance gave the buccaneers enough time to load their muskets and take aim. This was not fair either, the Spanish captain would have thought had he lived. Jacob too was sickened as through the trees he watched the escapees fall. Only a handful of Spaniards made it back through the stockade alive.

Jacob looked around, appalled at the carnage in which he had partaken. His gaze paused at the tree where his first victim had fallen. He then rushed toward him, armed this time with nothing but his leather bag, for he saw the caballero move. Jacob knelt down beside him in a pool of sunshine. The young Spaniard was breathing, and he was conscious. Jacob loosened his blood-drenched tunic so he could breathe more easily.

'No *quiero morir*,' said the soldier, grasping Jacob by the sleeve, as if by doing so, he would keep a hold on life. There was nothing Delpech could do except try to cover the wound. The rest was in the hands of the Lord.

But as he was rummaging in his bag, he felt a shiver. A shadow came over them, blotting out the sunshine. Delpech looked up and saw in horror a red-stained goatee, eagle eyes, and a short, curved blade smeared in blood. It came hurtling down and severed the lad's head from his shoulders. Jacob jerked back in disgust as blood spurted over his face.

'Wrong side, Doctor,' growled Captain Brook. 'Should be seeing to our lads!'

Jacob promptly threw up.

Any wounded or dying cavaliers were quickly dispatched in a similar fashion by blade. There was no sense wasting lead shot on an incapacitated foe. Brook would argue that it was only right to put them all out of their misery, nice and quick. And it saved the buccaneers from any vengeful encounters in the future. For as the captain was like to say: 'Dead men don't bite back!'

It was monstrous. It was inhuman. Jacob failed to find any justice in it. It seemed that all the lines that had so neatly structured his existence were becoming increasingly blurred.

However, Jacob's sense of survival enabled him to not dwell on the atrocities he had been part of. Instead he focussed on the buccaneers' wounds. These mostly consisted of deep cuts and slices into the flesh, except one mate whose intestines had spewed out from a lateral slash to his belly. Jacob recognised Steven, the lad who had come running into Jacob's quarters on the ship after Ducamp's fall from the rigging, the lad who wanted to learn to read and write.

Jacob held his head, stroked his soft young beard, and said a prayer as the lad stared into the sun, until death took him. The doctor then laid down his head, closed his eyes, and moved on to the next injured sailor.

*

The buccaneers had spent the night travelling upstream. Once outside Bayamo, they had planned to rest while waiting for de Graaf to take up position on the south side of the township. However, they had been surprised to find not only ambushes that forced them to take a fatiguing detour through wild woodland, but also a timber stockade and a company of cavaliers whom they had virtually decimated. And all for just five dead and a few dozen wounded.

Brook had no difficulty firing them up for a last attack, to finish the job while Lady Luck was still with them.

A plan was swiftly devised and validated by vote. Two teams of half a dozen crack shots took up positions. They gave cover to a third group of about a dozen men who made their way to the gate with powder and axes.

Jacob watched them stealthily cross the laboured field where Spanish bodies lay strewn. They met no enemy fire. Soon after reaching the gate, there came a loud explosion from the stockade, then a series of quick, successive axe strokes on timber, and the great gate was flung open.

The whole horde of roaring, fearsome men stormed across the field without a shot fired at them and poured through the open gate.

The town had never once been worried by assailants, and there had been no need to erect a stone wall. However, the mayor had told the townsfolk to die rather than fall into the hands of the lascars. So they locked themselves in their houses and fired shots from their windows, causing the buccaneers to halt and take cover. But Brook had dealt with this kind of nuisance before; from experience, he knew it was an easy one to resolve.

He gave the nod to storm houses at the edge of town and pull out the women and children, who were hiding under tables and inside cupboards. Two men were captured. They were knocked about but not killed. These were not soldiers. Any able-bodied cavaliers would have fled—as would those at the barricades as soon as they got wind of events. Instead Brook sent them to the mayor to tell him he would slit the hostages' throats and burn down the town if they did not surrender.

The mayor, entrenched in his residence with his retinue, returned a note, saying he had sent horsemen to Santiago, that a Spanish expedition was already on its way, and that the pirates would be annihilated if they remained.

Brook did not order the hostages to be killed. Instead he ordered a party of buccaneers to creep up and throw smoke pots through the downstairs windows of the mayor's residence. By noon, the buccaneers had taken over the whole town.

*

Captain Brook, who had no time for women with their silly screams and petty demands, put Captain Cox in charge of selecting the finest maids. The captain of the *Fortuna* then had them ushered to the beautiful salons of the mayor's residence, where the ground-floor windows had been opened to give the place an airing from the smoke. Old hags, ugly nags, and their sprogs were locked inside the church.

Ducamp and Blunt took charge of conducting the Spanish men to the edge of town, where they herded them into two wooden warehouses used for drying tobacco and storing cocoa beans. When they were done, Brook walked up to the warehouse under Ducamp's charge. In his thick, gravelly voice, he ordered the town's councillors to stand before him.

Five podgy, affluent-looking men, sweating buckets, showed themselves at the open doors. Of them, Señor Guiseppi Alonzo de la Firma del Barro Bravo stood erect and said, 'There is expedition coming here from Santiago. You stay, you will be *matados todos, todos*. Leave now, and you will save your life.'

Brook grabbed the man by the lapels. He brought him up to his face and said in a low, seething voice, 'You better think carefully where you've stashed yer coin, then! It might save your poxy lives. Savvy?'

He put the man down, stepped back outside, and gave the nod to Ducamp to lock the warehouse doors, which was promptly executed among indignant complaints in Spanish that the place was already like a bakehouse inside.

While the Spaniards were being left to stew in their

juices, a party of buccaneers set to work on what buccaneers traditionally did best. They built a long fire in the middle of the main square. And over the fire, they made an extra-long *boucan*—a wooden grill placed on wooden stakes—where they could roast vast quantities of meat. Other contingents of rovers went rummaging for drink and cold food to whet the appetite.

The methodical slaughter of animals, especially the pigs, would curdle the blood of the hardiest prisoner, thought Jacob, who was busy patching up wounds. He imagined the anxiety the wretched prisoners must be going through on hearing the almost human squeals. But he realised too that this was all part of the ploy to instil fear in the hearts of the townsfolk, to make them loosen their tongues. It would leave them in a better disposition so that the buccaneers could steal away as quickly as they had come. However, Jacob could never imagine in a thousand years of Catholic purgatory what would happen next.

TWENTY-THREE

THE PLAZA WAS soon a festival of many merry men, tucking ravenously into a feast of maize and meat, washed down with wine and rum.

A few hours later, once the sun's heat had abated, many of them had taken quarters in houses with good beds; others were at the mayor's residence with Captain Cox. Meanwhile, on the market square, Captain Brook summoned the five Spanish councillors to the shaded side, where the buccaneers had assembled a cosy array of seating.

The Spanish gentlemen, drenched in sweat, were visibly disgusted as they were escorted into the square, past pools of blood where animals were racked, gutted, and carved up. After passing the boucan, where dogs were stealing bones and half-eaten animal parts, they found themselves facing the snarl of Captain Brook, who was lounging in a magnificent armchair.

'Jack Taylor, frow 'em somink to eat,' said Brook, turning to one of the men at the boucan.

The sailor lobbed each of the Spaniards a pork chop from a dish. But either the gentlemen were not good at catching, or they were not hungry. They let the pieces of meat fall to the ground. After each failed catch, Jack Taylor feigned disappointment, which made his crewmates laugh out loud.

'We do not eat with thieves!' said the proudest of them in accented English.

Brook let his left hand, which was holding a bottle, drop to the side of his armchair, and motioned with the other for the white-haired Spaniard to approach, which he did.

'You've had enough time to think, Señor,' said the captain warmly. 'Now, you tell us where you've hidden your treasure, and we leave you in peace. That's the deal.'

'I take you to be a pirate,' said the Spaniard with pride. 'The vassals of the king of Spain do not make treaties with inferior persons!' But he must have sensed his dignity might be contradictory to his health this time, because he added, 'Soldiers on horseback will have already arrived in Santiago. You have no time to lose. If you leave now, you can escape the armada.'

However, this show of bravado and generosity did not have the desired effect.

'Pin him down, lads!' said Brook, businesslike.

The accompanying sailors who knew what this meant kicked away the man's legs from beneath him, and held him face up on the ground. A roar of laughter rose up from the drunken sailors lounging around the boucan. They were glad for some entertainment now that their bellies were full.

'Now what say you?'

'Never will I bow to filth!'

'Make 'im eat his own shit!' shouted out one mate. After another swig of rum, Brook put down the bottle, then pushed on the armchair and sprang to his feet. As he did so, he reached for an axe that was leaning on the side of the armchair. He swung it over his shoulder as if he were ready to chop wood.

An expectant silence fell around the marketplace that was turning orange with the late-afternoon sun. The surrounding flora filled the balmy air with sweet-smelling perfume that mingled deliciously with the savoury smell from the boucan. Captain Brook was now stomping around the captive held to the floor.

'Go now, *por favour*. Leave us in peace, and I will *personalmente* vouch for your safe passage,' said the Spaniard.

'We go when I say so, and that's when you've told us where you've hidden your poxy coin, man. *Entiendes?*'

'Never!' said the Spaniard, whose pride had got the better of him again.

In a burst of rage, Brook roared and cussed. He then swung the axe from his shoulder and, in a nifty loop, slammed it down on the Spaniard's forearm. The spectators let out a cheer of appreciation. The Spaniard let out a cry of horror. He clasped his handless arm, blood spouting out the severed end.

'That's what you get for slapping Captain Brook in the face!'

Brook tossed the axe aside and drew a pistol from his sash. He bent over the man still writhing on the floor, and grabbed him by the shirt front. He cocked his weapon and shoved it into his mouth. The captain then delivered one of his favourite catchphrases that never failed to captivate his audience. In a deep, seething voice, he said, 'If you don't feed me silver, I'll feed you lead!'

But the proud Spaniard, who prized honour and courage

above all things, could not bow down to a *ladron*, a vulgar thief.

'*Que el diablo te lleve!*' he said, and spat in the captain's face.

From experience, Captain Brook knew that the first sacrifices sufficed to get what he wanted, and the quicker they were done, the better it was for everyone, including the townsfolk.

Brook pulled the pistol away from the Spaniard's mouth and slowly stood up, still pointing with the barrel at an oblique angle. With a strange fascination, he observed the fear in the man's eyes, then squeezed the trigger. The onlookers roared out in hilarity and disgust. There was a mess where the Spaniard's head had been.

*

Jacob, who was sitting with Ducamp, had fallen into a deep snooze. Having become inured to the buccaneers' cheers, he had not woken when the town councillors were marched onto the other side of the square. He suddenly woke now with the sound of the shot. He turned his head to the scene taking place forty yards across the square. He could not at first fathom what was taking place.

The captain was turning round the four Spaniards waiting in line. He said: 'Like the man said, amigos, we have no time to lose! *Entiendes?*'

With a disgruntled shrug, the captain put his pistol back in his sash with its "brothers," as he called them. He then picked up the axe and curled his finger at the next councillor.

'What's it to be, amigo? Silver for me, or steel for you?' This was another one of the captain's catchphrases, and the audience reacted accordingly. They were enjoying the show.

The man, in his mid-forties, with a paunch from good living, was febrile, and had pissed himself. He made the sign of the cross and stepped in front of the captain.

'No *tengo nada*, Señor Capitán . . .'

Brook said not a word. He fondled the man's buttons with his razor-sharp blade, and popped them off one at a time.

'*Es la verdad. Solo soy médico.*'

'On the floor! Now!' shouted the captain. The man fell to his knees, holding his heart.

'My God!' said Jacob, appalled. He could hardly believe his eyes as he looked around for someone to react. But he only saw the engrossed onlookers, some drinking, others scoffing corn on the cob or meat, others just watching the show. Ducamp told him to keep calm and stay put.

'Lay him flat, lads,' said Brook, 'and spread him out!'

'Pwaah, fat bastard's shit himself!' said Taylor, which produced a few laughs and a crackle of applause as the fat man was thrown on his back. He began gasping for air, as though he were drowning. The spectators watched with bated breath. Taylor punched him in the face to make him lie flat.

'For the love of Christ, man, stop this insanity!' cried out Jacob, getting to his feet and breaking the unnatural silence.

Brook frowned and fired his bloodshot eyes in the direction of his interlocutor, who was moving towards him. Then the captain's eyebrows straightened.

'Ah, Doctor Delpech,' he said in a comradely tone. 'You wanna have a go?' He took a few unsteady steps forward to beckon Jacob closer. 'Sweet vengeance, Doctor!'

'I have nothing against this man or any other man here.'

'But he's a Catholic.'

'He is a Christian!'

'Come on, Doctor, five pieces of eight for every finger, fifty for every limb. And if you manage to make the bugger talk, I'll pay your indenture twofold!'

The captain's eyes were glazed over, unblinking, as he made his offer in all earnestness. Jacob read for the first time in his life the look of a madman, rapt in his hellish folly.

'Come on, Doctor, what do you say?' he urged.

Captain Brook was always glad to initiate a new member to his ways, and what better draftee was there than a doctor? What greater stamp of approval could there be for his love of inflicting pain and death? Not a stronger emotion was there as what one felt upon seeing a man's last breath; a doctor should know that. And there was no greater feeling than that of being the instigator of such emotion as pure terror. It overwhelmed by far all others. It was better than sex with women. It was the purest emotion he had ever experienced. It was the animal instinct of the predator, the confirmation of the sovereign force of the dominant.

Jacob had never thought such extreme madness could exist except in hell. He realised he was the only pillar of righteousness around. Deep down, he knew he had to act, or he would be as good as part of it. His Christian duty was to interpose.

Quashing his fear, he stepped forward and said, 'Captain Brook, I beg you to come to your senses, Sir. I beseech you in the name of God, cease this cruelty and hate, or it shall be your demise, Sir.'

'Hate? Who said I hate 'em? They might be Spanish filth,

but they've got coin, and lots of it. I can smell it. So how can I bloody hate 'em, Doctor?' said the captain, turning halfway to his audience, who laughed out loud.

'Sir, these men deserve human decency. I beg you to take hold of yourself. There are other ways to win respect.'

Had this French doctor not administered the mercury unction that gave him relief from his syphilis, Brook would have ripped out his throat by now. Instead he roared: 'I'll show you respect, Doctor. I'll show you how to get it from these dogs!'

'NO . . . NO . . . Wait!' shouted Jacob as the captain took a step back. Then he swung round and raised his battle-axe high above his head.

The Spaniard wheezed in horror as the incensed captain hammered down the heavy iron blade between his ribs. There was a thump, a squelch, the sound of smashed bones, expelled air, blood, and other matter, and the Spaniard gasped for air no more.

The captain turned to the remaining councillors. He roared: 'Tell me where you've put the poxy coin!'

Ignoring Jacob's continued protestations, which Brook put down to fatigue and a mild case of hysterics, the captain ordered the next man to step out of the line.

'By God. How can you stand there?' hurled Jacob at the group of sailors he had prayed with aboard the *Joseph*. 'This man is mad,' he said, with a stern eye for Quartermaster Blunt, who was among them. 'In the name of the Lord, I beseech you, stop him!'

Ducamp now had caught up with Jacob, and, taking him firmly by the arm, he swung him round. In a low but resolute voice, the bosun said in French, 'Are you out of your

257

bloody mind, Delpech? Your life is on a thread, man, and I won't let you lose it!'

Jacob said, 'You cannot be part of this. You cannot let this go on.'

'This is what the Spanish do, except they make it last longer. The captain puts on a show to force the others to talk.'

'Bosun,' called out the captain, twenty yards away, where his next victim was pleading on bended knee. 'Tell the bloody doctor he is upsetting our proceedings. Tell him to put a sock in it, for the sake of his health!'

'He's calmed now, Sir. Just not used to campaigning, Sir.'

As the bosun answered, the noise of marching boots made everyone's eyes turn to the south side.

'You can thank your lucky stars this time, Delpech,' said Ducamp as a mob came roaring into the square.

'I thank God,' returned Jacob.

It was the land contingent, headed by the tall figure of de Graaf.

Brook stood, legs apart, balancing the long shaft of the axe on his shoulder. As the Dutchman came nearer, Brook called out, 'You took your bloody time, man!'

'You were supposed to wait!' returned de Graaf, continuing his stride while his men flocked round the grill like vultures. They took meat while Brook's men handed them drink and threw more meat on the boucan.

'Monsieur,' intervened Jacob as the Dutchman came by him. 'Please, put a stop to this man's murderous folly. The town is won . . .'

'Take the man away, before I stop his yap!' hurled Captain Brook. Then he raised his axe with both hands and slammed the bloody steel blade into the blood-drenched earth by the side of the praying Spaniard.

The bosun again took the doctor by the arm, but to Ducamp's alarm, Jacob shook it free and continued: 'The town is won—'

Ducamp had no choice but to place his thick forearm around the doctor's neck. The man had already made his point. Now he was tempting the devil.

'Sun's turned 'is bloody brain, don't know his arse from his elbow!' said Brook.

De Graaf stopped and held up a hand. 'Let him speak,' he said.

Ducamp released his hold. Jacob put his hand to his throat where the bosun's arm had pressed against his larynx. He said, 'There is no need for callous killing. I beseech you, stop this torture. The town is won!'

Before the Dutchman could answer, Brook growled: 'We didn't come here for the bloody town, you soft prick!'

Then he turned to the Dutchman, who could now see the carnage. 'You know the score, Laurencillo. It's for the good of us all. Sacrifice a few of the bastards, and the rest will jabber, right?'

Meeting Brook head-on, the Dutchman said, 'Ned, I told you before, man, no bloody torture!'

Brook knew de Graaf's rage, and his short fuse for a fight. He was a big bastard too. Besides, the passion for butchery had left him; he had got his fill of killing for now. Any more would spoil the special pleasure it brought. So he just grunted his discontent.

'Apart from that, you've done a good job,' continued de Graaf, remaining pragmatic. 'Now leave the talking to me, and we'll be out of here in two days with enough coin to sink a bloody galleon!'

Without waiting for an answer, de Graaf lifted up the Spaniard by the arm. In fluent Spanish, he told the man to take him to the mayor.

'*El alcalde* is there, Señor,' said the Spaniard, pointing to the body parts of the first sacrificial corpse.

De Graaf looked back at Ned Brook with disgust and annoyance. Now, instead of one leader, he knew he would have to deal with several of the *regidores*.

'For crying out loud, man, you've blown the head off the bloody mayor!' said the Dutchman. Captain Brook simply scratched the top of his head.

De Graaf marched the prisoner over to the other councillors waiting in line. So that Brook could understand, he said each sentence in English, then translated it into Spanish to make sure the Spaniards also understood. He said, 'Tell your people to bring us their money and valuables. We want one hundred thousand pesos by nightfall tomorrow. Or we will burn the town and everyone in it down to the ground. We also want fifty cows and all the barrels of wine, tobacco, and cocoa in your storehouse. Be off!'

Jacob, who had followed in the Dutchman's wake, was wondering if burning a whole population alive was any better than Brook's methodical sacrifice of a few leading citizens. However, at least de Graaf's way gave the poor wretches a chance to come out of the raid with their lives and all their limbs attached.

The Dutchman turned back to Brook. 'Ned, man,' he said, 'I want you to string up the bodies so everyone can see the consequences of their stupidity. The mayor'll help his villagers see reason yet. We stumbled on soldiers along the way, got 'em all, but you can never be sure. We need to be in and out quick, man.'

TWENTY-FOUR

HUNDREDS OF THOUSANDS of flies swarmed over the battlefield where the caballeros had fallen. Birds, dogs, and even hens were digging into the broken flesh. And now, with the evening temperature, mosquitoes began siphoning blood from the living. Except for the two bodies strung up on display, the town square became deserted as the buccaneers took refuge inside houses or at the mayor's residence.

The drunken orgy had resumed in the salons and bedrooms, where the most pragmatic women accepted that they would do better to lead the game rather than be taken by force. At least this way, they were able to choose their partners, and avoid the ones disfigured by syphilis.

But this separation of mind and body was beyond many of the womenfolk. This was the case for one young lady who found herself being carried off to a room by a bull of a partner, much larger than herself. In his frenzied desire, he flipped her petite body over and bore down on her from behind, clutching her hips, her shoulders, and ultimately, her neck. 'Come on, woman. It's like shaggin' a sack o' beans,' protested the thick-necked sailor before letting her fall, inert and heavy onto the bed. The man, who was no stranger to such an occurrence, headed off for some refreshment, leaving the girl for dead.

*

Jacob had taken possession of the doctor's house. All the injured mates and their partners had left the premises except one. The young man, a cobbler's son from Bristol, lay dying of his wound on a mattress thrown down in the room that must have been where the doctor practised his surgery. There were medical instruments neatly laid out, and jars and ointments on shelves. The patient had been delirious, then chatty, and now he was unconscious again. Jacob did not think he would last the night; his buddy had also died, so no one was there to comfort him. Jacob had bound up his open belly. There was nothing more he could do.

He wondered if the battlefield tactic of putting the mortally wounded out of their misery was not so cruel after all. However, at least this way, the man had time to repent for his sins and commit his soul to God.

The battle had made Jacob see the fragility of life, and its futility without hope of life after death. All those men were born to parents who had no doubt shed tears of joy on the day of their birth. They were all born with fair souls as children of God. But then they had become corrupt and conditioned by hatred. Did not fate have a hand in that corruption, for no one chooses their birthplace or their station? There again, every man who had been taught Christian values was responsible for his life choices, be he born a Spaniard, a Dutchman, a Catholic, a Protestant. But Jacob pushed these thoughts to the back of his mind. He did not want to go into an inner dialogue about the fairness of faith, not while he was still in the void after so many deaths.

The house was comfortable. He entered the study, which was filled with medical books and collections of animals and insects that reminded him of his own father's house. He wondered what had become of his mother and sister. He only knew that they had fled Montauban before the soldiers had entered his beloved hometown. But he did not want to think about it.

He opened a cabinet and started sifting through drawings and personal papers of births and deaths and suchlike. It took him back to his own house. He also kept his wife and children's birth certificates in a walnut cabinet. But he did not want to dwell on those memories either, preferring to take refuge in the present.

Suddenly he felt a presence. He turned his head from the sketch he was perusing to see a dishevelled-looking young lady appear on the threshold. She must have entered the house from the rear. The cabinet was on the same wall as the door, so she did not see him immediately. She looked dazed, her clothes were torn, and her neck was red and blue. She was pretty, though, and Jacob knew where she had come from. He dared not think what went on at the mayor's residence but still felt shameful for it. Then she saw Jacob's reflexion in the glass on the wall opposite. She turned to him with a gasp of surprise, though no sound came out of her mouth. Her expression turned to indignation, as if to ask what he was doing there.

'I was admiring the drawings,' said Jacob. 'Is this your house?'

She had been abducted and raped; she cared not who this

stranger was. She only cared that he would not hurt her. He did not look as if he would. She was dying to sit down, to forget. But she remained standing, clenching the knife she had taken from the kitchen.

'My father's,' she said in Spanish. Jacob, who had studied Latin, found that he could understand Spanish fairly well.

There came loud voices from the street, drawing closer.

'And the melons, all soft and bulging like pigeons,' said a deep and joyful voice outside the closed shutters that led onto the street. 'You've gotta give it a go, man.'

'If we find her,' said a more fluty voice.

'She can't have got far . . .'

Jacob quickly crossed the study and opened the door that led to the surgery room. He nodded to her to enter quickly. She was unsure whether she could trust this man or not, but she had no choice. Moments later, there were footsteps in the hallway. Then two men staggered wildly into the brightly lit room.

'Oh, sorry, Doctor.'

'What do you want, Mr Griffiths?'

'Looking for a tart,' said a big fellow whom Jacob deduced to be one of Cox's crew.

'Right tasty 'n' all,' said the chirpy man called Griffiths.

'Well, you won't find a "tart" in this house. Only Mr Barret.'

Jacob prayed his patient would not wake up and give the girl away. In fact, he hoped he was dead.

'Oh, right. How is he then?' said Griffiths.

The doctor did not answer. He just left an awkward silence.

'Well, give 'im our regards, eh, Doctor?' said the big fellow. Then he turned to his mate. 'Come on.'

The men backed out of the room and left the house.

A few minutes later, Jacob opened the surgery room door. The young lady stepped out, still gripping her knife. She looked at Jacob with her big brown eyes, then said, 'My father is a doctor.'

'Yes,' said Jacob, 'I have used some of his instruments.'

'He was,' she said, correcting herself, 'he was a doctor, until someone put an axe through his heart.'

She crossed herself, then moved toward the hallway. At the door, she said, 'Your patient is dead,' and she went upstairs.

*

Señorita Ana rose at first light, the cleanest time of the day. The drunks and thieves would all be asleep. She had slept with her door locked, a chair wedged under the doorknob, her knife under her pillow, though she remained covered in her rapist's smell the whole night through. At last she was able to fetch some water up to her room and wash the sweat and scum from her body.

It was still early morning, and all was calm when she ventured out to find her mother, sisters, and brother, whom she knew to be locked inside the church.

The township was built according to the Laws of the Indies, which meant a rectilinear grid of streets was built around the plaza mayor. Ana now crept catlike under windows and wrought iron balconies that resounded with snorts and snoring of drunken raiders; now she darted like a gazelle across open spaces, until she came to the north side of San Salvador church. She scratched with a stone at the wooden door that was locked shut. At last someone scratched back on the other side, and she slid her note under the door. She wrote to her mother only that she had escaped. She made no mention of the horrible fate of her father, whose body she had encountered the night before as she crossed the square, after escaping through the window of the mayor's residence. In the darkness, she had been drawn to two figures, each ligatured on a cartwheel between two torches. Then she saw him full on, with a cleft in the middle of his chest. In a bid for her sanity, she had kept her mind busy with prayer.

Now she was desperate to know if her mother, young sisters, and brother were well. If they were dead, then there was no point praying for their safety. If they were alive, she would pray to the Virgin Mary and all the saints of the calendar to keep them safe.

In the torment of the night, wrapped in the smell of her ravisher, she had clenched hold of that hope of being in the bosom of her mother and siblings again. It was what kept her from thrusting her knife into her heart. Her youngest brother was only eight, her sisters three, six, and eleven. She realised she would not be able to face living again if anything had happened to them. She was their big sister; she loved them with all her heart, like a little mother. If they were gone, her life would no longer have any sense at all.

There was another scratch at the door. Then she heard a hushed voice that said: 'We are here, Ana.'

'Mother!'

'Are you well?'

'Yes, Mother . . .'

'And your father, have you any news of him?'

She could not lie to her mother, but she could not tell

her that he was killed. He, who had settled his family in Bayamo because it was far enough from the coast to be a haven from rovers and foreign armies; he, who had wanted a refuge so his children could focus on their intellectual understanding of God's world; he, whose altruism, love, and knowledge were unremitting; he, destroyed by men who smelt like goats and cared for nothing but their own sordid gratification.

'The men are locked in the warehouses, Mother. And you, how are you?'

The silence lasted two beats too long, and Ana knew her mother suspected the worse. Her voice was on the verge of breaking as she said, 'We are bearing up, my dear Ana, but the heat yesterday was unbearable for many of us, especially the old and the toddlers. I fear for your sister. We have hardly any water left. I pray to God the raiders leave soon. I do not know how we can go through another day in here.'

*

Ana decided there and then to live for something greater than herself. Now that growing into a woman had lost all its value, she was prepared to be taken again to protect her cause, for she could not lose her virginity twice. She suddenly became aware of the power of the charms of her carnal envelope, of her smooth and shapely curves, of her plump breasts that had grown so quickly during the past year, and which even in ordinary times men could not keep from ogling. She could now understand those women at the residence who had spoken to her of setting aside her body from her soul. The Lord would not abandon her in sin. Did He not forgive Mary Magdalene?

Yes, her mind was made up: she would be a whore to save the children. But she needed to do it with one of the men who could open the doors of the church.

A little later, she redressed in her mother's bedroom. As she passed her hand lightly over her soft breasts, she prayed to the Virgin Mary, who would understand. Then she knelt and prayed to God that He would help her in the name of His son.

'O God, please be there,' she said to herself as she left her room. 'Please be there!'

*

Jacob did not sleep easily on the couch in the study. He had slept with one eye open, wondering where he could bury Barret and the others, then wondering about the girl. Was she all right? Should he go to her door? But how would it be interpreted? Would she be vengeful, stab him while he slept? Then his interrogations and fretting had followed into scenes of horror, scenes of butchery and slaughter, of the face of the lad he had stabbed, of himself paralysed, unable to raise so much as a finger, or call out, impuissant to prevent the slaughter of innocent people. Then he saw a knife, the girl. He awoke.

She was standing over him. She was clean, her dark hair was soft and silky and held back with red ribbon, she smelt of perfume, and she was wearing a dress that made her look like a woman. She was truly beautiful, as Spanish girls often are when young, and she offered a shy smile. But what did she want?

'You were shouting,' she said softly in Spanish, with a motion of the hand.

'Oh. Yes,' said Jacob.

'I want to thank you for last night.'

It took him a moment to clear his mind of slumber, to translate the words. After she said it again, he realised she was talking about the sailors who had come looking for her.

'I am sorry about your *padre*,' said Jacob solemnly and slowly in French, slipping in any Spanish words he knew. 'I am equally sorry for the *alcalde*, and for all this killing.'

'The mayor was not such a good man. My father was, though.'

'I am sure,' he said, getting to a sitting position.

Ana sat down on the edge of the armchair opposite, poised and arching her back. She was determined to get this doctor to act for her. But how did you go about seducing a man? She had seen some women do it during events in Havana, where her father once had his practice. They smiled, empathised, laughed merrily at stupid jokes, and gave looks. It was an art that she had no time to learn. So how did you get a man to just lie with you?

'Can I do anything for you, Doctor?' she said.

She immediately regretted saying *Doctor*; it made her offer sound medical.

But Jacob had been a man about town when young. The olive-skinned girl was very attractive, and he knew she was after something.

'You are safe here. There is no need for you to act, my girl.'

'Thank you,' she said, slightly embarrassed. But a girl, she was not, and she kept up her pose, which was not without some effect.

Jacob noted her fleeting frown of disappointment, but he

270

could see too that she was resolute to get what she wanted. Did she want protection?

'Yes, you can help me,' he said, nodding toward the surgery room where Barret's body still lay. 'Is there a place where I can bury our dead, *los muertos*?'

'The churchyard?' she said.

'He is not Catholic,' said Jacob, who was suddenly aware how absurd it was to mention the man's religious denomination.

Ana realised that there was no point keeping up her charade; she would fare better talking straight. She knew not this man's intentions, but she was ready to risk all. Relaxing her posture, she said, 'There is a special place. I can help you, if you help me.'

As the pain returned around her pelvis, her hips, and her neck, she desperately told Jacob about the plight of the women and children locked inside the church.

Jacob listened attentively as the girl returned to her natural self, a serious, obliging, and beautiful young lady.

Using his hands and key words, he explained he would speak to the commander without delay. There was no reason why they should not be released and given refreshment. He would tell the commander that in return, the buccaneers could bury their dead in a proper grave. Brook would not care. But Jacob believed de Graaf to be of Christian principles even if he sinned like a heathen. However, the Dutchman would need reassurance that the bodies would not be dug up and fed to the crocodiles as soon as the buccaneers had departed.

'You must talk to Father Del Lome,' said the girl in her native tongue. 'He is strict about religion, but if he gives you

271

his word, he will keep it. You must tell him about our agreement.'

*

Delpech headed out immediately to the warehouses down by the riverside. That was where he would find the padre. But on the way, he was hailed by a sailor whose mate had shot himself in the foot. Jacob was obliged to lead the man back to the doctor's house, where Ana was hiding upstairs. At first, she was alarmed, wondered where she could run. But no one climbed the stairs. She quickly understood that the men had come to be treated.

Jacob extracted the lead shot, cleaned and bound the wound, and sent the man hopping with his partner. As he headed out again, he saw the girl on the stairs. 'Please hurry,' she implored.

He passed by parties of buccaneers escorting townsmen to their stash, and groups of five or six taking to the saddle on Spanish mounts, to venture out onto the versant and plunder farmsteads.

By the time he reached the warehouse built along the Bayamo River, it was already sweltering. The padre, a man in his sixties, was manifestly in no hurry to meet his maker; he was relieved to be offered a chance to step out of the inferno.

As the priest spoke only Spanish and Latin, the councillor who had escaped Brook's sacrificial torture offered to translate into French. Jacob explained that he was an indentured doctor who wanted to help the people who were suffering in the church. The padre told Jacob where they buried non-Catholics, and agreed that, if Jacob could save the women and children from further suffering, he would leave the dead rovers in their resting place.

The councillor took the opportunity to give Jacob his thanks for his intervention on the square, and now for saving those in the church where his own wife, mother, and son were also held. He said that he was aware that the doctor had nothing to do with these villains other than being indentured to them.

'I promise to give a good account of you, Doctor,' he said.

This left Jacob perplexed. And as he walked briskly back through the elegant streets lined with whitewashed houses, he wondered if the man really thought the town would be rescued by his countrymen. It hardly seemed likely, did it?

*

Within a half an hour, Jacob was standing in the governor's library. The windows were flung open; the shutters were half-closed.

Valuables and coin unearthed from gardens, wells, cellars, and cisterns had been trickling into the library all morning. The three captains were lounging on the comfortable seating, drinking and smoking while crewmates sorted the piles of gems, silver, and gold into casks for easy transport.

'You have no experience of campaigns, Monsieur Delpech,' said the Dutchman. 'It was in fact on my command that they be locked up. We cannot let any women or children roam about freely.'

'But, Sir, I beg you. The most vulnerable among them will certainly die of suffocation or thirst.'

'They're locked up for a reason, Doctor,' said Captain Brook. Jacob turned to face his captain lounging with a bottle in one hand and one leg swung over the velvet arm of his chair. 'And that reason be their own safety!'

De Graaf said: 'These men are predators. Many of them have wild imaginations and untamed curiosity.'

'Some o' these boys'll try anything once!' said Brook.

Outside, horses were drawing up in front of the building. Their snorting could be heard through the shutters. Brook got up, and looking through the shutter, he said, 'Have you ever seen a dog shag an old nag?'

'God forbid, I have not, Sir,' said Jacob.

'I have,' said Brook. 'On campaign, anything goes. That's why we lock 'em up!'

'They will suffocate . . .'

There came a bustling and footsteps in the entrance hall. Then in walked five buccaneers with a black slave.

One of them said, 'Picked him up three miles east.'

'De donde vienes?' said De Graaf.

'Santiago, Señor.'

The buccaneer then handed the Dutchman a piece of paper on which was written a message to the mayor of Bayamo. De Graaf translated the message out loud.

'Dear Mayor,' began de Graaf, who then flicked up his eyes to meet those of Captain Brook. The latter gave an innocent shrug of the shoulders. De Graaf continued. 'Dear Mayor Guiseppi Alonzo de la Firma and the people of Bayamo. The fleet is on its way to Manzanillo bay. They come with their mounts, so relief will be with you within four days of sending this message. Instructions are to delay payments, or only pay small amounts, to delay the raiders as much as you can. Signed, the governor of Santiago.'

'When was it sent?' said Cox.

'The fifteenth of the eighth month of 1688,' read de Graaf.

'Two days ago,' said Brook.

Jacob realised now what the Spaniard in the warehouse meant about giving him a good account. Somehow, perhaps from a different messenger, he had been receiving news. But Jacob said nothing, for there was nothing to gain from another dead Spaniard and a fatherless child. And in some respects, the Spanish fleet being on their way gave Delpech some cause for relief. Provided the captains withdrew, it meant the horrors he had witnessed would cease. Wouldn't they?

'What's the plan?' said Brook.

'Assemble the men on the plaza.'

'What about the people in the church?' said Jacob, seizing the space Brook left for thought.

'Give them scraps from the boucan and water from the well. No fresh cuts; we'll need all the provisions we can get for ourselves.' He turned to a crewmate and said, 'Trev, go with the doctor, fetch Rob and Two-Fingers, and smash the church windows . . . from the inside.'

'Thank you,' said Jacob, who knew this was as good a compromise as he would get.

'Doctor,' said Captain Brook. Delpech turned to face him. 'Remember to bring the medicines, right?'

Jacob knew what he meant and nodded his understanding. He then left quickly to draw pails of water from the well and fill baskets with cooked leftovers from the boucan.

*

Over two hundred buccaneers assembled on the main square. Brook spoke about the intercepted message; then de Graaf stepped forward. In a raised voice and a measured, slightly ironic tone, he said, 'Lads, I see no point wasting lives and plunder on a confrontation that would serve no purpose, other than the pleasure of killing Spanish soldiers!' There was a loud roar of laughter, mingled with *ayes* all round.

Along with a good stack of booty, De Graaf had attained his objective of taking the inland township, which would send a warning to the Spanish that he could strike anywhere. They would from now on think twice before raiding the west coast of Saint-Domingue, which the French Dutchman was commissioned to protect. Brook, Cox, and their men had also made a nice fortune for services rendered while thrillingly navigating close to death, sometimes too close. So it was unanimously voted to get out while the going was still good.

De Graaf then sent five horsemen to give notice to the mariners back at Manzanillo Bay, to sail the ship westward along the coast to where the *Joseph* and the *Fortuna* lay anchored at the cay. The rest of the raiders would travel down the Cauto River, which flowed into the bay a good twenty miles up from Manzanillo harbour. From there, they would continue by boat along the coastal shoals, under the cover of night.

Two groups of six townsmen were "volunteered" from the warehouses for the employ of the buccaneers. Under escort, these men were loaded into carts and put to the task of removing the barricades along the road to the embarcadero. And they did not dally.

*

Later that afternoon, de Graaf joined Jacob, who stood with his Bible over the dead sailors. They lay side by side in hessian sacks at the bottom of a large trench. Ducamp had shown up along with five score of maritime desperados.

Captain Brook had stayed in the library with the loot. He never went near a graveyard if he could help it, preferring burials at sea. Seeing his crewmates cramped six feet under only put him in the doldrums and made him feel bitter with thoughts that his life was destined to be short, riddled as he was with the pox. He would rather spend his time watching mulatto Joe dress in silk and pearls. Captain Cox had chosen to remain in the playroom, as he liked to call it, for a last fling with his favourite female company.

As agreed with the padre, the short ceremony took place on the burial ground reserved for non-Catholics. The factions of Christianity seemed more absurd to Jacob now than ever. Their rules seemed only to obscure the essence of religion, namely, belief in God and one's desire to be near Him by following the teachings of Jesus.

He had witnessed for himself how manmade religious rules only gave perfidious men a pretext to commit wrongness to the extreme, in the same way that absence of morality led men to commit unimaginable acts of cruelty.

Standing at the head of the pit, he read a passage from Matthew chapter V, which he had translated into English. He then turned his head to encompass the silent horde of rovers huddled around the trench from left to right. In a loud and resolute voice, he said, 'To live without God is to live without hope. And life without hope has no value. God brings meaning and morality to our lives. God. Is. Hope. Amen.'

He said it, of course, not for the dead, but for the sake of the living, in the hope that some of them would find the righteous path. His eyes settled for an instant on Ducamp to his right.

'Amen,' mumbled the horde of wayward sailors.

The slight breeze rose up from the north. The burial ground was suddenly polluted with the nauseating stench of putrid corpses. It came as a reminder of the scores of Spanish soldiers still strewn over the field where death had been sown.

*

The rest of the afternoon and the early evening were mostly spent carting provisions and saleable barrels of tobacco and cocoa to the embarcadero. From there, the cargo was loaded onto the buccaneers' boats, as well as pirogues and canoes that belonged to Bayamo boatmen, which increased cargo and seating capacity.

De Graaf negotiated with the councillors, who provided thirty "volunteers" to slaughter animals on the square and salt the meat which was then loaded for transport. It was at least an escape from the stifling warehouse, and the *vecinos* carried out the butchery diligently and swiftly to be rid of their assailants by nightfall. If the rescue fleet commander accused them of not delaying the buccaneers sufficiently, they had the perfect scapegoat. They would put the blame on Señor Guiseppi Alonzo de la Firma, their proud and now

278

faceless *alcalde*, whose morbid silhouette seemed to be bearing reproachfully down at them from his wheel. The governor of Cuba could hardly hang him for failing in his duty now, could he? Pity he had to die so atrociously, though, but then again, everyone had to die sometime, and anyway, he was old, and inflexible, and a tyrant. At least this way, his life was given meaning, and he would be remembered as a hero, instead of as an ignorant town official who had stupidly sent a battalion of cadets to their deaths. The doctor, on the other hand, was a tragic loss. He had not long since been coaxed to Bayamo from Havana to look after the townsfolk; the move had not provided him with the safe living they had promised. Nothing could be promised in this world where one day, the spectacles of Paradise filled you with wonder, and the next, a hurricane or a band of raiders could come and devastate your entire existence.

Jacob meanwhile busied himself by replenishing San Salvador church with water and what food he could salvage from the boucan. Now, when the rovers opened the door for him to deposit his pails and extra goblets, instead of hundreds of staring, frightened, wary faces, three ringless ladies stepped forward in dignified gratitude and took charge of the distribution. One of them was the doctor's wife, to whom Jacob had given a note from Ana on his first visit, to reassure them that the water was drinkable and the food edible, that they were not poisoned.

On leaving them for the last time, he told them he would pray to God to protect and deliver them. '*Adios, y vaya con Dios*,' he said.

The whitewashed buildings were now bathed in the orange glow of evening as he hurried back to the house where Ana was still hiding. The streets had taken on a frenetic air in the end-of-day gloom as beasts of burden, horses, and carts stole away with the last of the barrels. Jacob guessed the urgency was enhanced by the fact that no sailor wanted to be the last to see the ghostly chaos left in the wake of their rampage, or hear the spirits of the dead cadets as night encroached.

He passed the mayor's residence, where de Graaf, Brook, and Cox were standing outside, in discussion over the barrels of loot to be loaded for transport.

He crossed the plaza amid empty hogsheads, bottles, jugs, and piles of offal. The glowing embers under the boucan, the torches planted to give light, and the mass slaughter of animals, lent it a hellish hue.

The morning would bring to the townsfolk the terrible realisation of what had hit them, thought Jacob. They would have to come to terms with the weekend of rape, "consented" intercourse, killings, desolation, and stolen life savings and harvests. Jacob felt debased and ashamed to be part of it, despite his efforts to alleviate some of the horror. How could he dishonour himself further by taking a share of the spoils? It was not like stealing from the Spanish silver fleet at all, which transported treasures pillaged from the natives of these lands. This was an ordinary township with ordinary civilians who had no quarrel with the commanders of war.

A short while later, he pushed the rear door of the doctor's house and gave five syncopated knocks on the study table to let Ana upstairs know it was him. He went to the surgery room and hurriedly took the vials he needed for Brook and his crew. Then he went back to the study and sat on the sofa where he had slept—he had been unable to snatch any sleep in someone's bedroom. He picked up the wooden cross he had placed on a low table. He glanced over the six acorns he had stood in a line on a strip of wool.

The cross came from his own study, plundered and ransacked during the dragonnades. The acorns, chosen for their size and painted with faces, were sent to him from his son, Paul, when he was in prison in France. These were the objects of his cocoon of protection that gave him a reason each day to go on. They represented heaven and earth, and all he ever wanted. And they brought him comfort when God seemed to turn silent.

He placed the cross in his leather bag, even though, with deep regret, he realised that his prayer said to the desperados at the end of the burial had already been forgotten. He began putting the acorns safely in a writing case which he first packed with the wool.

'Your family?' said Ana, who now stood before him. He had not heard her enter. Now that she was in a more conservative dress, he could tell she must be no more than fourteen, barely older than his eldest daughter, Lizzie. Yet she was sharper than most adults.

'Yes,' he said solemnly. 'Me, my wife, my daughter Elizabeth, my son, Paul, this one's Louise who is with our Lord and her sister Anne, and this one's the newest member of the family. I hope to see them all again.'

'I hope you do too.'

'All is not so well in France, my homeland.'

'My father used to say the same about Spain. That is why he came here.'

'Ana, I have had to take some of the medicine from your

father's cabinet,' he continued, using his hands to give shape to his meaning. 'I am sorry, but I cannot do otherwise if I want to see my family again. You understand? Truly, I am sorry.'

'Don't be. It is nothing.'

'Of course,' he said, realising the insignificance of the act compared to the horror she had endured.

'My father would have gladly let you have the medicine you need,' she asserted slowly so that he could understand, which took Jacob by surprise. 'You gave me hope and morality when in my despair I was lacking. You could have taken what I had left, but you did not. My father would have liked you for that, and for what you have done to save the people in the church from thirst and the calenture.'

Jacob got to his feet. He took both her hands. He said, 'Keep your faith, Ana, and others will have faith in you. Take this as a reminder to keep your hope, and others will hope for you.' He placed the acorn that represented his precious Lulu in her hand. 'Small acorns grow into great trees, just like a tiny spark can light a beacon. I will pray that you become a tree of wisdom and a beacon of hope despite these atrocities, Ana. Your family will need you.'

Half an hour later, Delpech was riding on one of the last carts out. His heart sank as he left the devastated township and followed the dark road to the embarcadero, accompanied by the evening song of birds, the chirping of insects, and the howling of hounds.

TWENTY-FIVE

DE GRAAF HAD invited Jacob to sit beside him in his boat.

'I regret you had to bear witness to the horrors of war, Monsieur Delpech,' said the Dutchman in a low voice, while stretching out his long legs as best he could. 'But you must realise, it is an eye for an eye in this world. And this campaign was in response to far greater atrocities committed against our people.'

'A Christian would turn the other cheek, Captain de Graaf,' said Jacob, lighting his pipe.

The Dutchman let out an indulgent chuckle; then he said as if in banter, 'Have you ever seen a woman impaled? Or men burnt alive at the stake for heresy? Have you ever seen children picked up by the ankles and thrashed against the wall until their brains spilt out? Have you ever seen a man slowly sawn from his genitals upward? This is what they do.'

Jacob suspected that de Graaf was trying to give himself a good conscience and a clever pretext to attack and loot an innocent town. But he knew better than to argue with a man capable of leading a band of butchers without shedding a drop of blood himself. Instead he said, 'I have seen what men of war are capable of, Sir, whatever their nationality. If you continue to meet violence with violence, when will it stop? It is a virtue to learn to turn the other cheek and pray for those who persecute you, is it not?'

'That may work, Monsieur Delpech, if the offender has read the Bible and shares its virtues.'

It was a fair point, thought Jacob, puffing at his pipe as images of Elias Verbizier reeled through his mind.

'Besides,' said the Dutchman, 'if we abided by those virtues, you would not be able to recover your freedom and pay your passage back to Europe, would you?'

'I will take none of it!' said Jacob.

Fatigued, de Graaf preferred to let it drop, and made himself as comfortable as he could on his Havana hide until it was his turn to take the oar.

As the canoe slipped through the black, brackish water beneath the star-speckled sky, Jacob settled with his pipe. However, though it gave protection from insects and the foul tang of sailors, it could not wipe away the killing from his memory.

*

Travelling downriver would normally take a good deal less time than rowing up it. However, each craft also carried part of the spoils of victory. So instead of crossing the strips of land where the river snaked round parallel to itself, the buccaneers preferred to ride out the bends even though it added precious time to their return journey. And the closer the river got to the coast, the more it coiled like a Cuban boa. Sometimes it took half an hour to get to a point that was no more than a stone's throw across a strip of land. But it was certainly less strenuous than heaving barrels of provisions, crop, and plunder through marshland.

At one point, however, the water became so shallow and full of fallen branches that they were obliged to pull into the south bank. Then they had to carry their boats and cargo the short distance through the swamped woodland to reach the next navigable stretch.

The men in the pirogue that brought up the rear had been sneakily swigging as they drifted downstream. Instead of carrying the precious cargo separately like the crews before them, they got the notion to heave high their pirogue with the barrels still in it to save the hassle of lugging them. After all, it was only fifty yards to the next strip of water, and there were ten of them to carry it.

It turned out, however, that as they advanced carefully in the paling darkness of predawn, the main hindrance was not the cumbersome weight, but the nature of the terrain. The marshy ground was strewn with roots. One of the men tripped, sending another over with him. The false steps caused the boat to dip and tilt. The barrels toppled over to the ground. The one containing plunder had not been capped and hooped—given that it was soon to be emptied— and its contents spilt over the marshy bed.

Brook, who loved loot even more than his mulatto, was walking with the boat in front. He turned and saw the barrel of treasure a foot deep in thick, muddy water. He roared out: 'By Jupiter, I'll cut your bloody arms off if you don't put that barrel as you found it!'

The guilty party urgently lowered their pirogue to the ground. As if to prove the utility of their arms, they proceeded to frantically recover the spilt treasure, feeling around in the cold, murky water for any coin that might have toppled out.

Three boats up, de Graaf looked back and immediately guessed what all the fuss was about.

'For crying out loud! The lot of you drunk or just plain stupid?'

'Should 'ave waited till daybreak before heading down,' said Cox in the next boat up, thinking of the extra time he could have spent in the library in Bayamo.

'And we'd be in worse lumber than a beached whale!' returned the Dutchman. 'Because the Spanish aren't stupid. They'd have also sent soldiers across the hills on horseback!'

'Oh, yeah,' said Cox.

'Just pick up the big stuff,' shouted de Graaf. 'We gotta make it down before the day breaks over the bay!'

They salvaged what they could, leaving behind a small fortune to whomever would one day dig into the mud on the south bank where the river was shallow.

They soon caught up with the pack waiting further downstream on the river's edge. The whole band of buccaneers then rowed the rest of the way without another hitch to the river's mouth.

In the grey light of a misty morning, the seventeen-boat flotilla hacked along the coastal shoals until they came to the cay. Quickly and under de Graaf's careful eye, they heaved and hauled the takings into the holds of the three waiting ships so they could weigh anchor before the sun dissipated their cover.

'Rendezvous on Pinos Island for the count,' called out de Graaf from the epicentre of the circle of men, after a brief consultation with the captains.

As the men broke away to board their ships, the Dutch captain turned to Jacob and said, 'Monsieur Delpech, I am sure Captain Brook would not mind if you rode with me.'

'Like hell I would. You ain't stealing my doctor, de Graaf. He's indentured to me, and he's an invaluable member of my crew!'

'Then I will pay the indenture in advance of the doctor's share with interest, and I'll throw Joe into the bargain,' said de Graaf, shrewdly addressing the captain's two most delectable sins, which had a stronger hold over him than the virtues of a medical man.

'All right then,' said Brook at length, 'but leave the medicine with me.' The doctor and de Graaf agreed.

Deep down, the mulatto, who was wearing hoops and a silk scarf, didn't know whether to laugh or cry to be so esteemed by his new protector and multi-ethnic family. But all in all, he considered the services due were certainly worth the wealth and freedom that he could look forward to, and one day soon, he might even be able to jump ship.

Poor Joe's manifest enthusiasm would surely have been dulled had he not been ignorant, thought Jacob, of the sailor's ailment.

TWENTY-SIX

DELPECH WAS SITTING at the captain's desk, in the handsome frigate built for a sea prince.

De Graaf had invited him to share his cabin and use whatever space he could find, except the great mahogany table, strewn with navigational instruments and rolls of charts, that stood in the centre. Elsewhere was richly furnished with silverware, a fine French *glace*, and a Persian carpet. Delpech had strung up his hammock near a writing desk which enabled him to corner off a personal area. As the morning light flooded in through the stern windows, he wondered how a man could be so elegant and considerate and yet so ruthless. It was true, however, he had not actually drawn a drop of blood throughout the campaign. In fact, Jacob believed de Graaf's presence had reduced life loss. Yet given the man's authority over these battle-hardened cut-throats, including the obnoxious Captain Brook, there could be no doubt as to the Dutchman's murderous capabilities.

The deck outside the half-open door was losing its eerie stillness as it became animated again with predominantly French accents. Going by their cheerful banter, the crew

288

were returning from Pinos Island in even livelier spirits than they had left the ship, three hours earlier that morning. The reason for this, Jacob knew, was they had just received their share of the booty, worth over one hundred thousand pieces of eight, the price of a thousand slaves.

Jacob hadn't written a thing. His wooden lacquered pen case with its pastoral scene still sat unopened on the desk beside his Bible. He had been thinking a lot about his life, about his goal to recover his family, and about his spiritual objective.

He needed means to pay for his freedom and to return to Europe. Yet the Christian values to which he wholeheartedly adhered left him unarmed, and without resources to fight to recover his family. *Thou shall not steal!* And he had refused to take a share of the profit from the deaths, desolation, and robbery of innocent people. If he had, how could he qualify for a place in heaven?

A knock on the door brought him out of his introspection. *'Entrez!'* he said, turning round on his leather chair. His sunken eyes showed surprise when they met with the large frame of the bosun that filled the doorway. 'Ah, Monsieur Ducamp, have you jumped ship?'

The bosun advanced into the spacious cabin, whose wide array of stern windows offered an excellent view of the shore.

'Not yet, Monsieur Delpech, no intention of going north yet.' He was referring to de Graaf's imminent departure to Saint-Domingue, which meant circumnavigating the island of Cuba windward and included a detour northward to Nassau. 'I have come to give you this.' He held out a leather drawstring pouch.

Jacob got to his feet. Ignoring the bosun's outstretched

289

hand, he said, 'I am sorry, I distinctly told Captain de Graaf that I would have nothing to do with such ill-gotten gain.'

'It's not loot,' said Ducamp. The pouch of coin made a jingling thud as he dumped it on the desk beside Jacob's Bible. 'It is payment for the belongings I sold from your house in Montauban!'

'I cannot become a profiteer!'

'It's coin I had before, and it is not negotiable. Would you deprive a man of his first step toward redemption, Monsieur Delpech?'

Jacob glanced at the money bag. Was this not an answer to his secret doubts?

'By the grace of God, take it, man. You deserve it. You have been a light of good and a ray of hope to many of us here. And I can assure you, I have never seen a bunch of cut-throats stand so still as when you spoke at the funeral. Some of the lads want to know if it was from the Bible.'

Jacob gave a curt nod. 'It was, Lieutenant Ducamp,' he said. He twisted his torso to reach for his desk. Turning back with his Bible in his hand, he said, 'Matthew chapter five. Take it, please.'

'You are a good man, Monsieur Delpech,' said the bosun, 'and good men deserve to be free!' Taking the book, he held Jacob's gaze for a full second, an instant of mutual understanding which said more than all their pleasantries.

'It is written in French, not Latin. It is God's will that all men may one day be able to read the word of the Lord, and examine their conscience for themselves.'

Jacob felt a fleeting movement of the heart as the big man's expression lost its grim, battle-worn mask of ruggedness, and he saw the lad standing before him, humbled like a son, and with a sheen of hope as if, at last, he had received a long-awaited gift. 'May it help lighten your burden, Monsieur Ducamp. And may God stay with you!'

'I'll say it again, you are a good man,' said the bosun. 'If God exists, may He protect you and yours, Sir.' He bowed, then turned without another word said.

Jacob followed him with his eyes and watched him lower his head back through the cabin door onto the now bustling deck, and climb down the rigging to the longboat to join the *Joseph*. He was taking the Book of God into hell, thought Jacob. There was hope.

Sitting back at the writing desk, Jacob pulled out a sheet of paper from the desk drawer, then he opened his pen case. Five acorn faces stared back at him. He arranged them on the desk on the strip of wool. He then prepared his pen, drew ink from the well, and began to write.

My Dearest Wife . . .

TWENTY-SEVEN

ETIENNE AND CLAIRE Lambrois had stopped at Schaffhausen. Situated on the Rhine at midpoint between Geneva and Brandenburg, it bordered the minor German states of the Holy Roman Empire. During their spring travels, Claire had become overly fatigued, and Etienne had decided to make a halt for a couple of days.

The young couple had been given hospitality by the First Consul of the Magistrature, Monsieur Rhing de Wildenberg, who was only too glad to entertain them and give vent to his love of French culture. He had completed his tour of France as a young man and spoke the language fluently. Claire and Etienne had initially planned to rest just a few days, a week at most, but during a conversation at table, Etienne discussed his future plans.

It so happened that Monsieur de Wildenberg had a son-in-law who was hoping to expand his woodworking business, given the new sawmills and the expansion of the wealthy township. 'So one thing led to another, and here we still are,' Claire had told Jeanne, while sitting with Ginette in front of the dwelling that Etienne had been able to rent.

Situated close to a sawmill not far out of Schaffhausen, the squared timber-framed dwelling came with the added advantage of a large adjoining barn, useful for Etienne's carpentry activities. To everyone's contentment, it also now employed Jean Fleuret. It was the reason why Jeannot had headed directly for Schaffhausen instead of Brandenburg, Etienne having previously sent word inviting him to stop by on his travels.

During a discussion a little later, Jeanne learnt how the officials looking for Jeanne Delpech had not been prompted by the audacious pauper after all. As soon as the Fleurets arrived at Schaffhausen and informed Etienne and Claire of the boat tragedy, and that Jeanne was recovering in the village where Pierre was buried, Lambrois and Jeannot headed out in a cart to fetch her and Paul.

By the time they arrived in Nion, Jeanne had already left. Monsieur Gaugin explained to them her intentions, so Etienne sent out a message to officials along all the possible routes to stop her so that they could take her back to Schaffhausen by cart. But in Yverdon, they bumped into none other than Cephas Crespin, who told them that, not wishing to travel by boat, she had taken the land route through Payerme. This was confirmed by an agent of the Confederacy who had seen a woman in a green coat with a little boy.

'I assumed that green was a favourite colour of yours, and that you had naturally purchased another one of the same colour,' explained Etienne, over the dining table which stood in a separate room from the smoky cooking kitchen.

'We found the green coat, all right,' said Jeannot Fleuret, 'but on another woman!'

Lambrois said, 'When she described the person she bought it from as having mutilated thumbs, we immediately knew it to be the pauper.'

'And we knew something didn't tally righ' 'n' all,' said Fleuret, 'seein' as he'd sent us on a wild goose chase.'

Etienne explained how they hurried back to the track that Monsieur Gaugin had told Jeanne to take. They soon picked up the trail of a Madame Delgarde de Castanet. Lambrois, who knew Jeanne had a nobiliary particle after her name, had a gut feeling that they were on her path, which was confirmed when they asked at a pair of riverboats on the Aar if they had seen a lady travelling with a boy. By good fortune, a woman was able to tell them that she had travelled from Yverdon with a lady and a lad who had since headed to somewhere that began with *Schaff*, and that they had taken the road to Zurzach.

Lambrois and Fleuret ventured across country in the light of the moon, neither of them wanting to rest until they had found Jeanne and Paul. They arrived at Neunkirch a couple of hours after sunup and were directed to the place where Jeanne had left a note of thanks.

'There are too many coincidences,' said Jeannot with a glimmer in his eye. 'It can only have been an act of Providence that brought us to your aid in time, can it not?'

'Pity the wicked imp got away with your bag, though,' said Ginette.

Jeanne gave a contented smile and said, 'It is of no consequence. We are safe and alive, and we are here now among friends, aren't we, Paul?'

'Brave lad, too, taking on a full-grown man,' said Etienne, clasping the boy's shoulder blade.

'Aye,' said Jeannot, 'there be a courageous young man inside that heart of yours, me boy, that's for sure.'

'I did as Pierre would have done,' said Paul, with both hope and sadness in his smile. 'I am sure he was with me.'

*

Jeanne accepted to stay for the imminent childbirth. Lacking her mother, Claire was glad to have Jeanne at her side. She was reassured too that the Fleurets had decided that they could do far worse than to settle in Schaffhausen, where Jeannot would not lack work pertaining to his true trade.

One warm Sunday afternoon, Jeannot was sitting in the shade on the bench outside the kitchen, watching the children— Paul and his daughters, Rose and Aurore—playing in the meadow in front of the house. Jeanne sat down beside him.

'It is beautiful,' she said.

'Isn't it? He would have loved it here,' said Jeannot, rubbing the side of his big, tanned face. 'I do miss him. Can't help it,' he said, turning to her, his eyes glistening, his brow furrowed. 'I keep wanting to tell him I love him, but he's not there.' Jeanne placed a hand on his forearm, and pressed her fingers on his Sunday shirt. He continued, 'Why this sufferance, Jeanne? For what? For whom?'

Why indeed, she knew not. She too was sometimes given to ask: Why had her faith driven her from her beloved homeland? Why had her children been taken from her? Why did Lulu and now Pierre have to die? Had they not given enough proof of their faith? But she tried not to dwell on it, tried to live in the present and have faith in the future. It was the only way to move forward without the ground subsiding beneath her feet.

At length, she said, 'I do not know, Jeannot. But what I do know is that your Pierre and my Louise are with Jesus, that one day we shall be reunited in heaven.'

Jeannot placed his hand upon hers. 'Thank you,' he said. A solitary tear ran down the creases in his face. 'I needed to hear it. It is my one hope.'

*

Upon the general insistence, Jeanne agreed to winter in Schaffhausen at least until she received confirmation of Jacob's arrival in London, for she still had no certitude that he had gone there, that he had escaped even. She and Paul would thereafter take to the road again in better health.

The glorious days of summer soon gave way to the autumn chill. But the early snows in October were as fresh and beautiful as the summer meadows were warm and picturesque. Through the church, the group of immigrants integrated into Schaffhausen society—facilitated by the First Consul and Etienne's professional connections, as well as a general willingness to embrace their new home. 'I never thought Etienne would pick up the language so quickly,' said Claire one day while feeding her baby by the fireside.

Jeanne said, 'Just goes to show what a pleasant environment and good people can do to boost your willingness to fit in, doesn't it?'

'Bit of a struggle sometimes, though, ain't it,' said Ginette. 'I don't know if I'm ever going to make 'em laugh in German one day.'

In spite of the cold, Jeanne and Paul had also settled into the ways of a Swiss country town. They marvelled at the annual sleigh races, with horses magnificently harnessed and attired for the occasion, and Paul enjoyed activities in the snow with new friends. Jeanne helped with Claire's baby, who was named Jeanne Lambrois, and also at church despite the language barrier. In this way, with much relief, she looked forward to some kind of stability during the harsh, cold months in the company of people she loved.

But one clear and icy-blue day, she received the letter she had been praying for. The men were at work, Ginette was at her new dwelling, and Claire was lying down after the baby's feed. Jeanne sat alone to open it in the kitchen, where chestnuts were roasting in the hearth for the children who would soon be back from the schoolhouse. The tall case clock counted time as she set her eyes on the letter and read:

> *My Dearest Wife,*
> *I have encountered as many difficulties as atrocities, but by God's grace, having escaped my gaolers, I do believe my fortune has turned. I will not elaborate on the course of events that have enabled me to write this letter, but I am free, my dear Jeanne. I can imagine the torment you yourself have had to endure, and I long for the day when we shall be united again. So I will ask you, my dear wife, to join me in London, where I will meet you. I am told there is a Huguenot church there. That is where you will find news of my whereabouts, and you can be sure I will run to meet you as soon as I am given word of your arrival.*
> *My heart beats for the day that will bring us together.*
> *Your husband who loves you dearly, Jacob*

Jeanne kissed the paper that her husband's hand had brushed, and then pressed the letter to her heart. She gazed through the kitchen window at the winter wonderland of snow and ice that muffled the ambient noises and gave off a blue hue, now that evening was encroaching. Of course, she was elated; of course, she must leave at once. But apart from the local pathways which town valets had sprinkled with sand, they were snowed in.

Enjoy this book?
You can make a big difference

Thanks for reading book 2 of *The Huguenot Chronicles trilogy*, I hope you enjoyed it.

Honest reviews of my books help bring them to the attention of other readers. If you've enjoyed this book I would be very grateful if you could spend just five minutes leaving a review on the book's Amazon page.

Thank you very much.

Paul

ABOUT THE AUTHOR

Paul C.R. Monk is the author of the Huguenot Connection historical fiction trilogy and the Marcel Dassaud books. You can connect with Paul on Twitter at @pcrmonk, on Facebook at www.facebook.com/paulcrmonkauthor and you can send him an email at paulmonk@bloomtree.net should the mood take you.

ALSO BY PAUL C.R. MONK

In the HUGUENOT CHRONICLES Trilogy

MERCHANTS OF VIRTUE (Book 1)

France, 1685. Jeanne is the wife of a once-wealthy merchant, but now she risks losing everything. Louis XIV's soldiers will stop at nothing to forcibly convert the country's Huguenots to Catholicism. The men ransack Jeanne's belongings and threaten her children. If Jeanne can't find a way to evade the soldiers' clutches, her family will face a fate worse than poverty and imprisonment. They may never see each other again...

LAND OF HOPE (Book 3)

A 17th Century family torn apart. A new power on the throne. Will one man reunite with his wife and child, or is he doomed to die in fresh battles? Land of Hope is the conclusion to the riveting Huguenot Chronicles historical fiction trilogy.

Also in the The Huguenot Chronicles series

MAY STUART

Port-de-Paix, 1691. May Stuart is ready to start a new life with her young daughter. No longer content with her role as an English spy and courtesan, she gains passage on a merchant vessel under a false identity. But her journey to collect her beloved child is thrown off course when ruthless corsairs raid their ship. Former French Lieutenant Didier Ducamp fears he's lost his moral compass. After the deaths of his wife and daughter, he sank to carrying out terrible deeds as a pirate. But when he spares a beautiful hostage from his bloody-minded fellow sailors, he never expected his noble act would become the catalyst for a rich new future.

Other works

STRANGE METAMORPHOSIS
When a boy faces a life-changing decision, a legendary tree sends him on a magical expedition. He soon has to vie with the bugs he once collected for sport! The journey is fraught with life-threatening dangers, and the more he finds out about himself, the more he undergoes a strange metamorphosis.

"A fable of love and life, of good and evil, of ambition and humility."

SUBTERRANEAN PERIL
Set in the story-world of Strange Metamorphosis, this action-packed novelette offers a thrilling episode of a boy's fabulous and scary adventure of self-discovery. When 14 year-old Marcel leads his crew out of a dark and disused snake tunnel in search of fresh air, little does he know he is entering the labyrinthic galleries of an ant nest.

ACKNOWLEDGEMENTS

My special thanks go to Marc Bridel, secretary of the Huguenot Society of Switzerland, who welcomed me at his home and gave me invaluable information about the Huguenots in Switzerland. My supportive advance reader group gave me feedback and extra eyeballs once those of the editors' had passed over the manuscript. My thanks also go to my mother and brother who were a constant source of encouragement while writing this book. Finally, I thank Florence Monk, Anthony Monk, Dylan Monk and Lloyd Monk, who allowed me my nightly escapades into my study and gave enthusiastic advice when it came to publication.

Made in the USA
Coppell, TX
17 March 2024